"Dance with me." Leslie spoke softly as she gracefully moved into Augustine's arms in gentle rhythm with the soft dreamy music. Augustine's response had quickly turned to tender anticipation as he enveloped her in a soft reverent embrace.

"You know why I'm here, then?" he asked as his eyes probed hers deeply.

"Of course," she replied, pressing her lips close to his ear. Leslie moved her body closer to his and felt a gratifying response, silky and sensuous through the gossamer fabric of her robe. "You know I'm a woman with a mind of my own . . . perhaps not quite what you want," she teased him.

"No, perhaps not quite," Augustine replied quietly. "But then this is the age of freedom, and you've always known what I've wanted and needed from you."

"Yes," she agreed. "But I should tell you the one thing I need from you—I've chosen you as the man to give me a baby. . . ."

Dear Reader,

It is our pleasure to bring you romance novels that go beyond category writing. The settings of **Harlequin American Romance** give a sense of place and culture that is uniquely American, and the characters are warm and believable. The stories are of "today" and have been chosen to give variety within the vast scope of romance fiction.

The American territory of Puerto Rico is the setting for this distinctive story that examines the machismo of the Latin culture. Dorothea Hale writes from a keen observation of the heritage of her adopted homeland. Leslie is a perfect foil for the strong-willed tradition of Augustine Rivera Platos.

From the early days of Harlequin, our primary concern has been to bring you novels of the highest quality. **Harlequin American Romance** is no exception. Enjoy!

Vivian Stephens

Vivian Stephens
Editorial Director
Harlequin American Romance
919 Third Avenue,
New York, N.Y. 10022

A Woman's Prerogative

DOROTHEA HALE

Harlequin Books

TORONTO • NEW YORK • LONDON
AMSTERDAM • PARIS • SYDNEY • HAMBURG
STOCKHOLM • ATHENS • TOKYO • MILAN

To my children,
Aurea and Fremmito

Published November 1983

First printing September 1983

ISBN 0-373-16029-1

Printed in Canada

Chapter One

The bronze bust of Isabella the Catholic presided imperiously over the sunny garden tucked away next to the library of the Ponce Art Museum. Leslie Williams sat deeply engrossed in a remote corner, far from the general hubbub and bustle of the tourist crowds that flocked to this modern miracle of classical architecture in the southernmost city of Puerto Rico.

She looked up uneasily, puzzled and uncomfortable, and examined the nearly completed infant sweater stretched across the long slim knitting needles in her hands. She peered around the foliage that surrounded her shady masonry hideaway. Her eyes swept over black and white paving stones and searched the facets of enormous marble fountains as they splashed quietly. They echoed the silence, which had become inexplicably eerie.

The back of her neck prickled as she bent once again to the soft intricate creation on the needles, which would adapt easily to the knitting machines in her small factory studio if only, she thought to herself, she could just get this last little aggravating problem worked out.

She sensed that someone was watching her. Quickly she looked around, annoyed that her concentration had been broken. She glanced sharply toward the narrow door leading into the library and then scanned again the garden's quaint little paths. Slowly, almost as if in the pantomime of a well-rehearsed character camouflaging a fearful uneasiness, she began to reach for her knitting bag. A shadow fell over her and a soft masculine voice with a hint of a growl addressed her.

"Your work is lovely, senorita."

Leslie's eyes met those of a richly handsome man and she immediately felt the stirring of an uncomfortable, outrageous response. He stood straight and tall, an awesome man probably in his early thirties, impeccably dressed. There was a combination of dash and arrogant gentleness about him that was decidedly unsettling, and his words were warm and resonant with the refined sounds of perfectly spoken Spanish. His eyes, as they continued to pierce her own, were dark pools of sensuous emotion firmly forged around centers of steel.

"Do you come here often?" he inquired, again in Spanish.

"*Sí,*" said Leslie honestly, relieved that her hysteria was unfounded, but disturbed that her heart was beating so rapidly.

"I also come here often," he said.

Leslie looked at him in confusion.

Seeing her discomfiture and confusion, he quickly sought to make amends. "I'm sorry," he said. "I'm Augustine Rivera Platos, one of the patrons of this museum. I didn't mean to disturb you, but not many people appreciate the gardens and my curiosity was aroused when I saw you here."

As he spoke his great hand reached out to gently cradle the tiny creation on Leslie's knitting needles. He gazed at her admiringly. "I was struck by the incredible beauty of the scene," he admitted. "Forgive me, but I felt that I had to speak to you."

Completely at a loss now, Leslie looked at him in sheer incredulity. His familiarity, in spite of his flowery compliments, was disturbing and she resented her indefinable primitive response to him as she struggled to breathe.

Evidently amused by her reaction he continued in an exaggerated courtly manner. "I sincerely apologize for my intrusion and the impropriety of my introduction. I can assure you," he said with a little smile, "my intentions are completely honorable. Perhaps," he went on a trifle intimately, "the whims of fate will be kind enough to allow us to meet again, another day, in a more appropriate way."

His voice still resembled a soft, gentle growl. His eyes sparkled beneath black waving hair accented by a pencil thin moustache, giving a distinct impression of a World War II movie idol. He gestured a tiny salute as he turned to leave her and walked away with the rhythmic grace born only to the natives of the Caribbean as suavely and silently as he had come. With his retreat, his parting colloquial words, *"Hasta luego,"* "until then," reverberated around Leslie in the classic stillness of the garden and left her feeling uneasy.

As she continued to watch his aristocratic back disappear through the door she realized her concentration was completely broken. She ruefully surveyed the tiny garment in her hands, which for some strange reason seemed to have taken on an extremely personal dimension. Her heart slowed to a normal beat and inexplicably she felt as though she were creating something for a child that she herself would cherish forever.

Unconsciously Leslie again assumed a classic pose as she bent over her work and the needles began to click. As the stitches flew across the needles she tried to comprehend exactly what had taken place during the encounter with the admittedly attractive stranger. Subconsciously she made a mental note to tuck his name away as she finished and gathered her things together.

Slowly she walked through the door, entering the museum library, and went past glass cases of primitive displays. She paused for a moment in front of them, remembering her plans to examine more of these artifacts at one of several Taino Indian archaeological sites in the island. Her sketches of these artifacts had stimulated ideas for innovative ski sweater designs and she was looking forward to pursuing that creative avenue.

Strolling down the long corridor that skirted the Sala Europa, lined with magnificent portraits from some of the greatest masters in both the French and English schools, Leslie came to the *Portrait of a Young Woman* by Gainsborough and stopped to examine it a little more closely. The rich young girl was flawlessly executed, vulnerably innocent while also exuding a coquettish sense of power. She was seemingly unaware that she was being admired, perhaps in a deeply sensuous way. Although obviously much older, Leslie suddenly felt a special communion with the young woman in the portrait, as if she too were that young again in a wonderful euphoric way. Thoughts of the dark aristocratic stranger seemed to intrude almost naturally as she recalled the way his eyes had perused her only moments before. A few steps farther on she glanced at a mother and child in a classical pose and felt a warm and happy response. She barely noticed two large dynamic statues in polychromed wood symbolizing the continents of Europe and America and the natural ties of the island to both, as she passed on to the entry. Its radiant fountain and pool and two curving, ethereal staircases were illumined in a giant effusion of natural light and never failed to make Leslie pause as the white Parthenon beauty of the building both enveloped her and left her with a miraculous sense of awe and inspiration.

A few moments later, feeling completely renewed, she was on the way to her small hand-knit factory, Los Tejidos de María. She had loved the sound of those Spanish words, which translated into the blunter English, Maria's Knits, assuming correctly that the Spanish name would give her designs a certain flair.

As her small compact car made its way down the wide four-lane expanse of Avenida Las Americas past the Catholic University and the modern Santa María church, she was grateful for the air conditioning that effectively buffered her from the broiling tropical heat of early summer. With a practiced motion she turned down a small crowded street, swung across Calle Villas and headed out of town on Highway 10 toward Adjuntas where her factory was located just across the Ponce District line.

She wrinkled her nose in distaste as she made her way through the perennial dust created by the huge Ponce Cement Company. As the traffic grew a little snarled on the curving road she honked her horn and joined in the traditional foray that usually accompanied these situations and was essential if one were to survive them. Her patience was wearing thin as a large van with a loudspeaker blared out its wares accompanied by strident, tinny music with an insistent beat.

Leslie was growing hot and weary. As she glanced in the rearview mirror her dark eyes, peering from classic, beautiful features indigenous with fiery Latin American beauty, snapped back in reflection and reminded her of the Puerto Rican legacy she had inherited from her mother. Only her expressive, deep blue eyes and quick New York accent gave any indication of her American father's heritage. Her small trim body fit comfortably in the tiny compact car and she gripped the wheel unconsciously as the stresses of the incessant traffic took their toll. She cursed herself for forgetting the time of day and the rush-hour traffic.

As she drove on past Las Delicias and neared the El Madrigal housing developments with stacks upon stacks of small concrete pill-box houses the traffic jam dissipated almost instantly. She noted the drive to the

Ponce Country Club and thought about her plans to play golf the next day. She visibly relaxed as she drove on up the twisted mountain road. Gradually the cooler moistness of tropical rain forest foliage enveloped her. She rounded a curve and confronted two monstrous pillars that secured a wrought-iron gate at the portal of a winding drive that led to the ancestral home of her mother's family. It sat there in all of its grandeur, a throwback to an almost forgotten colonial age. She thought fondly of her home with its wide verandas and large airy rooms and the huge mango and avocado trees that shaded it as she drove past continuing to her factory just a few miles farther up the road.

Suddenly in remorse she realized, as she glanced at her watch, her mother had been home all alone for the entire day. Leslie had been so engrossed in trying to solve the problem of her design while at the museum that she had skipped lunch, which her mother usually prepared.

Quickly, with little regard to safety or other traffic, she made a tight U turn on the narrow two-lane twisting road and zoomed back through the gates toward her home. She was instantly reminded of its general state of disrepair, but she nevertheless loved it.

Leslie stopped the car with a screech and ran past the sunken remains of what had once been a swimming pool, then through magnificent French doors that opened out on a flagstone patio.

"Mama," she called. "Mama! Where are you? I'm sorry I didn't get home for lunch." She was greeted by a resounding silence that momentarily sent a shudder through her. "Mama?" she called again.

Leslie was devoted to her mother in the best traditions of both her Anglo and Latin heritage. She had the wonderful good fortune of wise and loving parents who encouraged her to think independently and to pursue her inborn talents vigorously. At twenty-eight she was a well-rounded astute businesswoman and artist with a real flair for knit fashion design. She in turn was devoted to her parents, basking in the security of love and mutual respect so rare in most familial situations. Her life was almost idyllic until about a year and a half ago when her father had collapsed on a cold city street the victim of an instant fatal heart attack. His death had devastated both Leslie and her mother, but Mrs. Williams, always somewhat frail since Leslie's birth, had been beyond consolation.

Fearing desperately that she was going to lose her mother also, Leslie had jumped at the chance when she heard about the opportunities afforded by the Industrial Development Program sponsored by the Puerto Rican government, more familiarly known as Fomento.

She would never forget the day she had met Magna Ruiz and first learned about it. She had been attending a cocktail party following a show featuring her designs when the vivacious woman came up to her.

"Have you ever considered going into business for yourself?" she began.

Leslie looked at her, a bit stunned for just a second. "No," she said as she responded warmly to the lively aggressiveness of this woman with the unmistakable Spanish accent.

"Well, you should," she said emphatically, "and you should do it in Puerto Rico!"

"What!" exclaimed Leslie, aghast.

"Surely you've heard of our Operation Bootstrap. It matches investment dollars in new manufacturing enterprises and gives from ten to twenty years in tax exemption."

"Well, no," said Leslie, "but you know it's a funny thing. My mother is from there and we...."

Leslie smiled fondly as she remembered the details of the conversation.

"I'm the director of Fomento in the southwest part

of the island,'' Magna had said later after expressing her deep concern for Leslie's mother. ''You've already created a name for yourself with your designs. Why not cash in on the whole manufacturing process? You can't beat this deal....''

That was all it had taken to get Leslie started.

Magna was a feisty divorcée with two children who made frequent trips to New York to coordinate the activities of her office with the branch office in New York. She never missed an opportunity to recruit new enterprises for the program she directed. They had become friends due to their heritage ties initially, but Leslie soon found herself drawn to this fiery woman who was not only warm and supportive, but fiercely independent too.

Leslie came out of her momentary reverie as the emptiness of the house abruptly reminded her of her concern. Her mother and two other aunts were the last of a once powerful and aristocratic family in Ponce, the Villarongas, and this country house was one of three that had been left to her mother and sisters years before. Leslie's father had insisted that they keep it, always remembering their dream to retire and spend their remaining years in warm, balmy Puerto Rico.

''Mama?'' Leslie called upon her commonsense to bring her momentary panic under control. Her mother had to be there someplace. Then Leslie saw the note on the huge dining room table that sat majestically beneath a great ornate chandelier.

Leslie Marie, my darling,
  Gerald is here from New York and I've taken him to the factory. We'll meet you there.
                                        Love, Mama

Tears of gratefulness sprang to Leslie's eyes. Perhaps her mother was at last beginning to take an interest in living again. Leslie had hoped that the combination of a change of scene and the return to her childhood home as well as active involvement in her small factory would help her mother to cope with her loss. Magna had been very sure that this was just the thing to revitalize her.

"You have to remember, Leslie, that although your mother loved your father very much and was totally dependent upon him, at heart she is a very strong woman."

"What do you mean?" Leslie had asked.

"Well, she comes from a very prominent family in Ponce. I'm sure they must have had plans for her. It must have taken a lot of courage to marry your father."

"I don't know," said Leslie. "Mama never talked about it. It seemed like she and Papa were just always one person. He was so strong and indomitable. We thought he was indestructible."

She swallowed as tears welled in her eyes.

"It will be good for both of you to come home to Ponce," said Magna as she patted her hand reassuringly. "You will have a huge family to support you."

Leslie had brightened at that. As an only child, while she had never felt any real need or desire to seek additional affection, she had always envied her friends who had brothers and sisters. For the first time in her life, particularly since the loss of her father, the thought of a family, her own children, began to appeal to her, but first she had to convince her mother that life was still worth living.

"Mama," she had said excitedly when the first sketches of the plant were made, "what do you think of these?"

"Oh, they're fine, dear, but really I know nothing about such things...."

Leslie sighed as she looked at the lifeless shell her mother was becoming.

"Mama," she had said again with great anticipation a

few months later, "we're going to Ponce to check out the family house and begin the construction of the plant. If you like, you can stay with Tía Isabel while I make all of the arrangements for our move."

Her mother had smiled brightly at the thought of seeing her sisters and other family members, but so far she had shown little more than polite interest through the months of construction, none at all when the machines and yarns came in and Leslie began training her workers. She took a perfunctory interest in the restoration of the house and listened politely as Leslie talked about the details of the new business, but she ultimately devoted herself entirely to Leslie's needs and nothing more. Now out of the blue her mother, on her own, had left the house and gone with Gerald to the factory. It was a good sign. Leslie was sure of it.

Quickly Leslie turned and raced back to the car and drove down the rutted drive in joyous unison with the put-putting enthusiasm of her little car as it bounced back to the twisting Highway 10. She whizzed around the curves careful to honk her horn while braking, then accelerating in the middle. It was a learned technique more appropriate for the Indy 500, but it allowed a car to get over these roads a good deal faster than the careful creeping speed the more prudent driver might embrace. Within moments she pulled up to her small factory.

She burst through the doors, racing past her secretary, Juanita, and literally tumbled into the great studio room as she stumbled over a newly arrived shipment of yarn. The soft whir of the electrically operated hand knitting machines and accompanying chatter of her workers greeted her. They were all surrounded by a great riot of colors protruding from the well-organized shelves of yarn that lined the walls from floor to ceiling.

"Mama? Gerald? Where are you?" She glanced

around, a joyous look of expectation on her face. To Leslie's surprise it was more than rewarded when she saw her mother in animated conversation with Leslie's aunt, who was an expert in crochet. They were arguing over the proper way to weave a garment together.

"Looks like maybe a little less doting on your part might help to bring your mother out of her shell."

Leslie whirled around. "Gerald," she cried. "When did you get in? I thought you were arriving tomorrow."

"Well, I guess I just got itchy feet and couldn't wait to see what you had accomplished down here."

He stood nonchalantly with his tie loosened and sport jacket flung over one shoulder, obviously an instant victim of the heat and humidity that affected even the most seasoned and acclimated person this time of the year. His tawny blond hair was ruffled and fell over his brow, giving his blue eyes a mischievous look.

As a well-known market consultant in the New York fashion world, Gerald Masters was an old friend—and probably came close to being the brother Leslie never had. Theirs was one of those rare and wonderful relationships between a man and a woman that shared all of the security and intimacy of warm friendship but had never been clouded by a physical attraction or passion. They had shared many joys and sorrows, including the pathos of lost loves, and often sought each other's approval whenever a current flame seemed to hint at something serious.

He was here now to see Leslie's new designs fully ready to take them back and promote them in all of the large department stores nationwide while also designing a sales program for her.

"You'll never believe how I got over here." He laughed as he gave her a warm comradely hug. "My Spanish, as you know, is terrible and the telephones here are outrageous so I decided to wing it and get here myself. I had an extra day and couldn't resist spending it with you and Doña María—you know how much I love your mother. Anyway I flew into San Juan and was then directed to Air Ponce. When I said 'wing it' I didn't know that's what I might be doing literally. Those little planes have only about twenty seats down each side like an oversize crop duster or something and then we literally bumped and dived over those mountains to the Ponce Airport. When I could open my eyes to look out, it was beautiful. The sun shining on those mountains with their dips and hollows must create every feasible shade of green. It's all perfectly blended and harmonious except for the wild colors of bougainvilleas, flamboyant, and Lord knows what else, but my God..."

Leslie was doubled over with laughter as she motioned him to continue.

"Then I looked for a taxi and somehow I wound up on a *publico* and that man drove worse than the pilot flew. The car was packed with people, but he knew exactly where to go. Everyone in town seems to know who you are, so here I am!"

"Oh, you poor thing." Leslie laughed as she wiped tears of merriment from her eyes. She could just imagine Gerald's reactions and gave thanks for his wonderful sense of humor.

"When I arrived, there was your mother worrying over your not being home for lunch. When she said you were in the museum working on a design I knew you might be gone for a while so, I hope you don't mind, I just insisted that she bring me up here. We called and had Juanita come and get us. Your mom has been over there with Doña Isabel ever since and I think she is about to take over the place!"

"Oh, Gerald," Leslie cried, "it's wonderful. This is the first time I've seen Mama like her old self since—"

She looked over toward her mother, who was so absorbed in her activity that she had yet to notice Leslie's arrival. Leslie's Aunt Isabel returned the glance warmly and gave Leslie a big wink. Clasping her hands in joy, Leslie went toward her mother and enfolded her in a great warm hug. "Oh, Mama, it's so wonderful to see you here. Tía Isabel and I can use your help."

"Well, I should think so," she responded with a twinkle in her eye, something Leslie had not seen in months. "Isabel is weaving this entirely wrong. I hope to heaven she hasn't been teaching the workers this way."

Leslie reached down for the garment and saw immediately what her aunt had done. She had deliberately used a grossly wrong technique to bait her sister's interest and it had worked. Leslie met her aunt's warm smiling eyes and gave her a grateful hug. This was just the type of thing the gentle, but firm matriarch of the family would do. She turned away before her mother could see how emotionally affected she was.

"Okay, Leslie, my sweet," Gerald said as he teasingly addressed his friend in his own personal way, "let's see those fabulous designs I've been hearing so much about."

Leslie laughed and grabbed his hand as she pulled him toward her designing studio and showroom. When they walked through the door it was like entering another world. The room was cool and serene in shades of blue and green accented with white. There was a well-lighted, comfortable area for designing and drafting in one corner and then a small partition that shielded it from a wide sunny showroom with comfortable rattan chairs and bright gleaming terrazzo floors.

Suddenly almost shy, Leslie hesitated before one showcase. "Well, really I'm just getting ready to start the adult line. I'm planning a trip while you're here to research some more of those Taino Indian designs that you liked for the ski sweater line and I've got several dresses and suits on the drawing board, but I'm just finishing up this project that for some reason completely captivated my imagination for a while."

She was pulling small garments from the case and laying them out lovingly. They were exquisitely made, beautifully created baby clothes.

"Why, these are...these are for babies!" Gerald exclaimed in startled confusion.

Leslie looked away, suddenly very self-conscious. "I know," she said. "I just seemed to have this compulsion to work with them. The women here, you know, love to make baby things and it seemed a good and simple way to train my workers. The results are so quick and then they turned out to be so much fun.... I just couldn't help myself."

Still astonished, Gerald sought to immediately make amends when he saw her confusion. "Forgive me, Leslie honey, these are wonderful. I'm not much on babies, but even I can tell that they are unique. I guess it just seems so out of character for you to work in this medium. Why, you've never shown any inclination at all to work with children's designs. But as always," he ended exuberantly, "your timing is perfect. Babies are very big and back in fashion again. All of the career women who delayed motherhood are suddenly having their families. They've planned everything very carefully and they want the very best for their little bundles. These will go over fabulously. I'll have to have a sample of each. This line alone could make a fortune."

His smile was mirrored on Leslie's face when suddenly her secretary burst into the room after discreetly knocking.

"Doña Leslie, forgive me for interrupting," Juanita said nervously, "but Senor Augustine Rivera Platos is outside in my office. He says he is a shareholder in Los Tejidos de María and he wishes to see Mr. Leslie Williams."

Chapter Two

"Who *is* he?" Leslie exclaimed. She was breathless as she recognized the name of the dark stranger in the museum. Her body was in the grip of a shaky inner trembling she struggled to conceal. She peered around the door and immediately affirmed her suspicions.

"Why, he is *the* Don Augustine Rivera Platos from one of the oldest families in Ponce," said Juanita. She nervously tapped the steno pad she had picked up in her confusion.

Leslie managed in those seconds to arrange her expression into a facsimile of polite interest, but not without a struggle and not before Gerald and her secretary exchanged puzzled glances.

"But what does he mean, *Mr.* Leslie Williams? Surely he can't be serious!"

"*Bueno,* I don't know, Doña Leslie," said Juanita. "I just know he is one of our most prominent men and he says he is a shareholder in the company."

As Leslie stepped to the door to take another look at the now familiar face she reflected briefly over her decision to incorporate her small company. Could this man, indeed, be one of those shareholders?

"Well, Juanita, show him in," she said with alacrity. "Take him to my office. Excuse me for a moment, Gerald, while I get this cleared up."

Leslie willed herself to sound calm as Gerald nodded

his ready assent, but the transition of her emotions was not lost on him. This agitated young woman struggling for sophisticated calm was totally new to his experience.

She was also totally new to Leslie herself. As she smoothed her clothes and prepared to greet this unsettling man she labored to control a bad case of stage fright. She forced herself to walk slowly and took several deep breaths as she finally reached for the door of her office and opened it with reasonably restored confidence. Her entry resembled that of an aristocratic chatelaine whose estate had just been invaded by unwelcome forces.

Her decision that day to wear her lustrous raven hair in a low chignon further enhanced the image. Classic high-heeled pumps and a tailored skirt gave her extra stature that for the first time in her life she felt she needed. She drew herself to her full height and forced herself to smile graciously as Augustine turned and stopped in midmotion. He was completely astounded when he saw who she was. He made an immediate recovery and greeted her in English.

"I beg your pardon, Mrs. Williams. I had no idea that your husband was connected with this company. What an incredible coincidence!"

"I am *not* Mrs. Williams and I do *not* have a husband," said Leslie coolly. "I am *Miss* Leslie Williams and this is *my* company."

Her eyes bore into his and challenged him to patronize her in any way. He returned her glance in momentary fiery confusion and then most assuredly gave in to patronizing amusement as he responded expansively.

"I see I have managed to annoy you again. I am, of course, amazed that *you* are responsible for the entire operation of such an intricate business."

Leslie looked at him sharply. "Are you implying that I'm not capable of managing this company?" As she spoke she realized she was probably making a strategic mistake, but she was annoyed—to such a degree that all of her momentary intimidation of a few moments before completely disappeared. "Since you're a shareholder, if you've taken the time to read the prospectus you should be familiar with my management capabilities—or were they impressive to you only because you assumed I was a man?"

Her eyes snapped and challenged him to answer.

"Indeed not," he responded calmly. His eyes raked over her roguishly and he took in every detail of her heaving breasts.

Leslie stared at him in wary silence as she visibly forced herself to calm down and meet his address on a more rational basis.

He continued unruffled except for a tiny clench of his jaw. "The prospectus is very impressive and I invest only in promising ventures, but since I have many holdings in the garment industry I had little curiosity about the actual product until I saw you knitting this afternoon. Believe me, I'm sorry that my clumsy blundering mistake about your gender has annoyed you so."

He had slipped back into Spanish almost unconsciously as his patience began to thin over Leslie's lack of reaction to his apology. His voice took on a steely tone. "You really seem to be a little oversensitive to my introduction. Have you reason to be so uncomfortable about the inquiry of a legitimate shareholder in this company?" His eyes regarded her coldly.

Fully aware of the importance of answering this challenge properly she was all business now as she responded in a deadly voice.

"There will be an annual report at the appropriate time. You are, of course, welcome to examine our records at any time."

She had enunciated her last words in staccato bursts

and inwardly chastised herself for overreacting. She really didn't know what had gotten into her. For some reason she was overly annoyed and bothered by the very presence of this man who truthfully had done absolutely nothing to merit such a reaction. Could she still be resentful over her initial hysteria when she had first become aware of his presence in the museum? It had been a frightening, momentary feeling that left her vulnerable and defenseless, ultimately resulting in her being totally intimidated when he made his presence known. She realized in sudden intuition that she was somewhat fearful of him while at the same time strangely attracted by his very arrogance. She comprehended at last that she was in the presence of true aristocratic Latin machismo.

Then sensing at last just how ridiculous this entire scene was, Leslie extended her hand and displayed her brightest smile as she sought to amend her irrational behavior.

"You know, you're right. I think I owe you an apology. I *am* being a little oversensitive." Leslie had to restrain herself from visually imagining herself behind a seductive Spanish fan ready to click castanets.

Augustine was clearly amazed at this sudden change in her demeanor. "No apologies are necessary," he said, extending his hand to meet hers.

His hands were warm and strong as he used both to envelop one of her own. Leslie felt his power and strength flowing to her and for a moment she clung to him, not wishing to release the strength she held captive there. His eyes met hers and she felt a special communion. She forced herself to avert her gaze as his soft words dispelled the feeling and returned her to reality.

"We have both apparently been the victim of some unfortunate misunderstanding that would best be forgotten."

He spoke with a soft humor and charm that touched

her from head to toe as she felt her blood warming throughout her body. She was momentarily flustered as she again met his gaze and quickly glanced away.

"Well, yes, perhaps so," she said, forcing a contrived cheerfulness into her voice, "but now that you're here let me show you around."

"By all means." Augustine moved gallantly to the door to assume the gentlemanly role of ushering her properly from the room. When they emerged, Leslie was surprised to see Gerald stationed close by, an expression of troubled concern obvious on his face.

"Leslie?" he questioned while his eyes silently inquired as to her well-being.

"Gerald," she said in an overzealous greeting, "I want you to meet Senor Augustine Rivera Platos."

The two men seemed to instinctively square off as each took the other's measure.

"Gerald is a marketing consultant, Senor Rivera. He and I are old friends as well as business partners."

"I see," said Augustine, switching easily back to English for Gerald's benefit. The inflection of his words, however, intimated something deeper. It was almost a paternal insinuation and suddenly Leslie found herself growing impatient with both of the men and their assumptions that she was some object in need of protection.

She spoke brusquely as she took both of their arms and began to guide them to the great studio room of the factory. "Shall we go, gentlemen?" They went down a short hallway and then stepped again into the studio filled with the sounds of busy knitting machines.

As they moved among the clatter of machines and voices the workers grew a little hushed. Over and over again Augustine's name was whispered and recognized around the room as the workers covertly watched his progress with Leslie and Gerald.

"You see," said Leslie as she motioned to one of the

workers to demonstrate, "these machines can knit one row in the blink of an eyelash." As she spoke the worker touched the electric pedal and sent the carriage whirring down through the designated needles. "I see," said Augustine somewhat musingly. "Then these machines are vastly different from those found in a standard knitting operation?"

"Yes," Leslie replied. "We're creating unique, high-fashion knits that will be exclusive but affordable. We think that requires the versatility of these studio machines."

As they continued on Leslie found herself growing annoyed again as Augustine continued to question, musing now and then over the validity of her concepts. Although he demonstrated a polite business demeanor time after time he parried words with her thrust for thrust.

Finally she spoke in exasperation. "Surely you understand," she said tightly, "the distinction between a studio factory and a garment mill. Our purpose is to produce classics that will be identified with our company."

"An admirable pursuit," said Augustine, "but one that may be a little naive."

She managed to maintain a calm exterior, but her eyes flashed defiantly and indicated her intense displeasure. More infuriating though, she felt powerless to defuse her emotions and grew inwardly more angry as she prepared to grin and bear it.

Seeing Leslie's distress, Gerald moved to rescue her from her volatile reactions. "Actually, Senor Rivera, my firm researched Leslie's proposal for this business and our studies indicated a very innovative concept that should succeed in every way."

Leslie looked at him gratefully.

Although Augustine was listening patiently, his expression was a noncommittal mask that managed to shroud even his smoldering eyes. He continued to exude a diabolical inquisitiveness.

"But you promote this as a 'hand-knit' factory. Is that not somewhat deceptive?"

"A point well taken," said Leslie as her eyes met his in an open challenge. "I can appreciate your concern, but all of our products are labeled 'studio knit,' even though," she said as she reached for a garment piece that was descending through the center of the needle beds to demonstrate her last point, "all of the pieces are hand woven together rendering them nearly seamless and perfectly handmade to the naked eyes."

Leslie looked at him pointedly. She was weary of this presumptuous man's ability to seesaw her emotions as though they were trifles to be bandied about. She purposely introduced her own note of arrogance. "I hope I have satisfactorily relieved any anxieties you may have with reference to our integrity." She drew herself up and continued patronizingly. "I can understand how a person of your standing in the community might be concerned."

She had sought to dismiss him and ended up pandering to him again. She was now seriously beginning to resent this man's influence upon her behavior.

Again Augustine looked at her in patronizing amazement and then unaccountably changed the subject completely. "You seem to have a real fondness for these machines," he said, his voice softening again to a low growl, "but when I encountered you this afternoon you were knitting by hand."

"Yes," she said with a hesitant smile, a victim of his charm in spite of herself. "Usually I create my initial designs by hand and the museum is a wonderful place to work out problems. I have a feeling though that in the future I'll be calling upon my latest acquisition."

Her face registered a sly little smile as she began to maneuver the two men to a small section in her design area that was also easily accessible to the business offices.

"But of course," said Augustine as he stepped into the adjoining room and gazed at her small office computer. "Most small businesses are using these today. I'm *very* glad to see that you have one."

Again Leslie's head snapped up. She observed him keenly, but she prevented herself from reading more into his comments than was actually there, acutely aware now of his ability to bait her. She forced herself to continue on enthusiastically. "Not only does it have the capabilities to do all of our bookkeeping, but it's a wonderful tool when I'm designing. All I need now are the body measurements and the initial sketch to create a pattern."

"Why, that's fantastic," said Gerald, honestly impressed.

"Yes, I'm sure it will be a big help to you in every way," said Augustine, "especially with all of its mathematical abilities. Women often find math to be tedious."

Leslie stood next to the computer beaming, but her smile faded. She was very proud of her factory and felt a wonderful sense of satisfaction whenever she walked through it. Not until this encounter with Augustine had anyone challenged the power she felt as the result of her accomplishments, but then, not until this encounter had she truly been aware of it or in fact ever defined it. Now she was acutely aware of it and felt a real sense of anxiety as though Augustine with his feigned superiority was trying to steal it from her. And yet she was strangely affected by him and felt intuitively that his recognition of her talents was terribly important. It left her feeling vulnerable and that made her nervous. She struggled to regain her usual sunny optimism, refusing to allow this insensitive man to further intimidate her.

Augustine was moving unaccompanied around the designing area into the showroom. He stopped in front of the showcase holding the baby clothes Leslie had shown so proudly to Gerald only a short time before. "I noticed," he said, as he gazed at her expectantly, "that all of the machines in the studio seemed to be producing small items similar to what you were working on in the museum."

"Yes," said Leslie, "we plan to produce a full spectrum of knits including baby items."

"Baby clothes," he said, nodding his approval. "How very appropriate." He looked her over with a satisfied gleam in his eyes. "Your sketches are very good too," he said as he leafed though them.

This was apparently the first thing from the entire tour of the plant that had really impressed him. "I can see," he went on, "with proper guidance that this business *is* very promising. With your feminine designing abilities and the selection of appropriate business acquaintances," he elaborated, "most promising indeed." He had a satisfied paternal smile on his face. "You can be sure of my continued interest in this enterprise from this day on. I have other connections who might also be of help."

I don't think so, thought Leslie to herself. *No! Not ever.* She could feel her agitation growing.

Gerald also sensed her disgust and anger and gave his complete sympathy. He looked at her questioningly and offered his most understanding glance, but she did not catch it. Her mind was seething a hundred miles away as Augustine continued to wander around the room.

Leslie had never shown the slightest interest or inclination to embrace the women's movement. She had never truthfully felt the need for it, but suddenly she had a devastating insight into its founding impetus. She recalled her deference to Augustine during the office confrontation when she had assumed the coy "senorita" role to smooth his ruffled feathers and her endurance of covert insinuations throughout this ridiculous charade. In an experience totally new to her she suddenly felt a rage over her need to react in this way, to this man, that she could not repress. How dare he categorize her so smugly! Before she knew it she heard her own cold words addressing Augustine across the small expanse of the room.

"Senor Rivera, I really don't think that you and I have anything to discuss that would be constructive to my business. I think we should discuss the sale of your shares in my company."

Both Gerald and Augustine registered astounded looks at Leslie's baffling, out of context outburst. She completely ignored their reactions as her rage demanded further expression. She was just about to order Augustine from the premises when her mother was suddenly at her elbow exclaiming in agitated surprise.

"Leslie, *mija* forgive me for interrupting, but I simply must know. The face...the name.... I must ask! Is this indeed, Senor Augustine Rivera Platos, the son of Augustine Rivera Gonzalez?"

"It is indeed, most gracious doña," said Augustine, breaking in expansively and obviously relieved by her interruption. He had intuitively attached the title of respect to her, surmising with her colloquial use of *"mija"* that she was Leslie's mother. "You must be— Of course! *La Familia Villaronga,* the beautiful María. The love my father never forgot!"

Leslie's face could in no way adequately express the shock this revelation caused her. She was speechless as her mother and Augustine swept them all along in their mutual discovery. Gerald was as disconcerted as Leslie simply because of the transition from English to Spanish, but soon joined in the happy melee, which was, by its very nature, infectious.

"In spite of his love and devotion to my mother," Augustine continued as he addressed Leslie's mother, "my father always carried you privately in his heart. He spoke of you to me in his later years just before his untimely death a few years ago. This is indeed a pleasure, a wonderful, coincidental pleasure."

Could this be? Leslie thought to herself desperately. Could her mother actually have been romantically tied to the father of this impossible man?

Leslie came out of her shock just in time to hear her mother enthusiastically inviting Augustine to a party she had apparently just decided to hostess on the next Saturday night in Gerald's honor. "You will, of course," Leslie heard her mother finish in simpering enthusiasm, "bring your fiancée, Philomena Munoz Villa. I read in the newspaper only recently of your engagement. I wondered then if you were—" She stopped then, a little flustered and embarrassed, as she met Leslie's shocked and accusing eyes.

"But of course, Doña María," he said. "I'm honored by your invitation. Until then"—he glanced at his fine gold watch—"I shall be thinking of you often." He spoke to both Leslie and her mother. "I'm sure Philomena will also be happy to accompany me."

His speech was flawlessly suave and served only to further ignite Leslie's feelings of rage. With the mention of Philomena she suddenly felt an inexplicable sense of revulsion bordering on betrayal. How very like him, she seethed to herself, the perfect Latin gentleman feigning roguish interest in all of the feminine gender while his faithful, all sacrificing fiancée waits quietly in the wings.

Leslie would have none of it, she fumed, none of it, and she would see to it that he stayed completely away from her business. He was after all only a shareholder and at the bottom line this was *her* company. Her eyes were fiery and defiant as he walked out the door. She had one unflinching thought as his artistocratic back disappeared. She *must* buy back those shares. She wasn't about to allow him to interfere or have any part of her business.

Chapter Three

Leslie couldn't believe that her mother had actually invited that reprehensible man to their home, but it didn't matter. She would find a way to stop this, but she had to do it without hurting her mother. She had waited too long to see Doña María begin to enjoy her life again and she didn't have the heart to upset her now.

Why, she asked herself vehemently, did he have to show up just when her mother was beginning to live again? Why was Leslie's own well-planned, well-managed life suddenly so complicated? She sighed as she heard Augustine's car leave and vowed to find a way to prevent the devastation his introduction promised. She shuddered to think of him interfering in her factory operation as she took Gerald's arm and headed wearily back toward her office.

The entire plant was quiet now except for Doña María's excited chatter with Leslie's Tía Isabel. Leslie felt a sense of annoyance and chastised herself for not being glad about her mother's excitement.

"I don't know about you," Leslie said to Gerald, "but I'd like a glass of wine, which I'm sure must be a terribly unhealthy indication, but honestly that man is enough to drive anyone to drink."

She smiled up at him ruefully, hoping his usual sense of humor would come to her rescue and save her from the terrible depression that was rapidly descending upon her.

"You're not kidding," he said with a boyish, affected enthusiasm. "That guy is not only from the eighteenth-century school of chauvinism, he's practically the keeper of the light in a Cro-Magnon cave. You'd better be careful or he'll be trying to give you something to use those baby clothes on."

"Oh, Gerald." Leslie laughed, grateful for his humor and friendship. "How silly you are."

"Maybe so," said Gerald, "but I swear I've never seen such a gleam in a man's eye at the mention of baby clothes. Now, personally, I'd rather visualize something under one of those sexy sweaters you're designing or better yet, how about a knit bikini with a ravel in it?"

"You're too much," she laughed again, her usual good spirits completely restored. "There are times when I think you definitely have a one-track mind and half the time it's off its trolly!"

"Yeah, well, I'll bet you a dollar to a doughnut you haven't seen the last of ol' Augustine there. He's definitely got plans for you and this place—Philomena or no Philomena. Seriously," he said, all laughter gone from his voice, "you'd better watch him carefully. I wonder just how many shares of stock he does have in your company."

A few moments later as Leslie filled narrow glasses with chilled wine from the small refigerator she kept in the showroom for her clients Gerald's last question echoed in her mind and she made a mental note to check out that very thing.

As she reentered her tastefully furnished office her mother's lively chatter once again reminded her of this unwelcome complication. "Mama," she said as she broke into the schoolgirlish giggles of her mother and aunt, "surely you can't be serious that that man's father was a serious love interest of yours?'' There was a shaky, strident edge to her laughing challenge that she could not totally conceal. Her mother, ever perceptive to her daughter's emotions, was instantly concerned.

"Leslie, *mija*, forgive me. I didn't mean to upset you."

"You aren't upsetting me, Mama," Leslie said a little too quickly. "I'm so happy to see you beginning to enjoy yourself and it's wonderful that you've decided to give a party. I guess I was just a little amazed at the coincidence of your knowing—"

"Mija," said Leslie's mother as she turned her daughter gently to face her while Isabel and Gerald looked on. "You are feeling protective of your father's memory and I'm happy to see that you care so much, but Augustine's father was once a great friend of mine— much as Gerald is to you. When we were children Augustine was always there caring for me and protecting me."

Her eyes were shining as she settled into a chair and the memory swept her away. "I remember when we started to school, to kindergarten. You know the children have always worn uniforms to school here, and he was so handsome in his khaki shorts and tie, but oh, so bad."

She gave a little sigh and shook her head, but as she looked into Leslie's eyes, Leslie could almost see her mother's face growing younger with the memory. She met Tía Isabel's eyes and watched her nod her head. The eyes told her to stay quiet and listen; this was good for Doña María.

"Had our teacher not been a nun who was used to handling the devil himself, Augustine would have been totally unendurable." She smiled. "But she handled him. Oh, but she was strong." Another sigh escaped her. "But she was gentle too. We always had to take a nap on a little rug we had brought from home. The first day I was afraid and began to cry because I was away from my mama. Oh, I will never forget.... Augustine grew quiet and began to watch me, then he rolled up his rug and came over next to me.''

She laughed and there was a definite twinkle in her eyes. ''You know, of course, the boys were not allowed to sleep with the girls.''

They all smiled.

''But he would have it no other way,'' she went on, ''and from that day on Augustine was my protector. We were inseparable. I depended on him for everything, and you know''—a touch of pride in her voice—''many of our teachers in later years felt that I was responsible for the kindness and chivalry Augustine developed. Oh, he was something—totally impossible one moment and then a well of kindness the next. He could never stand to see anything or anyone suffer. It would enrage him into an angry defense.''

Doña María looked around a little self-consciously as her fingers created a pleat in her skirt. ''I have a feeling,'' she said softly, ''that the Augustine we met is just like him.''

Leslie could feel herself growing increasingly uncomfortable as her mother continued with her contemplation.

''As we grew older there was talk of marriage, and our families would have wished that that should happen. It would have been an impressive alliance. Our children would have been Rivera Villarongas. For a while we did discuss it, but we were very young. Then I got an independent streak—I don't know where it came from—and I went away to school in New York,'' she said as she returned fully to the present. ''I met your father and never thought of another man again. Seeing Augustine was almost like seeing the son of my brother and I feel a close tie to him.''

There were tears in her eyes and Leslie could not bear to see her mother suffer in any way. Surely this one additional encounter with Augustine at a family party would not hurt her. When her mother was a little stronger she would find a tactful way to exclude him from their lives. For the moment though she wasn't going to trouble her mother with the infuriating details of her earlier encounter with Augustine in the factory and her fears of his intentional interference in her business affairs.

"Well, *mija*," Leslie's mother continued enthusiastically, "we must begin. We have a great deal to do before the party."

"I guess we do," said Leslie. "This is going to be just the usual word-of-mouth, informal gathering, I assume?"

"Of course," said Isabel, chiming in. "We want Gerald to have a good time while he is here so he must meet the entire family."

Leslie's and Gerald's glances met in perplexed astonishment and then they both broke into laughter. "Well, I guess," said Leslie as she now began to truly appreciate the sparkle that had returned to her mother, "Gerald, you are definitely going to get a dose of the local culture. I hope you're ready for this."

"Ready and willing," he said as he began to maneuver all of them toward the door. "But right now I'm looking forward to the grand tour of this famous Villaronga estate!" They laughed as they bundled into the two small cars belonging to Leslie and her aunt and headed for the Villaronga estate a few kilometers away.

Leslie awoke the next morning feeling a wonderful sense of luxurious laziness. She had decided last evening to indulge in something she had not done for a long time: She was taking the day off. Hearing this, her mother had quickly seized the opportunity to commandeer the car so she could shop for the party, and before Leslie knew what was happening she had talked Gerald into chauffeuring her.

Leslie was nearly overwhelmed by her mother's sudden emotional recovery. Doña María had come home last evening, made a few strategic phone calls, and quickly set into motion the foundation for the party invitations. It looked as though there would be a general outpouring of the entire family.

Feeling the need to sort through her emotions of the day before, Leslie was glad to have a day to herself. Gerald had always enjoyed her mother's company and was delighted with this chance to sample the local scene, although Leslie had warned him that except for the Spanish language the stores and shopping centers were identical to those stateside.

"Great," he had said with his unfailing humor, "but you can't tell me that Doña María is not also familiar with the market I've heard so much about and the town plaza. I'm sure," he said, giving the older woman a comradely hug, "she can show me some interesting sights. Truthfully I don't think it will hurt you at all to rest up a little. You look a little tired to me."

Leslie smiled. "I think you're right. I could use a little time to just think. I really appreciate this."

"No problem," Gerald said, "but there is one little catch. I'll expect a candlelight dinner with that famous fricassee of yours when we return."

"You've got it," she said as she gave him a playful swat when he went through the door. Isabel had agreed to drop him off at the Holiday Inn on the western outskirts of town. Leslie was again momentarily sorry that so few of the rooms in the house were habitable, but on the other hand it was probably best to avoid the gossip that his staying here might create. There were times when she missed the free and easy ways of New York.

Then on the other hand there were times when she was appalled by the current moral permissiveness with its own unique pressures and restrictions. She had basically always respected her parents and their values. They had given her no reason not to, and ultimately she felt that was the more prudent way to live.

Leslie continued to think of her parents fondly as she pulled on leisure clothes. It was becoming less painful now to think about her father and she often enjoyed reminiscing about her happy and secure childhood. She had never honestly had to deal with any real stress or tragedy until the past year. The confidence she had enjoyed since childhood had carried her through the first bumpy years of her career and it still seemed to sustain her adequately throughout the confusion and upheaval resulting from her decision to begin her own business. She had felt vibrant and alive and supremely satisfied with the entire operation until yesterday when the appearance of Augustine Rivera had drastically challenged her serenity.

The thought of him triggered her memory and she stepped to the phone and dialed the number of her New York stockbroker.

"Harold," she said a few seconds later as the direct dial signals clicked through, "I was wondering if you could check the status of my account. I've had some rather unsettling—"

"Funny that you should call," he said. "We just got something in from the SEC about a large block of your stock. Hold on a second and I'll call it up."

Leslie waited patiently as she mentally pictured him operating the computer console on his desk.

"Damn!" she heard him utter and pulled the phone away from her ear. "Would you believe," he went on in disgust, "this thing is down again!"

"What do you mean?" asked Leslie.

"The computer's on the blink," he said, "but listen,

this is important and I'll get back to you. I can't quite remember the particulars from the top of my head.''

"Well, does the name Augustine Rivera mean anything?'' she asked with a bit of a sinking sensation.

"No, can't say that it does," Harold said, his voice still obviously tinged with annoyance over the computer breakdown, "but your monthly statement is on the way out. Seems to me like it had something to do with a conglomerate.... Can I get back to you?''

"Sure," said Leslie, "but I'm not in the office today.''

"I'll catch you first thing in the morning," Harold said. "In the meantime watch for that statement.''

"Will do," said Leslie a little uneasily, but then she had learned what she wanted to know. The mention of Augustine's name didn't seem to represent any sort of threat, although something about the conglomerate didn't seem to sit right either.

"You're paranoid," she said firmly as she hung up the phone. She decided it was time to start to recoup some of her earlier serenity and take a walk through the surrounding hills and valleys with their dense green foliage. As she left the screened veranda of the house and skipped down two flights of wide concrete steps, Augustine Rivera again occupied her thoughts.

Leslie had never given much thought to the men in her mother's heritage although it was one subject her mother had been articulate about, speaking often of their alleged double standard and the expected submissiveness of the Latin women. Certainly Magna had had plenty to say about it, Leslie recalled ruefully. Her friend was invectively derisive of her former husband who had expected her to accept his penchant for a mistress or two.

"That scum," Magna had said venomously when she and Leslie were at lunch a month or two after their first meeting and Leslie was really seriously considering the Fomento program. "Do you know he had the gall to suggest that we stay together for the family and the children!"

Her eyes had snapped as she looked at Leslie and lowered her voice. "You know I watched my mother suffer through each of my father's affairs—she had no choice. Divorce was a total disgrace then and women were expected to put up with them, but no more," she had said vehemently. "The modern Puerto Rican women are just like their sisters in the States. Years ago we began to educate ourselves and we have a high ratio of doctors, lawyers, and other professional women, but even if we are housewives and mothers we don't stand for this anymore."

Leslie had looked at her friend and couldn't resist a bit of fun. "But I always heard that Latin men are so fiery, yet so charming," she had said teasingly.

"Ah, that they are," said Magna. "I will always love Felipe.... I can't resist him, but I won't," she said firmly, "put up with such nonsense!"

"You mean you still...?"

"Oh, no, no, no," said Magna with a wave. "I am strong. I have my needs, believe me, but when I knew for sure he would never change I divorced him immediately and when I did I broke my heart!"

Leslie had looked at her friend in astonishment. The other woman returned her gaze sadly. "I will always love him," said Magna sorrowfully, "no matter what other relationships might come my way, but I have to think of my self-respect and my children. I live a very respectable life in Ponce, but believe me, my dear, take my advice. Come to Puerto Rico and start your business. It's a wonderful place to live and work, but never, never get involved with a Latin man. They'll break your heart every time."

But in spite of her mother's comments and Magna's caustic bias, Leslie had frankly run into little opposition or surprise from the government officials and business community at large when she first initiated her project; all of the men had proved to be perfect gentlemen, showing honest respect for her talents.

Perhaps that was why this entire chauvinistic encounter with Senor Rivera, she said to herself with exaggerated emphasis, had been so shocking and infuriating.

As she walked on in the moist haze Leslie was grateful for her loose fitting cotton clothes, but soon realized she should have covered her legs as the *mimis*, a particularly annoying and vindictive tiny mosquito indigenous to the island, began to cause her acute discomfort. As she waved the insects away though, she was enthralled with the vivid greens and bright splashes of color that surrounded her. She recognized many ferns and plants growing naturally that were more familiar to her as hothouse ornamentals in the north. Wide plantain leaves waved gaily in the breeze and their tattered pieces tickled her face when the persistent breeze blew them in her path. She paused as she recognized *gandules* growing wild and made a mental note to remember them at Christmastime when *arroz con gandules,* rice with this special savory pea cooked with chicken stock, was a favorite dish.

As her hands ran over the slender leaves of the plant she recalled Augustine Rivera's hands and skin, which was like living teak. The slenderness of his mustache framing arrogant, petulant lips beneath shining amused eyes came to mind. Before she knew it she drifted into a daydream that saw her floating toward him and clinging to him in a cloud of spun copper that seemed to provide the proper smoldering aura to support his leonine magnetism.

When Leslie realized what was happening she jerked herself back to reality and was thoroughly annoyed with herself. She brushed at the darting insects viciously and suddenly felt as though their itching, stinging bite was a fitting punishment for such ridiculous thoughts. Quickly she turned, wiping perspiration from her forehead, and headed in another direction over what seemed to be an overgrown path. She kept the pointed triangular garrets of the sprawling wooden house in her sight as she moved steadily up a rocky course. When she reached the summit, she stood in the streaming sunlight and felt the uniqueness of her power as a woman.

She had a trembling, primitive intuition. She, and she alone, was the cradle of creation. That was her and every other woman's power and she was not about to let a man such as Augustine Rivera challenge it or take it from her.

Leslie looked all around. There was a huge spreading flamboyant tree with a riot of bright crimson blossoms to her right. She was amazed that she could see the entire distance over flat green sugarcane fields to the Caribbean, which lapped the shores of Ponce and clearly revealed its outline. It was beautiful and quiet here. It was hard to visualize the struggle against utter, abject poverty that went on daily in those cities and *barrios* below, but it was also reassuring to know that this was one place that was successfully fighting back. By providing not only work for the islanders, but a generous employee shareholding program as well, her factory was a part of that effort. As she stood there proud and defiant in the tradewind breeze she was glad to be part of it.

Moments later she scrambled down the hill and made her way once again toward the house. She was grubby and sweaty and the *mimis* had made her more than a little uncomfortable. She was really sorry that the swimming pool and garden off the drawing room and patio had not yet been restored, but a long, leisurely bath would have to substitute. Upstairs in her spacious room, which boasted an antique mahogany four-poster covered with an elaborate crochet spread made by her mother many years before, she closed the glass louvered windows and switched on the air conditioner installed in a shaded wall. As it began to hum she felt its instant coolness and dropped her rumpled clothes into a pile. They landed on an elegant Persian rug that accented the gleaming hardwood floor. She looked up to the high-vaulted ceiling and stripped the last of her lacy undergarments from her body. She reached for a silky knit robe of her own design and carried it brazenly over her arm as she meandered nonchalantly down the hall, totally nude.

The sunny bathroom with bright splashes of color housed a spacious antique bathtub. It was once the hallmark of modern convenience. Slowly she stretched and listened to the sounds of the tropical *campo* far different from the country sounds of the north. She laughed as tiny lizards darted about and remembered her initial horror of them until her mother had chastised her and told her what a household friend they were. The tiny nocturnal tree frog unique to Puerto Rico was making its melodious *"coqui"* sounds early as she stepped to the open window. It framed the opulent green surroundings and the steamy heat enveloped her, but she decided not to use the air conditioning . She wanted to enjoy the outdoor feeling during her bath.

Water gushed in from the ornate, antique faucets and began to rapidly fill the great white tub, which stood six inches from the floor on lion's feet legs. She went to the cupboard and selected a crisp citrus scent, which also had overtones of a sensuous musk, and poured it generously into the tub. With a sigh she stepped into the swirling waters and submerged her head in abandon as she reached for her favorite shampoo and began to wash her long hair.

The water soothed her tense muscles, but the insect bites began to antagonize her again. Leslie decided to ignore them and went on enjoying herself as she thought about the pool downstairs and decided to make it her next priority. She thought of floating around in its cool expanse in the middle of the formal gardens created there so many years ago during the gay madness of the twenties. She could just imagine her mother as a young child then, the pampered darling of a rich and powerful family. But times changed and dreams could be so swiftly altered, she thought.

Leslie must have spent nearly an hour just lying there dreaming of what might have been. As her thoughts floated in a satin web of mist she began to think of an elegant seductive design for a very special dress. She could visualize it as a shimmery fine knit shaped in clinging gores designed to emphasize a beautiful bosom. She added an intricate open pattern of lace and crochet over the high empire bodice and added popcorn stitch accents to the airy sleeves. It was a dress made for dancing and she saw it descending an elegant spiral staircase as the woman with upswept hair stepped into the arms of a dark, smooth, and velvet man who whirled her beneath shining chandeliers and nibbled around the edges of her dainty ears decorated with clustered diamond earrings.

It was a pink dress—perfect for the skin of the islanders. It was perfect for the man too—revealing exactly what he wanted to see. She envisioned his smiling eyes with a peculiar flickering flame behind them illuminating the straight narrow nose with slightly flared nostrils as his pleasure turned to passion. She lifted her lips to meet his and realized with a start that she had done it again—she had allowed Augustine Rivera to invade her thoughts and the theme was now becoming more than a little disconcerting.

Leslie raised her legs and began to quickly scrub in short hostile movements as her painted toenails splashed in the water and accented her annoyance. She washed the rest of her body in a flash, then stood, and the water streamed from her, leaving her cool and refreshed in spite of her annoyance. With a bright-colored bath sheet she patted her skin dry, then wrapped herself expertly in its luxurious absorbency, fastening it beneath her arm, and reached for an additional towel for her hair and swept it into a turban.

As the steaminess of the room began to immediately dissipate the cooling effects of the bath she dropped the heavy wet towel and reached for the loose silky robe she had brought with her. She tied it around her kimono style and languidly retraced her steps back to her now very cool room. In fact it was too cool. As she pulled the towel from her hair she realized these were perfect conditions for the much feared *munga*, the Puerto Rican flu, which knew no season and spared no one. She decided to return downstairs to the patio to dry her hair in the sun.

She was sitting on the low wall next to the empty pool humming a catchy island tune as she brushed her hair with long strong strokes and felt it rapidly drying in the warm breeze when she heard an unfamiliar sound break the silence.

"A woman brushing her hair is always beautiful, but a woman brushing her hair in the wind is a masterpiece."

Leslie whirled around and met Augustine Rivera's admiring eyes and was momentarily speechless.

"I'm sorry," he said, "I didn't mean to startle you. I went out to the factory and was told I might find you here. When I found the door open and no one about, I was troubled and came in to be sure everything was all right. I didn't mean to intrude, but when I saw you sitting there looking so beautiful, I just had to express myself. In that pose you really should be on a pedestal or in a portrait created by a grand master."

Although his expression was appropriately contrite

and respecful Leslie looked at him in astonishment. Yet she also felt a very real softening toward him and sensed he was addressing her sincerely. Then for no reason that she could readily fathom, she very much wanted to be in control of this pretentious man with the ability to feign such humility. She was immediately aware of his recognition of her state of undress and she moved with a deliberate feline grace as she turned to answer him.

"Locked doors have never impressed me very much. I've always felt if anyone wanted to come in badly enough they could always find a way." She smiled up at him coyly and seductively. "But then we're so far from the dangers of the city, I find it hard to think of any dangers out here."

"Rest assured that there are! Many of us are still inclined to believe that our women should be protected."

"How archaic." Leslie laughed. "You're obviously still a debonair gentleman of yesteryear. The only thing really dangerous out here are these dratted *mimis*."

As she spoke she laid her hairbrush aside and reached for the lotion she had brought with her. Extending one of her shapely legs, she began to smooth its soothing coolness over the tiny angry welts that peppered her limbs. She was more than aware of the effect she was having on him as she heard him gasp softly.

His eyes raked over her in a spiritual passion of the senses. Then he stepped closer to her and his eyes glittered with a hard light as he apparently considered his strategy and decided to retreat.

"Apparently I've come at an awkward time. I only wished to discuss the possibility of arranging a small show for some of my other business associates who I'm sure can be of real assistance to you, but that can wait. Again please accept my apologies. I really am not in the habit of invading a lady's privacy."

"That's really perfectly all right," she said. "I don't

see any problem with that. Since you've taken the trouble to come all the way out here, I see no reason why we can't discuss it. Just give me a moment to change and I'll be right with you.''

"By all means," he said bowing in insidious submission. "I'd be delighted."

Leslie brushed past him, pulling her robe snugly to her bare body, and felt his eyes outlining the hardness of her nipples, which had grown taut in the excitement of their exchange.

Chapter Four

She was back in moments, but in that time she had had time to pause and think. Leslie was shocked by her reaction to Augustine's unexpected appearance. This was a man whom she had vowed to remove entirely from her existence just yesterday, yet she had only seconds earlier plied all of her seductive charms to induce him to stay.

She had put on a cool sundress, which accented her slim waist. Her hair was pulled back casually with a ribbon and her feet were encased in strappy sandals. They made a clatter on the wooden floors of the house as she returned to the terrace, echoing her embarrassed confusion.

Augustine greeted her politely before she had a chance to speak. "I imagine Gerald and your mother are out preparing for the party."

His voice was sociable and congenial in the manner of a correctly polite gentleman. His eyes astutely appraised Leslie from head to toe and they reflected a flame preserved in a wall of iron as the soft musical notes of Leslie's voice wove a tenuous gossamer web of polite communication between them.

"Yes, they are and it's wonderful to see Mama so full of life again."

She smiled and gave him a polite submissive nod. It

was if they both, through mutual agreement, had decided to forget their initial meeting of a few moments before. It was an exercise in expected good taste and manners, but the vibrations of those earlier fiery moments still reverberated throughout the room to produce a background scenario more sensuous than the softest music and candlelight could ever hope to be.

Leslie flushed as she searched for appropriate words, acutely embarrassed now by her earlier seductive display. She was sincerely glad Augustine had chosen a safe subject, indicating he was more than skilled in handling difficult situations smoothly and easily.

It was a skill Leslie had once felt she possessed, but it seemed to elude her when she was in his presence. He always managed to be in command, except, her subconscious intuition suddenly telegraphed, when she chose to exercise her woman's prerogative and issue a primitive challenge—the mating challenge.

It was a blunt realistic definition of what had begun the initial struggle between man and woman. She had the ultimate power to make him perform at her bidding, and he in his rugged slavery to machismo felt the uncontrollable need to steal that power and in so doing rob her of her very uniqueness.

It was a pointed, thrusting insight that brought Leslie to a momentary halt as the anger for all of the generations of fearful female submissiveness once again overwhelmed her. She must conquer him. Her survival as a complete woman depended upon it.

Augustine had watched her, his eyes autocratic and eagle sharp, as Leslie transformed in seconds from a demure, chaste woman into the challenging seductive woman of a few moments before. It gave her an air of irresistible mystery that attracted him beyond his wildest imagination as she turned to address him again.

"Now, you mentioned something about a show?" She spoke with a direct businesslike primness.

"Yes, but we can discuss it another time. You obviously are relaxing today."

"No, really it's okay." She moved inside to a high-standing ornate liquor cupboard in the corner of the room. "Would you like something to drink? A glass of wine or rum?"

"Yes," he said, his expression visibly brightening, "if it wouldn't be too much trouble. I'd really enjoy a rum and water."

"Of course," said Leslie. "Do you want lots of ice?"

"Please," he said.

His eyes were warm and liquid now as he again openly admired her with a gentle humor.

While Leslie prepared his drink and poured a glass of wine for herself, she gathered her resources to deal with the exotic, unfamiliar feelings this man created within her. She watched him carefully, beneath discreet eyelashes, and sensed an inner little-boy vulnerability that he kept safely hidden except in rare moments, and it had a surprisingly softening effect upon her.

As she handed him the icy amber drink he looked at her with a warm, philosophical gaze, then his eyes perused and savored the color of the liquor. "Rum, properly aged, is like life," he said. "You have to hold it in your hand, look at it and feel it, sense it and then enjoy it—but whatever you do, never abuse it." His words were intimate and personal.

Leslie looked at him and their eyes met. He raised his glass to her in a salute. In that moment Leslie felt she was glimpsing an eloquent, gentle inner man and in yet another poignant insight she wished fervently she could know that man.

She could feel herself beginning to relax and wondered if it was the wine that caused it. Whatever the cause, she was glad. She felt comfortable now. The business discussion of a few moments before was seemingly forgotten as Augustine settled into his chair and apparently prepared to continue with his philosophical discussion.

"Life here, you know, is very sensual—almost too human," he said as he gestured with his hands in unison with his words. "Too sensual in many ways to define. You *should* take the day off. It's uncivilized to work just for the sake of work. Here we work when we need to, or when we're happy or inspired, but we're not afraid to relax either."

His voice had been warm and personal as he leaned forward, drawing her closer to his revealing thoughts. He took another swallow of his potent drink and savored it as he smiled at her.

Leslie was somewhat at a loss to reply to this unexpected lesson in Puerto Rican philosophy, but she was not too surprised by it. This type of dialogue was, in many ways, a national pastime. A certain poetic introspection seemed to be a part of everyday life and was employed in accordance with the whim of the moment. She was touched by Augustine's words.

Leslie wanted very much to be a part of this island and this culture, which in her grandest dreams melded comfortably with her father's stateside customs. It was in many ways not unlike the many other ethnic pockets that made up the entire United States, and it was no secret that many in the island hoped that one day soon they too would be a state so they could fully enjoy the benefits of their United States citizenship. It was, however, also a volatile subject and one that shadowed the foundations of all the island's political parties, one of which cried for independence. Innocent philosophical discussions had a way of evolving into these subjects.

Not wishing to become involved in what could prove to be an intricate conversation, Leslie rose and moved toward the veranda and its cooling breeze. The shadows were falling, bringing with them a refreshing balminess accompanied by the whisper of the wind through the surrounding leaves. She realized that Gerald and her mother would be coming soon and she had promised to prepare dinner.

Leslie went toward the kitchen, which was another large airy room in the old house. It had a wide opening to the dining and patio areas. There was a modern outdoor table and chairs on the veranda, which looked directly to the counter next to the stove in the kitchen.

"I'm sure you will understand, Senor Rivera."

"Please," he broke in, "call me Augustine. Surely we are friends by now and, as your mother indicated yesterday, we are practically family."

"All right," said Leslie with a delighted smile. "I'm sure then you won't mind if I begin to prepare dinner." She gestured toward the patio chairs. "Just make yourself comfortable there on the veranda and we can talk about your business associates while I'm working."

"Oh, no," he said. "Perhaps I should leave."

"Not at all," said Leslie. "I'm really enjoying our conversation."

As the words spilled out of her almost routinely she realized in amazement that she really was enjoying his company.

"Please, just sit down"—she gestured again to the veranda—"and finish your drink. This will only take a few moments. Mama and Gerald will be here soon and I know Mama would be unhappy if she missed you."

"Well, if you insist, Senorita Williams," he said in mock submission.

"And fair is fair," said Leslie with a tinkly laugh. "My friends all call me Leslie."

"As you wish," he said with a nod, "but surely that's not your only name. What does the M stand for?"

"Why, Marie, of course. I'm named after both of my parents."

"Ah, I see then the practice of naming one's offspring after the father is not a uniquely Latin one, although it is a distinction usually saved for the firstborn son in our families.''

She flashed him a congenial smile and was really glad that they had managed to totally relax in each other's presence. Perhaps she had been more tense than she had realized, resulting in a grossly exaggerated negative reaction to him on that first day. This day of relaxation had been a good idea and now she had a new friend.

Leslie was happy and began to hum a little tune as she stepped to the refrigerator and retrieved the chicken her mother had thoughtfully cut into pieces and seasoned with spices and lemon juice. Augustine watched her intently as he continued to enjoy his drink. She had visibly mellowed and there was a hint of velvety gentleness about her.

As she continued to banter with him in mundane comments about the house and her mother's plans to restore it, she quickly chopped vegetables and sautéed them in an electric skillet. A savory smell began to permeate the entire house as she added more ingredients and stirred the entire simmering concoction with a wooden spoon.

"Ay, que huele!" said Augustine as he left his chair and came to stand beside her in the kitchen. He was tall and standing so close he seemed to give Leslie a towering sense of comfortable protection.

"What are you cooking? That smells like a *sofrito,* as fine as any I've ever encountered in this island!"

His words were tinged with amazement as he lifted and kissed his fingers with enthusiasm.

"Chicken Fricassee, Puerto Rican style," she said enthusiastically. "My mother always prepared both Anglo and Latin meals. This was one of our favorites."

"Well, it's wonderful! You could run a restaurant as well as a factory," he said with admiring humor.

As he talked Leslie added the cut-up chicken pieces and stirred them to coat them with the hot *sofrito* paste.

She noted his eyes watching the action of her breasts against the unnatural confinement of her dress as she stirred. She flashed him a meaningful look tinged with humor as his lips pursed instinctively. Then she turned to reach for a can of beer, which she opened with one swift gesture.

"What are you doing?" exclaimed Augustine, suddenly alarmed. "Surely you are not going to ruin that wonderful mixture by adding beer?"

"I am," said Leslie, once again feeling a little of the earlier challenge. "That is my own special touch and everyone loves it."

"No, no, no," he said in expansive mock horror as his voice softened to a cajoling note. "Wine. You must add white wine with a touch of sherry—even water would be better."

"Yes, yes, yes," said Leslie, mocking his exaggerated speech. "This is really quite wonderful." She poured the entire can in with practiced ease.

Augustine clutched his heart and stepped away in feigned pain. "What have you done, what have you done?" he sighed in real pathos.

"I've created a masterpiece," said Leslie as she laughed at his exaggerated performance. She quickly added a sliced potato and a handful of green olives stuffed with pimiento. Then as the crowning touch she dropped in a large bay leaf and brought the entire contents of the pan to a boil.

"There," she said as she reached for the lid and lowered the heat to a slow simmer. I'll just leave this for half an hour and it will be wonderful."

"There are some things better left to the natives," Augustine said drolly.

"Just you wait and see," said Leslie, clearly enjoying this exchange, in which for once she was the declared victor. She *had* done it her way.

Augustine continued to stand next to her, watching

intently as she browned some slivers of salt pork and prepared white rice in the traditional Puerto Rican way by first sautéeing and then boiling the ingredients together. When she finished and placed a large plantain leaf over the steaming concoction they continued to banter. She lifted the lid from the fricassee and grandly offered him a taste of the fragrant sauce. His expression was one of sheer wonderment as the delicious blend delighted all of his senses.

"I don't believe it," he said, truly amazed. "That's just amazing. You're right. It's delicious! But beer," he said in derision, "is so bourgeois."

"So common," said Leslie, chiming in. "Sometimes a woman knows best," she said teasingly, but there was a touch of mockery in her voice too. "When it has simmered it will really be fantastic," she continued, "and then it can sit for a time and wait if dinner is late for any reason. All in all it has always seemed to be a perfect dish for this culture with its crazy sense of time."

"You are an amazing woman," said Augustine as he stepped closer to her. His eyes glittered. "An enigma I can't resist!"

His lips came crushing down on hers as he swept her into his arms. His voice was soft and gentle as he nibbled her ear and growled her name in a dizzying confusion of all her senses.

"You are a woman," he said, "a real woman and you should have a woman's name."

His lips nibbled gently and urgently, forcing her own to open in response, welcoming his parrying, thrusting tongue. Suddenly Leslie realized she was about to make a disastrous mistake.

In the twinkling of an eye she had almost voluntarily submitted to the pressure of this man's dominating power. She had placed herself in a traditional submissive role and he had moved with swift vengeance to take advantage of her. She struggled to pull herself away as the thought of his fiancée suddenly flashed across her mind. She was consumed with an insufferable rage as she raised her fists to fight back his persistent, continued advances.

"*María*," he whispered, "*María*.... You are a madonna made for love."

His arms held her prisoner as he enveloped her with his masterful passionate power.

Leslie was incensed beyond words not only by his uninvited advances, but also by this arrogant insistence of changing her name, yet she fought not only him, but herself as well. Her body, bare beneath the skimpy sundress, clung to his and was seared by the fire of his thighs and the trail of his hands as he drew her closer and closer. It took every effort to let him know that she was serious. She did not, in her mind, want his advances to continue, but her body did. His hands moved over her hard and insistent as he drew her closer to him. The palm of his hand on her lower back guided her in a rhythm of ancient response and melded her to his animal strength. Her anger and struggle seemed only to excite him as he covered her face and neck with warm caresses and said her name over and over again.

Suddenly, just as she was about to panic completely, afraid that she was going to be a victim of her own responses, she heard the familiar sound of her little car's motor in the distance as it made its laborious way up the drive.

"Augustine, please!" she said breathlessly. "Mama and Gerald are coming. Please, they must not find us like this."

"Oh, but of course, *niña*," he said as he stepped away from her reluctantly. His words were tender but the motion was so automatic that Leslie was sure that he had been in a compromising situation such as this more than once.

As her own panicky words echoed around her she

was again chagrined as he continued to look at her in smoldering passion. It was obvious that he had incorrectly assumed she was as annoyed by this interruption as he was. All of the rage generated by his previous actions came crushing back, magnified beyond comprehension.

She turned from him, unable to look at him, and knew she must find a way to crush him and destroy him. His threat was too great. He would take her and use her, steal her very essence and then she would be nothing.

Within seconds she heard her mother entering the front door, laden with packages and gushing out the details of her day's adventures with Gerald. They both came to a surprised halt when they saw Augustine and Leslie together, although the latter two had managed to return to some semblance of a respectable scene.

"Augustine," cried Leslie's mother. "What a pleasant surprise."

She looked momentarily at Leslie with a small hint of a troubled expression, but she soon overcame her anxiety as she bundled Augustine into the other room to once again discuss her younger years in the island when she had known his father.

Gerald's eyes had darted around, wary and concerned since his entry, and he was not so easily deceived as Leslie's mother.

"Leslie, honey," he said as he turned her toward him. "What's going on here? Did old brother Gerald arrive in just the knick of time to save the damsel in distress?"

He had meant his remarks to be funny, but when Leslie's eyes met his they were venomous with hatred.

"That bastard," she said. "That lousy chauvinistic, two-timing bastard! Someday I'm going to kill him with a knife so sharp his screams will be heard for miles!"

Chapter Five

"Leslie, for heaven's sake!" exclaimed Gerald. "What's gotten into you! I've never heard you talk like that."

He was clearly shaken by the wicked vehemence of her words.

Realizing her voice had dropped to a violent guttural whisper, more suitable for an animal than a human being, Leslie was immediately embarrassed by her outburst. Gerald was right. She never talked or acted like this. She abhorred violence and sought constantly for serenity in her life. It was that man, that terrible man who drew her to him, who wanted to destroy her, and she was frightened because she knew now he had the strength to do it.

As she made hasty amends to reassure Gerald that she was all right, Philomena, a woman she had never met, but with whom she now felt a strange sympathetic kinship, came to mind. Her anger took on a razor edge due to her struggle to conceal it, but she managed to smile brightly as she addressed Gerald.

"Oh, it's nothing," she said with a note of falsetto, "you know how infuriating that kind of man can be. Somehow he just seems to bring out the worst in me."

"I guess," said Gerald in obvious relief, "but maybe I'd better keep an eye on you just in case. What's he doing out here anyway? I told you, you'd better watch out for him."

Gerald's questions suddenly reminded Leslie of the earlier call to her broker. She knew now she must find out the exact extent of Augustine's interest in her company. From what she had just learned she thought it was safe to surmise that he couldn't have more than a few shares, but after his actions just moments before, more than ever, she had to make an effort to retrieve that stock from him.

As Leslie heard her mother so obviously enjoying Augustine's company in the next room, she realized for the sake of appearances and more importantly not to disturb her mother, she must go in and continue to play the gracious hostess role.

She went to the refrigerator to refill her glass of wine and offered one to Gerald too. He nodded ready assent and then they both went out to the veranda and insisted that Doña María and Augustine join them as well. Her mother had already prepared herself a cordial and renewed Augustine's drink.

Augustine's eyes kept returning to Leslie with a satisfied gleam of anticipation. He perused her entire body as though she were an object belonging to him. She was vastly uncomfortable and her rage continued to feed as she went on treating him cordially. It was obvious that he mistook her gestures as further invitation and she made a vow that should he return to claim that invitation, he would leave vanquished and beaten. Those thoughts gave her some sense of satisfaction as she participated in their continued banter.

Moments later Augustine arose to leave. Her mother remonstrated and invited him to stay for dinner.

"No, really, Doña María, I've already had a big meal today and as wonderful as the fricassee smells, Philomena is expecting me. I have something very important to discuss with her." He looked pointedly at Leslie. "She may be able to help Leslie. She sits on the board of a very large charity called Ayudalo that specializes in providing workers from the underprivileged classes for local industry."

His gaze was direct and congenial, but Leslie was appalled. It was happening. Already it was happening. He definitely had plans to interfere in her business and after his actions of a few moments ago he had the audacity to mention his fiancée's name in front of her! He was insufferable, as insufferable as any man could be. She felt a black bitter gall in the back of her throat as he made his departure.

"I'll be seeing you again," he said to Leslie as he bent to kiss her hand. "I'll call to arrange the showing. It's been a delightful afternoon, Doña María." He gave her a familiar kiss on the cheek, traditional for greeting and parting among family and close aquaintances. "May peace be with you, Senor Masters. *Buenas noches.*"

Gerald and Leslie stood silently as he continued out the door with Leslie's mother. Her mother sincerely seemed to have taken Augustine into her heart as the son she had never had. It was uncanny and unreal and left Leslie feeling very sad because she knew her mother could not stand another emotional blow so soon after the grief of losing her husband. Somehow there must be a way she could protect herself from this man and her mother as well.

She turned to Gerald with an overly enthusiastic smile. "Have I got a dinner for you," she said with false bravado. As she said the words she realized the fricassee had taken on a whole new meaning to her. Never again would she prepare it without thinking of those searing kisses and her own outrageous response. It was something she really must forget....

Leslie was in her office the next morning long before anyone else. After taking a day off she was almost driven by a feeling of guilt, not to mention anxiety. Actually she had been completely unsettled ever since Augustine's departure the day before.

The phone rang and she immediately recognized the garbled echoey signals that indicated a transatlantic call gone amok. She heard the faint voice of her broker and then frowned as static drowned him out.

"Try again, Harold," she shouted, hoping he might hear her. She toyed with the thought of calling him, but realized that would tie up her line should he try to call back. So far she'd only been able to get one telephone line for the factory. She sighed and glanced through her mail and noted the statement from the broker hadn't arrived yet either. Something about that whole thing was very unsettling and the frustrating call had just intensified it.

Almost as if an omen dramatizing her worst fears the phone rang again with a piercing shriek. Thinking it might be Harold, she answered it herself.

"*Buenos días, Los Tejidos de María.*"

"María!"

She gasped. The soft growl was unmistakable.

"Augustine!"

"Yes, María. My goodness, you're in early today!"

"Well, not really...."

She heard Juanita coming into the outer office and suddenly felt like she needed to camouflage in two directions. Augustine's voice was like intimate friendly music, but she was irritated with his continued insistence of changing her name.

"I found our conversation yesterday most enjoyable," he said softly.

Leslie felt herself flushing from head to toe. The hint of sly innuendo in his words was undeniable. She immediately focused on those mad moments when her body had responded to his, consumed completely by a wild and hot fire. She could feel her hand trembling as she gripped the phone desperately.

"I was wondering," he went on, "if we might arrange a showing sometime today or tomorrow."

Leslie chided herself as relief washed over her. She had immediately assumed from the intimacy in his voice that he was calling to follow up on their tryst the day before.

"Certainly," she said, her relief obvious as her entire countenance relaxed. "You're thinking of both a plant tour and a fashion show?"

"Yes, exactly," he said.

"No problem. We're always prepared to entertain clients a few at a time."

"Fine," he said with his special expansiveness. "There will be about fifteen people. Would two o'clock today be convenient?"

Leslie paused for just a second. Fifteen was much more than the one or two she defined as a few. They would have to scurry, but it could be done.

"Well, sure," she said as the panic wheels of organization began to immediately revolve in her head.

"Wonderful! I'll see you then," he said, "and María...."

"Yes," she said absently.

"I can tell by the sound of your voice, you're exceptionally lovely this morning."

Leslie caught her breath and her heart quickened into an erratic pace. She hung up the phone in confusion after mumbling some sort of a good-bye.

"Juanita," she called as she began to immediately rush around.

The call from the broker was forgotten completely.

It wasn't until Leslie was rearranging the rugs in the show area to form delineated walkways for the modeling that she realized how very accommodating she was being. In her relief over the absence of further intimate pressures from him she had failed to see what was actually happening. As she filled a large coffee urn with water it suddenly dawned on her.

"My God," she said out loud. "You only met him a few days ago and he's already cracking the whip around here!"

A trembling wariness immediately enveloped her.

"Well, what's done is done," she sighed, but she realized then she must indeed be more careful. This was setting a very bad precedent. He hadn't even given her a reason for bringing these people in. She didn't know if they were clients, prospective shareholders, or what.

She went in and had a little talk with her workers and then asked Juanita and Tía Isabel to assist her with the modeling assignments. Quickly she went through her stock and chose a wide array of designs from her past work, selecting a very flattering low-necked summer sweater peppered with delicate open work for herself. Looking the part of a haute-couture moderator, she greeted Augustine at precisely two o'clock. He was alone.

"Well, where is everyone?" she asked, a little agitated.

"Oh, they'll be here in about an hour," he said.

"But you said—"

"My dear, we always say two o'clock if we hope to begin at three. Everything usually starts an hour late."

"But I could have used that extra hour!"

"I'm sure you could," he said in total nonchalance. "That's why I'm here now. Now, let me see, what do you have planned?"

He was moving on as though he were the proprietor.

"What have you chosen for yourself?"

Augustine turned and perused her from head to toe and his eyes turned to molten metal liquid. She felt herself growing warm.

"Oh, I'm not planning to model."

"Why not?" he asked, his disappointment obvious.

He was reaching through the selections she had hung in the showroom. He chose an elegant sheath with a low décolletage. "This would be so lovely on you, and oh," he sighed as he came to a sleek gathered swimsuit, "this too."

"Don't be ridiculous," Leslie said. "It wouldn't be proper. Someone has to moderate."

Suddenly his eyes lit up as he walked briskly across the room. He had seen a beautiful peignoir set she had left in the closet. It was a silky, revealing, diaphanous creation that only a truly skilled knit designer could have created.

"Certainly you're going to show this," he said. "You must wear it."

He had retrieved it and was holding it next to her. "María," he breathed as his lips softly brushed her cheek in an intimate growl, "only you could do this justice. I must see you in it."

"I don't think so!" she said sharply as she recoiled from his caress, but unconsciously her fingers touched her face and felt the track of fire still evident there. Her eyes cracked with anger.

"Ah, María," he said with a patient patronizing smugness, "I can't tell you how lovely you are when you're angry."

"Oh, how cheap and cliché," she said, really annoyed now. "Look, I'm running a business here, not some high-class bordello. I'll choose the fashions and conduct this showing if you don't mind!"

"But of course, María, of course," he said stepping back. Augustine shrugged, palms up in insidious submission, but Leslie knew this was only a temporary retreat.

His intentions were clear. He was here to take over and she had to do something immediately to stop him. Almost as if a godsend her mother suddenly appeared.

"Augustine," she cried. "How nice to see you again. *Mija*," she said, turning to Leslie, "Juanita called me and said you could use some help."

"Yes, Mama," she sighed. "Why don't you and Augustine check to be sure we have enough wine. The people should be here soon."

The amusement in Augustine's eyes was also tinged with a hint of respect as he allowed himself to be maneuvered from the room, but not before he touched her one more time, allowing his fingers to hover close to her breast.

Within the next few moments, Gerald too arrived along with most of Augustine's guests. They were well-spoken men and women, most executives in other related garment businesses. As she met them Leslie realized these were indeed important people, most from the upper echelons of the island society who could most assuredly be important business liaisons for her. Augustine really was being very good to her, extending his contacts and influence in a most supportive way. Magna was also a part of the entourage.

"Cuidado niña," said Magna at Leslie's elbow after watching another of Augustine's long-range perusals. "Remember what I told you about Latin men..."

"Oh, for heaven's sake," said Leslie with impatience. "I wish people would stop calling me *niña*. I'm not a little girl!"

"Umm, touchy aren't we?" said Magna appraisingly. "I think this is already more than I thought."

"Magna—"

"Relax," said Magna, laughing. "You don't have to prove or deny anything to me. Good luck with the show."

She turned and joined the others as again Leslie went through the plant much as she had with Augustine the first day they met. She was fully aware of his presence as he hovered close to her just within the margin of her instinctive territorial presence that made her ever cognizant of him. She could sense his eyes as they raked over her despite his noncommittal expression above crossed arms.

Finally Leslie seated the guests and adjusted the lighting. She began first with a slick set of colored slides illustrating her sketches and proposed ideas. As the guests relaxed with their wine and nibbled cheese and other appetizers she turned on soft, subtle music and continued with a polished, flashy presentation that Juanita and her aunt handled beautifully for her.

She herself was again impressed with the quality of her designs as her confidence and trust in her abilities and instincts returned in full force. There was applause when she finished and everyone in the room rushed to speak to her personally.

Augustine hovered in the background, but she was never, for a moment, unaware of his presence. She could feel him dressing and undressing her as thoughts of her fashions on her body flashed through his mind and projected existentially to her. It was as vivid as if she were thinking the thoughts herself. Gerald too was excited and there was no doubt now, her mother was also permanently hooked.

"Oh, Leslie, darling, I'd almost forgotten how beautiful your work is," Doña María gushed.

"Yes, very beautiful," said Augustine as he appeared by her side again, "and we must all work together to be sure it is successful."

Leslie snapped to attention as her eyes met his.

He returned her gaze with a smoldering smugness.

"Those ideas you have for that ski sweater line," Gerald broke in robustly. "Fantastic! We need to follow those up before I leave."

"We'll see what we can do," Leslie said, laughing. She was flushed and excited, grateful now that Augustine, in spite of his rather pushy presumptuousness, had arranged the show. She was fired with enthusiasm and turned to thank him.

"Really this was a wonderful idea," she said.

"But of course," he said with just a touch of humor. "I've been known to be right a time or two in my life."

Her smile faded as the threat of his charisma teased her like a cold talon. Although he spoke softly his eyes glittered with satisfaction as again he swept her body into his mind and claimed it as his own.

She caught her breath and stepped away.

"Yes, well, it has turned out very well." She had to force herself to continue now. "I...really appreciate it."

"My pleasure," he said.

He took a sip of wine and before they could say more someone had hustled him away, but the spirit of his eyes stayed to haunt her and Leslie could feel that now familiar unsettling anxiety beginning to form again.

"Why the long face, cupcake?"

She smiled and cleared her head as Gerald once again came to her rescue with his unfailing good humor.

"No long face," she said.

"No?" said Gerald.

He watched Augustine's progress across the room.

"Well, I hope not," he said as he gauged her expression carefully. "I still think we'd better watch that guy."

"Oh, come on," she said. "I'm a big girl now. I can take care of myself."

Leslie linked her arm through his and began to converse with her guests. Soon she was again flushed with excitement, but in the back of her mind she wondered if she hadn't spoken too glibly. Gerald was right. She'd better be careful. Augustine was a powerful man and he was obviously used to having his own way.

Chapter Six

From the moment that Gerald and Doña María had returned from their shopping they had all been busily preparing for the party to be held on the next Saturday night. Leslie was grateful because it left her no time to think about her unsettling encounters with Augustine during the past few days.

That night the house was gay with noise and laughter as a current popular island song with an insistent Latin beat blared out. Time after time she heard enthusiastic, boisterous *"Ehhh chicas!"* as guests recognized one another. They stopped in exaggerated shock as they opened their arms to one another in a traditional greeting of hugs and kisses on the cheek. Over and over again her mother was enveloped in this special outpouring of love as the house grew crowded with dozens of people, many of whom Leslie had never met before.

They had prepared *pasteles, arroz con pollo, lechón*, and a variety of other traditional island delicacies as well as hors d'oeuvres and traditional stateside dishes of ham and potato salad. The buffet was completely informal with all of the guests helping themselves and assisting in replenishing when something disappeared.

Several of the men had brought *güiros*, the native musical instrument made from a large gourd that they rasped with a large comblike utensil in rhythm with the infectious music. The men looked like festive *patróns*

in their colorful *guayavera* shirts, the tropical answer to
the heavy sport coat, and *pavas*, wide-brimmed straw
hats.

The current bright colors and folkloric prints in
bright and breezy full-skirted fashions of challis and
cotton blends were perfect compliments for the pre-
dominantly honey-toned skins of the excited chattering
women who swirled around the room as they replen-
ished their men's drinks and enjoyed their own as well.

Although Leslie frequently wore her own designs,
she also enjoyed the excitement of other fashions as
well and by no means restricted herself to her own knit
specialities. For the party she had chosen one of her
prettiest long summer dresses, which was a combination of elegance and informality, perfect for the hostess
of a Ponce upper-strata social gathering. She had piled
her hair high, leaving only a few teasing tendrils, and
completed the outfit with tiny black dancing slippers
and accents of gold jewelry sparkling with a tiny diamond or two here and there.

Over and over again she was greeted with delight and
sighs of admiration as everyone in the family offered
their congratulations and best wishes for the success of
her business and complimented her and her mother on
all that they had done to restore the old estate.

Everyone seemed to naturally gravitate toward the
cool verandas and she heard the familiar click of domi-
noes as several of the men set up tables and began to
play their favorite pastime near the empty swimming
pool on the flagstone patio. As the full moon played
over the scene adding to the gay light of lanterns and
tiki lamps lit to deter the *mimis*, Leslie once again made
a mental note to check into the restoration of the pool
and garden.

There was a sudden surge as joyous cries of greeting
magnified in unison and Leslie instinctively knew Augustine had arrived. There was a general shifting as

everyone made an effort to greet him personally while he moved, smiling and benevolent, through the crowd. She saw her mother run to greet him joyously. He searched over the room until his eyes at last sought out her own and compelled her to return his dark, hypnotic gaze. Quickly she looked away and maneuvered to remove herself as far from him as possible, but not before she had noted the rakish tilt of his *pava* and the beautiful scrolling of his *guayavera*, which accented his tight trousers.

His hips moved in a suggestive rhythm as he exuberantly embraced the spirit of the party and began dancing into the room, changing partners at random as he advanced. His laughter was hearty and boisterous as others joined in clapping their hands and shouting *"oles"*. He moved in a low seductive rhumba as he held a willing, adoring partner an arm's length from his body. His eyes were riveted piercingly to hers and his face was pursed in severe intensity. Then he released her with a great yell and joined the others in shouting laughter.

His commotion was rivaled only by that of a sultry siren who had been following close behind him. It was several seconds before Leslie realized that this must be the Philomena she had heard so much about and sympathized with in the past few days. It was glaringly and instantly apparent that her sympathies had been more than a little misguided as this haughty aristocratic woman with finely honed, aqualine features and dark, snapping eyes moved around the room in a flurry of exotic color, greeting and hugging men and women alike in an excited husky voice.

She was a swirl of pure silk crepe de chine and a heavy scent exuded from her suggesting an insistent seductive heat as heavy expensive jewelry punctuated all of her motions. Children who had been playing close by shrank back as Philomena flaunted her voluptuous attractiveness. The men around the room openly admired her as she swung her face-framing hairdo in abandon while her eyes scanned the room in search of new conquests. Her long slender arms reached out again and again to touch an admiring man while their mates instinctively drew closer to them in an unconscious protective gesture.

Leslie had little time to reflect on this disconcerting entry as Gerald and Juanita came in the door. Juanita had very happily consented to pick up Gerald and now she began to introduce him around and Leslie moved away from the boisterous commotion.

She could still hear Augustine's shouts and laughter as he continued in abandoned enjoyment of himself. He was a direct contradiction of her initial impression of him. This was a child she was seeing, but a very dangerous child. That could be his most lethal weapon in demolishing her defenses and she vowed not to let him near her again. In passing, as she attempted to dismiss him from her thoughts, she noted that Augustine and Philomena seemed little more than polite acquaintances who happened to arrive together.

Suddenly as Leslie was walking through the door she saw Philomena fly across the room. An annoyed grimace lighted her features. She had seen Augustine talking admiringly to a young, nubile girl who was strikingly beautiful. The girl was gazing at him in adoration when Philomena appeared at his side and swooped him away in a flurry of possessive motion.

A moment later Philomena left him in the company of some older harmless *duenna* and then turned her attention back to other conquests at the party. Leslie couldn't help it; she watched the entire scene with a rapt fascination. She noted a strikingly handsome man, equal to Augustine in many ways, watching Philomena with a patient intensity. Leslie remembered being introduced to him. He was Don Fernando Aguila, a cousin of hers and another wealthy and powerful man in the throes of a nasty divorce that was soon to be settled, according to local gossip. She recalled now that Magna had mentioned him a time or two also and she regretted that her friend was away on one of her frequent trips and therefore unable to attend the party.

Leslie was newly surprised as she watched the antics of the players in this unfolding scenario. Don Fernando walked easily over to Philomena after watching carefully for just the right moment. To Leslie's amazement the strident woman she had witnessed in a possessive rage just seconds before visibly softened as Don Fernando's arms went around her and they moved in a slow dreamy rhythm. His eyes as he gazed over Philomena's head and held her brow to his cheek told the whole story. Leslie wondered anew at Philomena's strange alliance with Augustine, which obviously had nothing to do with the basic fundamentals of true love and the woman's apparent ignorance of the feelings she was sharing with her dance partner at that moment.

This was almost more than she could stand and Leslie felt the beginning of a nagging headache. Everyone was singing and dancing in abandon when yet another person arrived amid wild shouts and laughter. Leslie's Uncle Pepe had arrived with *jueyes*, land crabs especially fattened and oysters in the shell. All of the men surged toward him in anticipation of a ritual feast in which they were dominant in the preparation as well as consumption. Leslie smiled, knowing that the party would take care of itself, and headed for her room to find some aspirin.

When she reached the top of the steps, she was drawn by whispers and laughs from her mother's dimly lit bedroom. She recognized the voices of several young women and it was obvious that they were admiring a baby. Leslie quickly downed some aspirin in the bathroom and then stopped to join her cousins in admiration of the baby.

As she stepped into the room the women were gathered around the young mother, who was changing the baby from fancy party finery to more comfortable night sleepers. As Leslie gazed down on the infant who lay happily gurgling, the baby rolled and curled herself into charming contortions. For some reason Leslie felt a pang of longing and she inexplicably had a compelling desire to touch the child and hold her. Memories of her feelings as she created the baby clothes suddenly overwhelmed her.

The child was exceptionally beautiful with a rounded face, well filled out contours, and a rosy blush emphasized by the pink of ribbon in her hair and the color of the nightie. As she cooed and gurgled she met Leslie's eyes and smiled joyously as though happy to see her.

"Oh, how lovely," said Leslie to the proud mother. "How old is she?"

"Six months," said the young mother as she gathered the child up and began to walk and rock in a soothing rhythm. The child was wide awake and gave no indication of going to sleep soon. She continued to gaze into Leslie's eyes while the mother moved around the room, humming gently.

"May I hold her?"

Leslie knew she had spoken the words, but it seemed as though they had come from someplace far away from her own body. She could not really recall ever holding a baby. She was appalled as the mother beamingly and proudly relinquished the child to her. But as the softness of the child filled Leslie's arms, the child's tiny lips brushed against Leslie's neck and sent chills of delight through her. Leslie felt an incredible, almost foreign, sense of fulfillment unlike any other she had ever known, except, her mind beaconed again, when she had created that first baby sweater, but then, that was really more of a happy hope. This was joyful fulfill-ment. The baby squirmed and beat her little fists as she continued to gurgle and smile.

"She likes you!" said the mother. The mother was very young and Leslie could see that she really wanted to get back to the party.

"Well, why don't we just take her back downstairs," said Leslie, laughing. "I'll be happy to hold her for a while."

The permissiveness of a society that revered its chil-dren was readily apparent as the mother happily acqui-esced. "Well, if you're sure you don't mind," the young woman simpered. "She certainly doesn't look as though she is going to go to sleep soon."

"Not at all," said Leslie with a delighted laugh.

She continued to hold the baby as they all exited from the room. When she reached the bottom of the steps, Leslie was utterly amazed by the debacle that met her eyes.

While she had been upstairs, her Uncle Pepe had continued with the preparations for his contribution to the party. He and the other men had rapidly set up a kettle over a small well-banked fire next to the flag-stone terrace. Water in it was rapidly coming to a boil and they were in the process of dropping large gray crabs into its contents, while in the kitchen some of the women began to prepare the yucca, sweet potato, and several other starchy root plants indigenous to the is-land, which they would mix with the crabmeat along with vinegar and oil. Other wives and girl friends stood to the side giving the men, now well covered with large cloth bibs, gay encouragement as nippers and small knives were brought out to dismember the cooked crabs.

They sat in groups around tables like ancient tropical chieftains as they savored their rum and waited in great expectation. As the men began to enthusiastically prepare the cooked crabs it was immediately apparent as to why they assumed what might seem to most a servile role. A glistening pile of crabmeat began to slowly grow on each table, but an equal amount was consumed by the workers. Leslie smiled as she realized how very much those starchy vegetables would be needed to extend this well-known island delicacy. The festiveness of these grown men enjoying themselves in such a primitive way was infectious and Leslie felt a very special affection for her mother's people.

As the baby continued to wave her fists and gurgle in her ear, Leslie shifted her weight and felt her gaze being drawn to another table. The men and women were downright rowdy as they enthusiastically split open the oysters that lay on a bed of chipped ice and guzzled them down, raw on the half shell with a squirt of lemon juice.

Augustine was in the very center and he was a picture of absolute debauchery as he reveled in the teasing and banter that accompanied this traditional feast. Over and over again the crowd made reference to the special aphrodisiac qualities attributed to this delicacy, and women and men alike laughed boisterously as oyster after oyster slipped down their eager throats.

Leslie had no idea of the picture she made as she stood watching in amused fascination, but she soon became aware of Augustine's reaction as he stopped in midmotion and stared at her in lustful fascination. The look was not lost on Philomena, who sat next to him. Her gaze turned malevolently toward Leslie, and Leslie was embarrassed as her own reactions to Augustine's charismatic magnetism began to betray her.

She turned quickly to find the mother of the child and made arrangements for a playpen, but not before she saw Augustine make his excuses to leave his place at the table. Moments later the baby had been safely and happily deposited in a shielded corner of the room and Leslie's arms suddenly felt empty and lonely as she continued to gaze at the child's perfection.

Always practical, she insisted she was probably seeing the child as the perfect model for the many tiny things she had designed during the past few weeks. She was startled as Gerald and Juanita appeared by her side and commented on her fascination.

"Wouldn't she be a perfect model for our new line of baby clothes?" Leslie said breathlessly to both of them. "Can't you just see what she would do for them?"

Gerald looked at her carefully and then quickly relaxed a momentary puzzled expression. "Sure, honey," he said with a little laugh, "but have you ever heard that all work and no play...?" He punctuated his words with an appropriate expression. "Forget that factory for just a moment and relax," he continued. "This is supposed to be a party not a work session."

He teased and chastised her with his usual skill as Juanita watched them both carefully. A perceptive Gerald quickly included her also as he turned to her, smiling. "Isn't that right, Juanita? I think I may need to give you some instructions about teaching your much too serious boss here how to play. It's obvious that you people certainly know how," he ended as they were again swooped away by someone who wanted to initiate Gerald into his manly duties with the crabs.

Leslie laughed as she watched them disappear. She looked reluctantly away from the baby and then smiled as she realized the party was a great success. Her mother was having a wonderful time and several times Leslie saw her in earnest conversations with Augustine. They seemed to end in enthusiastic smiling, head-nodding assent and hugs of excitement.

Again Leslie was sad and annoyed at the same time. She wondered why fate had dealt her such a complicated set of circumstances. Why did this man from her mother's past and Augustine have to be the same person? How was she going to handle this charade without hurting her mother or compromising her own values? There was an answer and she would find it, but right now she just wondered why.

Perhaps her life had been too sheltered and this was her first real taste of adversity. Maybe adversity was needed to make her stronger, capable of realizing her full potential as both a woman and an artist. Perhaps, perhaps not, she thought philosophically, but to her disciplined, organized mind it was a comforting thought because it put the whole thing in the context of challenge. That was something she understood.

Leslie could feel herself beginning to wilt as the noise and heat of the evening began to take their toll. Tiny beads of perspiration formed on her upper lip and in the small of her back. She looked longingly toward the whispering leaves of the surrounding foliage as they waved in the evening breeze. Methodically she began to make her way through the crowd, stopping to greet many along the way, until she was at last at the edge of the swimming pool. She went on to a secluded corner of the garden and stood for several moments breathing in the cool night air while sounds of the party went on behind her.

She heard something rustle and was not in any way surprised when she turned and saw Augustine there. She realized that he had been in her thoughts subconsciously all evening and sooner or later this encounter would take place.

"You are very beautiful tonight, María," he said with his now familiar voice.

He moved close and greeted her familiarly with a light kiss on the cheek. "We've not had a chance to greet each other properly," he said with a knowing, mischievous smile as he looked around noting their seclusion.

In spite of her resolve Leslie felt herself warming to

his touch and she immediately felt threatened. She looked at him for a long moment, mustering an icy control, and then spoke very deliberately.

"My name is Leslie," she said. "Leslie Marie."

Her eyes were fiery with challenge, but Augustine had been more than a little mellowed by both the drinks and the image of her holding the baby only a few moments before. He refused to rise to her challenge.

"You know," he said as he looked around the garden and completely ignored her rude retort, "the swimming pool should be restored as well as the garden. My father told me this was once one of the most beautiful patios in Ponce... You know, because of his memories of your mother, I feel I know you very well."

Ay cariña, he thought, *such a beautiful woman should be taken care of....* He could feel himself responding to her, but he was a persistent man who was well practiced in his use of time and charm. He waited perceptively for just the right moment to continue, obviously a man who enjoyed manipulating a high-spirited woman, savoring her responses as the air became laden with fiery vibrations.

"I have connections at Ponce Cement," he continued. "I'm sure I could arrange—"

"That really won't be neccessary," said Leslie, breaking in with a small tight smile. "I've already decided to make the pool and garden my next priority. I'm sure I can handle all of the details myself."

She was a picture of bristling hauteur and ruffled plumage.

"As you wish," he said with a small nod as his eyes roamed over her in obvious anticipation, "but the offer remains, in any event."

Then he paused as though searching for just the right words.

"I want you to meet Philomena," he said at last,

"but before you do I want you to know that I'm going to make changes in my personal plans. I haven't discussed it with Philomena yet, but I'm sure she will agree. I've waited far beyond the usual age for marriage, and our engagement was more of a mutual agreement to make our parents happy and unite two old families. In the meantime I'm sure if you make friends with her she can be of great assistance, as I mentioned yesterday."

As he talked Leslie was once again overwhelmed with his total lack of sensitivity. She had just witnessed him, for the past hour, warmly interacting with dozens of people, yet he apparently failed to see the nature of Philomena's attraction to him. He was a coveted prize and not one she would readily give up. He greeted Leslie as though she were a prize he'd already won and failed to see her obvious resentment. Surely he had to be wiser than this. All of her intuitive warning bells went off as she realized he must be attempting the most ancient of ploys—the story that the other woman would soon be gone so she, the newly chosen lover, could begin taking her place right now.

Her contempt for him was total as he stepped toward her with an expectant gesture. Before she knew what was happening she felt his lips brush softly over hers as he gently, almost reverently, lifted her chin and caressed the vulnerable softness hidden beneath while his fingers trailed down her neck.

"We have so much to discuss, *niña*, my dear little one."

Shivers and fire instantly collided and racked Leslie's body as her angry, astonished eyes met his. She struck back immediately.

"You really must think that I'm a total idiot," she said through gritted teeth. She moved purposely into the open again. "How could you possibly speak to me and act in such a preposterous way? Philomena is an exciting, attractive woman and it is more than obvious that your relationship with her is quite serious."

"I'm glad you see it that way," said a heavily accented, husky voice in English. "Augustine and I are most assuredly looking forward to great happiness," said Philomena with an ingratiating smile. She had apparently arrived only in time to hear Leslie's last few words.

Leslie flushed in confusion as the other woman continued imperiously. Augustine looked on solicitously as though this were a perfectly normal scene.

"I'm sorry we've not had the pleasure of meeting before," Philomena went on, "but your home is lovely and is going to be even lovelier when you have finished your restoration." She spoke with a polite and calculated charm as her eyes raked haughtily over Leslie.

It was more than obvious to Leslie that Philomena was still glowing from the attention she was receiving from Don Fernando. Leslie saw him hovering in the background, but Philomena was also pandering to Augustine, behaving the way he would expect her to. Nevertheless there was also a cold undercurrent of fury in her words that sent an icy shiver through Leslie. She wanted only to be away from this woman as quickly as possible.

As Augustine stood looking on benignly, Philomena continued. "Augustine has told me you might possibly be interested in some of our people from Ayudalo. It's his pet charity, you know. He looks on it as one of his ways of saving our people, who have for too long been 'slaves to the indignities of welfare and poverty.'" She quoted him in an affected overdramatic voice and smiled at him patronizingly. "We must make arrangements to have lunch and discuss this someday soon." She looked at Leslie in simpering condescension, which she effectively masked as she placed a cigarette in a small elegant holder and held it to her lips, indicating to Augustine that she needed a light. Their eyes met and he smiled at her in reward for her commendable behavior.

How very appropriate, thought Leslie in acute irritation as she watched the two of them together. *They are exactly right for each other.* Leslie turned to leave them as another of the guests approached to call something to her attention, but not before Augustine followed her for a few steps and caught her arm to detain her.

"Remember what I said, María," he said softly. "I'm very serious. My plans *will* be changed. I want you to understand that."

His eyes were almost hypnotic as they bore into her own, but she withdrew her arm swiftly as she was once again consumed with rage. She could sense Philomena's possessive eyes on her back. She was appalled by Augustine's outrageous, utterly dishonest conduct. Echoes of conversations with Magna filled her brain. As the sounds of the party continued gaily in the background she wanted only to be as far away from Augustine and his haughty lover as possible.

Chapter Seven

Leslie was still tired from the party when she returned to work Monday morning. But, she mused, the continued radiance of her mother had been well worth it. She thought this in spite of the fact that the continued presence of Augustine Rivera and his interference in their lives was growing more complicated. Leslie realized that the longer she waited to discuss this problem with her mother, the worse it was going to be. She had listened in agony as every other word of her mother's seemed to refer to him when she relived the party over and over again on Sunday. With the new Machiavellian twist introduced by Philomena and Augustine's blatant disregard for decency Leslie knew she must do something soon before it was too late.

The excited chatter of her workers broke into her reverie. One of them had won a small amount of money in the national lottery, which nearly everyone in the island used as the springboard for their dreams.

"You should use your money for shares in Los Tejidos," said Juan Pacheco. "In the long run your money would be invested in a sure thing."

Leslie looked at this valuable employee. He was an older man who carried himself with great dignity. He was exactly the type of person she hoped would benefit from her idealistic shareholding program.

"Already," she heard him go on, "I'm planning for

Juan Junior's college and a new house for my Emma someday.''

"Your house is wonderful," said Leslie as she gave him a grateful smile. "It was painted so lovely last Christmas, really quaint and beautiful in your little barrio in Adjuntas.''

"Oh, yes, I know," he said a little shyly. "It's always been in my family, but it's so small and it's wooden and sitting on stilts. Emma deserves a modern house someday.''

Juan's words gave Leslie a very good feeling. "Well, I certainly hope all of your dreams come true," she said with real affection. "And I thank you for the boost you're always giving this benefit from our company.''

"I am a practical man, Doña Leslie," he said with a hesitant smile. "The odds of ever winning big money in the lottery are small, we all know that. I think you are offering an opportunity we are foolish to ignore, but I must admit," he said with a twinkle in his eye, "I still buy a lottery ticket or two each week.''

"Of course," she said as she matched his humor, "a wise man always covers all of his bases.''

"That he does," Juan said with a little wave as he went off to his duties in the stockroom.

Leslie felt real affection for this man and most of her employees and she walked with a happy jaunt to her office after this exchange. She quickly glanced through the mail and her last words to Juan became an insistent echo. The statement from the broker had arrived and she glanced at it hurriedly. She screwed her face in annoyance as she tried to decipher the intricate columns of computerized information that filled several pages.

Obviously she needed time to go over this carefully and probably she should give Harold a call too since they'd never been able to make a good connection since his last call, but Gerald arrived then and she remembered their plans. As she greeted Gerald she noted the name R.B.R. Juarez Ltd. in several places. That must be the conglomerate, she thought, probably local. But surely if there had been anything serious the broker would have sent her a wire or something. This could wait and obviously by the size of this report Augustine was in good company. She hadn't even seen his name yet. She'd take care of this when she returned.

Thinking he would enjoy the outing as much as she would Leslie had planned her trip to go to a Taino Indian archaeological site while Gerald was there. It was on the other side of San Juan near a town called Loíza. It was named after a woman chief. Leslie was fascinated that the early primitive people who originally inhabited the island had women chieftains. She wanted to learn more about these ancestors and also look for unique ideas to complete her ski sweater line.

It should be a fun trip and on the way they could probably take time to see the usual tourist attractions. Leslie was looking forward to a rousing "work and play" good time.

"Don't you think, though," Gerald paused as they both caught their breath after laughing hilariously over yet another incident from the party, "that it would be a good idea to take Juanita along? You're going to be taking notes and conducting pretty extensive research. Couldn't Tía Isabel take her place for a few days?"

Leslie looked at him astutely and then broke into a big grin. "Why, you big devil," she said accusingly. "I do believe you're up to something!"

"Not at all," he said in mock offense, but he couldn't hide a tiny quiver that tinged his eyes and lips.

"I don't see why not," said Leslie in continued perceptive amusement.

She laughed with Gerald and they continued to make their plans. When she informed Juanita of their intentions a few moments later, she was momentarily confused and looked away from Leslie in an almost guilty confusion. But when she saw Leslie's genuine desire to have her along she blushed and grew excited, then immediately began to instruct Isabel in her duties.

"Take lots of note and sketch pads," Leslie instructed Juanita. "I want to get everything I need in one trip if I can. We'll probably be gone for several days."

Leslie and Gerald had brought their luggage along, so Juanita quickly made arrangements to pick up her own. But at the last minute Leslie decided to make a quick stop to be sure her mother was all right before they got under way. To her instant dissatisfaction as she pulled into the drive she noted the presence of a big dark car next to the house and quickly surmised that Augustine was already there.

"Mija," her mother cried breathlessly as she came rushing down the steps. "I thought you would be gone by now."

If Leslie hadn't known better she would have almost sworn her flustered mother was hiding something. Augustine was close behind as Doña María explained with an obvious tinge of agitation that he had stopped in for lunch. As if to give credence to her words Augustine wiped his fingers with a napkin as the last crumbs of a fried plantain chip disappeared between his lips in what was to Leslie a rather gauche accommodation of himself.

He certainly hadn't wasted any time in making himself at home, she thought heatedly.

As her mother again assured her that everything was all right Augustine also chimed in exuberantly.

"Go, go. Have a good time. Tía Isabel will soon be here and I'll stop in often to ensure their safety."

It was almost as if he were pushing her out of her own home. A flush of irritation washed over her. She wrinkled her nose in distaste. She had the distinct feeling that her life was being tampered with and she was powerless to stop it without disastrous results. It was a conflict becoming all too familiar as she weighed her mother's health against her own sense of distrust.

As Gerald began to make impatient sounds Leslie gave her mother another hug and turned to leave, not sure now that she should go. She had the most uncanny feeling, but before she could identify, let alone voice her disquiet, Augustine was herding her back to the car. His great hand grasped her elbow firmly.

"Ten cuidado, niña," he said softly as he looked from her to Gerald. "I'm glad to see you are properly chaperoned."

He nodded toward Juanita. A little smile played around his lips, but his eyes were serious. He kissed her with the traditional farewell *beso* and nuzzled her cheek with his forefinger while his eyes searched hers expectantly and roved over her body appreciatively. They dwelled at the point of cleavage displayed by the low V of her tailored blouse and moved on to the roundness of her hips below her neat waist.

Leslie could feel herself rising to the bait of his blatant mischievousness. Then she quickly realized how silly it was to allow him to upset her. By now she should be used to him. With a shrug she walked away, gave a last little wave, and they were off.

They left Ponce a few moments later and headed out on the Autopista Las Americas, the grand super highway that swept through the mountains in a breathtakingly beautiful drive from Ponce to the city of Caugas. Slowly Leslie relaxed as within a half hour they were enveloped in the grandeur of the drive. She reflected on their plans. They had decided to stop in the scenic Old San Juan area and stay for the night. Then they would continue on along the wild and rugged Atlantic coast to the town of Loíza Aldea the next morning, planning to arrive at the dig around eleven o'clock. The anticipation of what she hoped to find at the ancient Indian site as well as Gerald's unfailing enthusiasm and humor began to excite her. The car seemed to fly aloft into the dazzling blue sky as it conquered yet another of the vast green summits and then went hurtling down the well-designed incline. Before she knew it they were approaching the busy intersections of Rio Piedras.

With Juanita's expert guidance they were soon in the glittering Condado area with its huge beachfront hotels and casinos. They stopped in a tree-shaded parking lot close to La Fortaleza and elected to walk the short distance to the medieval streets of Old San Juan. After walking up and down several of the hilly, narrow streets with their unending number of tourist wares, Leslie had examined several needlework specialty shops as well as the Museo Del Indio, which included many of the artifacts she was interested in. Then she suggested that they refresh themselves in a street side café near the Plaza de Colon with its imposing statue of Christopher Columbus. There was a definite aura of the past all around them, but there was also an irritating note of modern entrepreneurism that made her feel a touch of sadness.

Shadows were beginning to fall when they finally came to the visitor's entrance to El Morro with its long winding road through a beautiful green meadow. They were frankly tired and the long walk looked exhausting. They decided to try to see this interesting landmark on their return home. After immersing themselves so thoroughly in heavy, intimidating Spanish history they really felt the need for a change of pace, so they headed back to the Condado area, but Gerald quickly demurred when Leslie mentioned the casinos.

"I came down here to escape big-city glitter," he said as he wiped his perspiring forehead and gave thanks for the air conditioning in the car. "How about something totally different?"

Quick to assist, Juanita shyly suggested that they dine in the Swiss Chalet Restaurant in nearby Santurce.

"Sounds like just the ticket," said Gerald as Juanita once again gave expert directions.

A half an hour later as they dined on delicious Swiss specialities, they were having a wonderful time, but as they laughed in boisterous, good-natured delight, for some reason in the back of Leslie's mind she kept seeing the picture of Augustine entering the party just the night before last. She found herself involuntarily smiling as she speared a tasty morsel of food with her fork and realized that after their theatrical farewell he had been in her subconscious for the entire afternoon.

In reflection she realized when they had reached the gates of El Morro and she had looked out over that great field leading up to that fortress standing in majestic silhouette, she could just imagine him striding around those ancient, unconquered walls. Then she thought of him as he sat philosophizing on that fateful afternoon before his disgraceful behavior. The thoughts gave her an unsettling, almost nostalgic feeling.

If she hadn't known better as she watched Gerald and Juanita enjoying their wine and having such a good time, she might almost have admitted that she missed Augustine. She could almost think tenderly of the man she had seen briefly who had a combination of childlike charm and was prone to sage, grandfatherly introspection. She could feel a soft mellowness welling within her until suddenly she drew herself up sharply, shocked that she had once again allowed herself to drift into a ridiculous and dangerous daydream. This man was at this very moment, she was sure, conniving to take over her business, very possibly her life in a very deceitful way.

Quickly Leslie forced herself to return to the scene at hand as the waiter brought the lucious dessert cart around. She joined Gerald and Juanita in discussing the best place to stay as they enjoyed demitasse and pastries. Again Juanita suggested a little motel close to the ocean that would be directly on the way to Loíza Aldea. They agreed on a festive note and departed the restaurant immediately to be sure they arrived in time to get rooms.

The next morning, remembering her bout with the *mimis* just days before, Leslie prudently dressed in a loose, comfortable cotton-blend smock and slacks ensemble, which gave her a carefree relaxed look. Knowing they would spend most of the day in the outdoors, she had advised Juanita to dress accordingly. Nevertheless with her hair pulled back in a neat chignon and the addition of fashionable sunglasses and gold stud earrings Leslie was still a picture of modern sophistication.

Soon they were making their way toward the town of Loíza. At last, after following special directions, they came to the archaeological site that was their destination. They stepped out of the car with a sigh of relief and as Leslie looked around she felt as though she had entered another world totally removed from the one they had just traveled in. Dr. Juan Bonilla, an archaeologist from the Puerto Rican Institute of Culture, was coming to greet her with an extended hand, commenting that she was right on time for their appointment.

Slowly Leslie gazed around, allowing the atmosphere to penetrate her totally. She was barely aware of her polite greeting to the archaeologist and introductory remarks defining the reason for her visit as she wandered around the humid grassy area until they came to the messy brown indications of the actual dig.

She listened intently as Dr. Bonilla began to enthusiastically acquaint her with Aloíza, the most famous woman chieftain of the Tainos who had sat on her throne in this very site. Her territory extended throughout the northeastern section of the island and was bordered by that of another chief, Agueybana. Leslie was surprised to learn that another Taino site existed so close to Ponce near Tibes. She made a note to check this out.

"Now, as hard as it is to believe," Dr. Bonilla explained, "the original inhabitants of our island, which the Indians called Borinquén, were often ruled in matriarchal societies."

As Leslie stood there in that quiet green expanse surrounded by mountains, the drama and history that had occurred there completely hidden, she did not find this revelation hard to believe. She could feel the vibrations from hundreds of years before and suddenly she felt a very real kinship with those ancestral sisters.

"Actually," Dr. Bonilla went on, "these were extraordinary women inspired by the 'earth mother' concept. They often fought alongside their men and helped provide the food. They chose the men they wanted to love and indeed, loved at will, but they would lie with them only for certain periods when it pleased them."

The professor had a mischievous twinkle in his eye as he related this intimate tidbit, then he went on.

"In general, though, these women ruled with gentleness and friendliness. They were natural masters and the men didn't seem to protest. I think it was a very relaxed society in which all were equal."

As the professor talked he led them to a large open tent with several displays of newly found artifacts. Leslie stooped to more carefully examine the items and noted that they were for the most part stone and hardwood carvings as well as objects in terra cotta and other ceramic materials that depicted some aspect of life in a symbolic rather than naturalistic style.

"Unfortunately," Dr. Bonilla continued, "the pure and naive form of matriarchal government was completely blasphemed by the introduction of the Spanish conquistadors shortly after the island's discovery by Columbus. These men were generously welcomed into these primitive societies and the women were greatly taken by them. It's terrible to imagine," he said regretfully, "the ruthlessness with which they must have been vanquished. It was here on the banks of the Loíza River that gold was discovered and that was the final blow to the Borinquén culture, but not before," he added brightly, "they had a real taste of the power of Aloíza. She was magnificent. First she fought them, actually taking some of them prisoner, and then she chose her men almost ceremoniously, ultimately making them all her slaves, conquistador and Indian alike."

"How do you know that?" Leslie asked in surprise. "I understood there were very few accurate records other than these artifacts being unearthed now."

"Oh, there are some," he said, "but really, I can feel it," he said with fervor. "The spirit of Aloíza is here and it's magnificent." The professor paused. "You know," he said musingly, "I think that original Taino spirit still lives in our women and I rather like it."

Dr. Bonilla's face had taken on an almost peculiar gleam as he appraised Leslie admiringly. Again she was struck by this knack for philosophic introspection.

She intuitively understood this cultured man's interpretation of the vibrations most certainly in existence there. She could feel them all around her too as she reached for a sketch pad and began with Dr. Bonilla's respectful and polite permission to sketch some of the objects he had mentioned and more specifically identified.

There were stone-carved *cemis*, strange heads representing protective spirits, and puzzling large stone collars yet to be given a utilitarian label, as well as pottery and low stools called *duhos*. The latter were carved from a dense black wood and decorated with insets of gold leaf.

They seemed to have an abstract geometric quality and a classical perfection of proportion. Leslie realized immediately that her presumption that this site might inspire unique ski sweater designs was right on target. The patterns were perfect as was the setting and general atmosphere of the place. She could imagine a perfect blending of the sun and these primitive patterns contrasted sharply by the white of snow in a totally alien environment as she began to sketch her own interpretations.

Juanita and Gerald seemed to have wandered off, busy with their own preoccupations. As Leslie continued to wander around, sketching busily, she could not help but identify with the ancient Taino women: the true, original Puerto Rican women, independent, with the freedom to mate and have children by a man of their own choosing and inclination. It was a refreshing concept uncluttered by convention. She could well imagine the initial response of the first conquistadors who did not worship "mother earth," but on the contrary conquered her.

Before she realized it, Augustine had once again come to mind. How very appropriate, she thought as she became aware of the intrusion. He was in fact the very embodiment of those historic intruders and suddenly she knew exactly how her ancestors must have felt. They must have instinctively plied their most seductive defensive measures and Leslie agreed. In this spot at least they must have reigned supreme. She could sense it and identified with it strongly.

They spent the entire afternoon and evening at the site, leaving early the next morning. Leslie stopped in Loíza Aldea and bought a beautiful Taino amulet designed to be worn as a long dramatic necklace as a memento of the trip. She felt a warm sense of pleasure as she held it in her hand. When they traveled back toward San Juan their conversation was animated and full of great anticipation as they discussed the ski sweater line.

"I really can't tell you how excited I am about your ideas for this new line," said Gerald. "This trip was a marvelous idea and I'm really fascinated with that site."

So was I, thought Leslie to herself musingly, but she laughed, sure that there was a trace of double meaning to Gerald's words as he and Juanita continued to obviously enjoy each other's companionship. Juanita seemed to be a little shy about it and often looked at Leslie furtively, but Gerald more than made up for her with his exuberance.

I really must tell her to relax, Leslie thought fleetingly.

Moments later they were discussing El Morro and decided they had ample time to make the visit they had postponed on the first day of sight-seeing as well as the beach if they spent another night in San Juan. Gerald could catch an early flight out the next morning and save himself the bouncy trip over the mountains in the small plane.

"You only live once," Gerald said to Leslie, "and I don't think another day of relaxation will hurt you one bit. Give your mother a call. I'm sure she won't mind."

A short time later Leslie was talking to her mother and she couldn't believe how excited, almost flighty, her mother was. She was more than happy to hear that Leslie was having a good time and encouraged her to stay. Everything was fine at the plant. Tía Isabel had managed just fine.

"Oh, and, Leslie," her mother gushed, "when you get back we, er, I have the most wonderful surprise for you."

She broke off almost as if someone were cautioning her, and Leslie was momentarily puzzled, but then dismissed it. She said good-bye after telling her mother where they would be staying.

Deciding to really throw caution to the wind, they had made reservations at one of the big glittering beachfront hotels on Ashland Avenue in the Condado. They checked in and then sat around the pool and sipped creamy piña coladas. Later they set off for an afternoon on the El Morro grounds. It was a giant, almost mind-boggling fortress jutting out into the ocean—the personification of medieval grandeur. Dramatic, impregnable, and interesting. It was a fascinating place for a fertile imagination.

As Leslie walked and climbed, fitting neatly into the small guard stations designed for much smaller people four centuries before, she again felt a great sense of history. She was well aware of the spirits of the conquistadors who manned and built this massive rock. The spirit and essence of Augustine was here. She could feel it. Now, after visiting the Taino site, she well understood the basis for her instinctive conflict with him, but the heavy, intimidating atmosphere of the fortress served to inspire rather than intimidate her. *Aloíza had known how to handle the conquistadors and so do I*, thought Leslie.

Tired and totally saturated with history, they made their way back to the hotel where they quickly donned bathing suits for a relaxing swim. Gerald and Juanita were in the pool as thoughts of Augustine again returned and Leslie remembered their volatile encounter next to her empty pool the night of the party. Almost as if an apparation come to life he suddenly was next to her, sitting down at the table.

"Augustine!" she exclaimed. "What are you doing here?"

"Well, I had an appointment with the governor at La Fortaleza this afternoon so I thought I'd come over and try to catch you this evening."

She looked at him warily. There was a smug, little-boy mischievousness about him.

"Your mother told me where I might find you," he said in response to her look.

Leslie could feel herself growing tense as the thought of how close he was growing to her mother agitated her again, but she was determined not to let him ruin her day.

"Well, now that you're here, what do you have on your mind?"

"What do I have on my mind?" he asked, clearly puzzled over this turn of phrase, as Leslie fell easily into her colloquial New York idiom.

"Yes, you must be thinking about something," she went on.

"No, I just thought we might have a drink together.... I missed you."

She looked at him and her insidious thoughts insisted upon clothing him in the armor of the threatening conquistadors. Her thoughts while in El Morro came flooding back, as did her knowledge of Aloíza.

"I have to get back to Ponce," he said. "I have a meeting in the morning, but perhaps we could all have dinner together."

His voice was soft and gentle, but his eyes were demanding as they took in the skimpiness of her bathing suit.

Leslie was suddenly self-conscious as the smart bikini she had thought nothing of wearing now made her feel very vulnerable. At the same time his fascination was obvious, almost bordering on slavery, and she decided to enjoy herself. Within moments they were joined by Gerald and Juanita and soon they were all having a festive time.

After an elegant dinner Gerald relented and they decided to make the rounds of the noisy glittering clubs and casinos.

"Come with me, *niña*," said Augustine as he pulled Leslie close. "Stay by my side. You will be my luck tonight."

Again Leslie was amazed as the little boy she had

seen at the party stepped forth. She had changed to a slithery dancing dress, which was comfortable and revealing, and now felt sparky and happy, honestly enjoying herself.

Augustine draped a light shawl around her shoulders and allowed his fingers to linger over her bare arms. "We're going to have a wonderful time tonight," he said as they swooped through the door and allowed the insistent beat of the tropics to envelop them.

As they stepped into the elegant lounge of one of the clubs Augustine took her into his arms and began dancing toward the terrace. She whirled around with him in a seductive tango and the stars were mirrored in his eyes. He held her close and then threw her away in a wide arc as every muscle in his body coordinated with hers.

Gerald and Juanita were laughing in wild abandon as he gave his own interpretation to the sexy music. In the background they heard the shouts and clicks, indicating the proximity of the casinos.

"This is my lucky night," said Augustine. "I can feel it!"

Leslie laughed, a willing victim of his enthusiasm. His arms were strong as he held her close and danced slowly to a dreamy beat.

"I'm so happy when I'm with you," he said softly.

His eyes met hers and spoke eloquently to her innermost being. She could feel herself responding and was momentarily disconcerted as his tenderness touched her in a treacherous way. In a way she almost wished he would be nasty again. In the long run her response to that was far less dangerous.

Leslie flushed and looked away, but she could feel herself being drawn to him. They walked through the great doors into the noisy, brightly lit casino and she immediately sensed a change in him. It was almost as if he were an animal readying himself for battle.

"Pick a number," he said as he plunked a large roll of money on the roulette table.

"Oh, no," said Leslie, "I'm no good at this sort of thing."

"You don't have to be good," he said with a little laugh. "It's all luck, and luck is with us tonight. After all, she allowed me to find you, didn't she?"

Leslie shook her head over this questionable logic. They stayed at the roulette table only a few minutes and true to Augustine's premonitions came away winners.

Gerald was having a wonderful time, but after losing a few dollars decided he liked watching better than playing.

Bolstered by the roulette, Augustine decided to try cards. As he played, Leslie saw a cunning look take over as he astutely gauged his plays. She could see that he was an excellent strategist. Somehow that left her with a great feeling of uneasiness and a little shiver went through her. She was having such a good time that she had almost forgotten how dangerous this man was. She remembered now and took steps to disengage herself from him.

"Augustine, isn't it getting late for you to get back to Ponce?"

"No, María, not at all. I flew over in my plane. Don't worry, I will be in Ponce early in the morning. I have a feeling that tomorrow is going to be a *very* special day."

There was a sly, mischievous look about him, but Leslie didn't pursue it. They were seated in the club again and the feature show of the evening was coming on. When a slick well-known performer stepped to the microphone they were soon swept into a make-believe world as show girls and singers gave a polished nightclub performance.

Augustine was never more than inches from her. His

hands traveled over her at every opportunity and he whispered into her ears and nibbled her throat as they danced. Gerald gave them a quizzical look now and again, but Augustine always managed to look chaste and innocent on those occasions and Gerald was really so enraptured with the effervesence of the evening that he paid them little attention. It was obvious that he and Juanita were in a world of their own.

Leslie was alternately wary and then touched. Augustine was a fascinating enigma in these surroundings. Finally mellowed by the drinks, she relaxed and gave in to the beat of the music.

As they danced on into the night she felt as though she were in a dream. When again they were beneath the stars she readily followed as Augustine led her down to the beach. Shoes in hand she walked along comfortably in the haven of his shoulder as he pulled her close and gazed at the moon.

The waves were wild as the tide came in and lapped at their feet. It was only natural to be kissed in such a place and she responded in abandon as she felt her ardor growing.

"Oh, María," said Augustine as he held her next to his heart, "I wish we could be like this forever."

As he showered her with light kisses Leslie was sure she was in a dream—another one of those persistent daydreams. It was perfectly harmless. Augustine was a wonderful person. She must have been terribly mistaken about him.

Before they knew it, it was 2 A.M. Augustine left them for the airport, and it was a tired couple that saw Gerald off the next morning. Sighing, Leslie sat back more grateful than ever for the easy drive home over the new highway.

She was tired and irritable as the full implications of the evening before came back to haunt her in the glare of the morning light. After dropping off Juanita, telling her she would see her in the morning, Leslie at last pulled up to her home.

She sensed something different, but barely noticed the trodden grass and remnants of brown paper bags near the back of the house. As she headed in that direction to enter through the flagstone patio she stopped in shock as the sound of moving water gaily gurgling like a babbling brook came to her ears. It took a moment for her to register the full scene. The swimming pool had been totally and completely restored during her absence.

Chapter Eight

Leslie stood in stunned silence. It took only seconds of deduction to figure out what had happened. She quickly recalled her mother's breathless fluttery voice and the mischievous, almost conspiratorial conversations between her and Augustine at the party. This was all his doing. He was openly and blatantly interfering in her affairs and involving her mother in a fiendish, underhanded way.

How very cunning, she thought, to do something that would require her utmost gratitude.

Anything less would indicate a severe lack of graciousness on her part. But she would have none of it. In her mind this was an outrageous intrusion and she would not stand for it.

"Mama!" Her voice was strident with anger as she stalked into the house.

Doña María was in the kitchen absorbed with a piñon casserole of ground meat, eggs, and plantain. She looked up in surprise as Leslie burst into the kitchen.

"Mama, how could you do this?"

"Oh, Leslie," her mother greeted her excitedly, not immediately perceiving her daughter's agitation. "Isn't it wonderful? I knew how much you wanted to restore the pool and Augustine had friends from Ponce Cement who owed him a favor. This is a special gift to you...."

Her voice trailed off into confusion as Leslie's contorted, angry face looked at her accusingly.

"Mama," Leslie said in a deadly monotone, "men such as Augustine Rivera do not give gifts or favors without getting something in return. How dare he use you in this way!"

"But, *mija*," her mother said in confusion.

Doña María had wilted before Leslie's eyes and she was immediately contrite.

Haltingly her mother went on.

"Augustine is a dear friend of this family. He knows how hard you work and he wanted you to have a place to relax as much as I did. It cost him nothing."

Leslie was speechless.

"Really, *mija*," she continued, imploring her daughter to understand, "this is a beautiful gesture. You are in a different society now. You don't have to be so independent here. Friends and family enjoy doing things for each other and share whenever they can."

Sincerely sorry now that she had hurt her mother, Leslie realized that she could not argue with this rationale without completely destroying her mother's newfound zest for life. It was apparent that she had already caused considerable damage as she watched her mother worriedly wringing her hands. In dismay she also realized she had waited too long to discuss the problems concerning Augustine. Now it was too late. To attempt to discredit him in any way now would leave her mother feeling unbearably guilty. All of her recent progress could be destroyed.

No, I'll have to handle this another way. The source of the irritation should be the recipient of it anyway, she thought vehemently.

With an effort Leslie hid her churning emotions and held her arms out to her mother.

"Oh, Mama," she said softly, "of course you're right. It is a nice gesture. I guess I was not only surprised but momentarily angry at the thought of the unplanned expense that would be difficult right at this moment."

"Then it's all right?" her mother asked hesitantly.

Doña María visibly brightened as she searched her daughter's face for approval and was rewarded.

"Yes, Mama, it's all right," said Leslie with a sigh.

But inwardly she was still raging as she looked over the beautifully restored pool. It had transformed the entire garden area and was as peaceful and soothing as she had thought it might be.

"I really must go and thank Augustine," Leslie said carefully. "Do you have any idea where I might find him, Mama?"

"Oh, yes. He's in his office in the plaza. He's waiting to hear your reaction."

"Well, then we shouldn't keep him waiting," said Leslie. Her snapping eyes belied the smooth calmness of her voice. "I'll go immediately to tell him what I think, but please, Mama, don't call him. I want to surprise him."

"Well, okay, *mija*." She headed happily back to the kitchen. "I'll finish the piñon and save it for dinner. It's one of Augustine's favorite meals, you know, and I thought you might enjoy it too."

Oh, so he's been here so often that she even knows his favorite foods, thought Leslie venomously. When she was finished with him today she doubted he would feel so free about visiting in the future.

As she angrily stalked to her car a tiny insistent throbbing was beginning in the back of her head and as the car bounced back to the highway she called Augustine every vindictive thing she could think of while she drove with vengeance down the twisting mountain road toward Ponce.

When she came to the city's central treelined plaza she entered the one-way street that went around the old square with its turn-of-the-century, two-story buildings. She passed the famous firehouse Parque de Bomberos twice before she realized she was literally running in circles.

She quickly checked her anger as she willed herself to calm down enough to locate a parking place in one of the narrow side streets. It was late in the afternoon when she stepped out of her car, but the heat was still like a blast furnace and quickly refueled her animosity as she set out to find Augustine's office.

As she walked, her mind was storming. She mentally tried to calculate the cost of the pool restoration. There was no way it could have been done for nothing, she fumed to herself. In added frustration she realized she had no way of making an intelligent calculation, but it didn't matter. She wasn't going to be indebted to this man in any way. She fished through her purse and she continued to walk until her fingers located her checkbook. She was tapping it in rhythm with her angry steps as she came to a gleaming mahogany railing that lined a long porch on a buff-colored building, half a landing above street level. As she looked up at heavy ornate doors with an imposing gold sign indicating the holdings of the Rivera family she unhesitatingly stomped up the steps and burst through the door in an almost unholy clatter.

Her entry was a rude intrusion upon the hushed calm of the dim wooden interior laden with restored Victorian influence. Seeing no one in the receptionist's chair, Leslie continued on. She opened a heavy door covered with carved squares and strode into Augustine's office without knocking.

"How much did it cost?" she asked through gritted teeth.

Her appearance had been victimized by the ravages

of her trip and the heat. She grabbed at wisps of hair and dabbed at the perspiration that flooded her face, giving emphasis to her obvious anger.

Augustine looked up in startled surprise. He was entertaining a client, but Leslie continued with her tirade.

"How dare you attempt to buy my mother's affection and interfere in my affairs!" she exploded in low, guttural vehemence. "How much did it cost?"

She waved the checkbook in front of him. Her eyes were wild with anger.

"Tell me! I want to pay you immediately!"

Augustine came out from around his mammoth desk, disturbed but solicitous, as his client looked on in confusion.

"María," he said, "there must be some terrible misunderstanding. Please calm down so we can discuss this rationally."

"Forgive me, Senor Gomez," he spoke in Spanish, switching from the English of Leslie's outrageous address. "Perhaps," he said meaningfully, "we can continue our business tomorrow. There seems to be some kind of an emergency."

"But of course," said the other man, rising politely.

He looked Leslie over appreciatively, indicating respect and man-to-man amusement for this kind of trouble. His exit just infuriated Leslie all the more and she turned on Augustine again.

She looked around the room and quickly noted the ornate, sumptuous trappings including a large chandelier. True to his word there were pictures of her mother as a young woman standing next to a man who bore a striking resemblance to Augustine.

"You don't care about my mother," she hissed. "Your first loyalty will always be to your own. How dare you trifle with my mother's affections and interfere in my affairs!"

"Leslie, María, please! I don't understand what you

are so upset about. When I mentioned to your mother my connections at Ponce Cement she thought restoring the pool would be a wonderful surprise. It was all her idea! I couldn't refuse her. I hold your mother in my highest esteem, which has nothing to do with my mother. Surely you have a better understanding of our culture than this?"

He ended in gentle chastisement.

"You could not possibly have restored that pool for nothing," said Leslie as her reason began to slowly return.

"But I did precisely that," he said patiently. "I have some connections, and a favor or two was owed to me. The filter was the only expense and your mother insisted on paying for that from her mad money. All in all it was a congenial way of repaying a past favor—one that weighed heavily on the mind of my friend and made your mother happy. It was an act of kindness for all concerned. I'm terribly sorry that you are so disappointed."

Leslie could feel herself wilting in embarrassment. Actually the restoration of the pool was a marvelous gift and she was reacting outrageously.

"I'm afraid I owe you an apology," she said hesitantly. "I'm very sensitive about being indebted to anyone and I guess I unfairly felt that you were forcing your will upon me through this... favor."

"You are tired, *mija*," he said. "You must learn to relax more. We had such a good time last night." He smiled.

As he spoke he placed his arm around her in a kind fatherly way and continued in a soft reassuring voice.

"Please don't be upset. It's not good for you."

For a moment Leslie felt as though she were enveloped in the warmth of her father's protective arms and then an insidious rush of blood began to pound through her veins as Augustine's touch lingered on her arm. She could feel herself responding as he continued to look at her tenderly.

Slowly, almost as if mesmerized, their lips came together in a sweet, innocent caress. It was a wonderful communing of the senses and she felt herself yearning for more. His lips sent trails of fire over her face as he swept her disheveled hair back and devoured her lips. Suddenly the strident ring of the telephone pierced the heavy background silence of the room. They pulled away softly, in complete contrast to the insistent phone. He left her reluctantly, patting her hand and grimacing over the interruption as he went.

Leslie was completely disoriented. She had no emotion to react to Augustine's actions or her own unguarded responses. As she sipped a cool drink he had thoughtfully provided after answering the phone she readily agreed when he suggested that they stroll around the plaza. She felt nothing when he casually and proprietarily suggested that she tidy up before leaving. She was suddenly a chastised, extremely embarrassed little girl.

As she combed her hair and tidied her makeup she touched her lips in wonderment. She had actually enticed his caresses, responded, and invited more. Although they were in truth incredibly sweet she realized she had made another regrettable error in judgment. In spite of the good time they had had the night before she didn't for one minute believe her initial, intuitive deductions were false.

In sudden insight she realized that Augustine was really enjoying himself. She had reacted exactly as he had thought she would. He may not have anticipated her volatile visit, but nevertheless he loved it. With these thoughts tentacles of her rage again teased her and restored her original resolve.

She returned to Augustine's office exuding confidence and charm. To her satisfaction he was momentarily discomfited by this rapid change in her demeanor, but quickly met the challenge of her psyche as he took her arm to lead her through the door.

They strolled slowly, making idle chitchat as though the chaotic scene of just a few moments before had never happened.

"Tell me," said Augustine companionably, "was your trip to the dig a success? You were so lovely yesterday, I really didn't think to ask."

"Oh, yes," she said, "but I must admit after our partying last night I'm exhausted. I didn't know there was another Taino site so close to Ponce."

"Yes," he said. "You must be talking about the site near Tibes, the throne of the great chief, Agueybana. He died fighting the enslavement of his people..."

His voice had faded into the now familiar introspective silence.

As they continued to stroll, the heat of the day seemed to be passing and the entire plaza was softened.

"This great chief, Agueybana, was a man, then," said Leslie, breaking the companionable silence. "I take it he didn't live during the period of Aloíza, who frankly fascinates me?"

"Ah, yes," said Augustine in genuine amusement as they crossed the street, "I can see how you would be taken with her. There is a wonderful legend about her, but Agueybana Guarionex, and several others—I can't remember all of them—came later and led some of the last battles to save the Taino and Arawak culture. Historians insist it was completely destroyed by the 16th century but," he said with a sage gleam in his eyes, "all of us who truly loved Borinquén know those ancestors live on in our *jíbaros*, the people who live in our mountain towns, and all of us, even the *hidalgos*, the descendants of those original Spanish conquistadors. It's the true source of our national pride."

His voice had assumed that now familiar soft, reflective tone. He went on almost as if talking to himself.

"You know, once this was an island of huts. Most had a chicken in the yard or fish from the sea. The people cooked rice and beans. They had a plantain tree in the yard and grew native fruits and vegetables. The children laughed and played naked in the front yard. They were poor, terribly poor, but they were free. They provided for themselves. Today the very poor must depend on someone else to care for them and they are slaves to welfare and crime. That's why," he ended with passion, "the Fomento program must be taken seriously. Those factories must be well-managed, profit-making ventures."

Leslie looked at him sharply and then realized he had simply made another philosophic transition, practically forgetting her presence.

As they walked by one of the many park benches scattered throughout the well-manicured formal gardens she noticed that Ponce, as in all other island towns, had its traditional old philosophers who sat on their patriarchal benches in judgment of everyone who walked in the plaza. They behaved with great dignity as though they had great moral authority. She smiled as she pictured Augustine among them forty years later.

They passed the tall, distinguished statue of the patriot Morell Campos and ambled toward the Cathedral of Our Lady of Guadalupe on paths that led to pools and fountains. They were designed to accommodate many strollers out for their evening walk while also providing privacy for lovers.

As he took her arm and guided her across the street, coming out in front of the city hall, Augustine asked Leslie specifically about the results of her research. He had continued to be solicitous in the way of a man who could confidently afford such actions.

Leslie could feel herself relaxing and responding warmly to him.

"Oh, it really was wonderful," she said. "I've made

lots of sketches and I think the ski sweater line based on them is going to be fabulous. I can't wait until the new machines we've ordered get in so we can execute a few of the designs and see them come to life."

"You will definitely be hiring more people then?"

She nodded.

He pointed to one of the numerous fresh sherbet stands, famous for ices that tasted exactly like the fruit represented. "Would you like to try one?" Augustine asked.

Leslie nodded.

They leisurely ate their sherbets while sitting on a park bench and again Leslie felt herself communing with Augustine in an easy comfortable way—amazing in view of her anger just an hour before.

Again as if in a dream Augustine placed his arm around her and gently kissed her. He gazed at her musingly as he ran his fingers along the softly lighted planes of her face.

"You were so lovely last night," he said. "When I have everything straightened—"

"Augustine, please," she protested. "This is a public street. What will people think? You forget yourself and who I am and where we are!"

Although her earlier reserves were again intact she was flushed and responding in spite of herself.

Augustine merely smiled in affectionate amusement.

"Soon," he said in complete confidence as he continued to nuzzle her neck, "there will be a right place and a right time, *mi corazón,* and I know exactly who you are."

His eyes were embers smoldering with the patience of a hunter who knows his quarry well.

Leslie knew she should be more angry, but somehow the fiery response just wasn't there. It was as if she were emotionally bankrupt after that earlier exhausting scene. The truth of the matter was that she was rather enjoying herself and somehow that seemed perfectly all right.

Perhaps, she thought to herself musingly, *these are the times when the spirits of our Taino ancestors meet*.

Augustine had just said there was a little *jibaro* in all of them and they both loved the country. She smiled wryly. In its own way it was a comforting thought in spite of the fact that Augustine was obviously a *hidalgo*, a direct descendant of the ruthless conquistadors.

A little later they returned in mellow companionable silence to Augustine's office, only to be greeted by the haughty Philomena as she waited in toe-tapping impatience.

"Really, Augustine," she fumed, "when you make an appointment with someone you might make an effort to be on time."

Their nebulous rapport was instantly shattered and Augustine seemed to guiltily recall that he had indeed made a date with his haughty fiancée.

"Yes, Philomena, I have something of great personal importance to discuss with you, but for the moment it can wait. Senorita Williams has graciously paid a call to my office and this would be a marvelous time to discuss Ayudalo with her."

He beamed at both of them, clearly satisfied with his expertise in handling a potentially difficult situation.

Leslie could feel the agitation of the other woman from across the room, but Philomena amazingly hid it from Augustine as she feigned a simpering charm and greeted Leslie with a cold kiss on the cheek. Her long nails grated on Leslie's arms and spoke a vicious language of their own.

"But of course!" she gushed in false enthusiasm. "Ayudalo is my life."

She settled herself into a plush chair, crossing her long legs seductively in Augustine's direction as she busily filled her cigarette holder in a practiced motion.

"Tell me," she said, "what kind of people do you need?"

Leslie flushed, feeling distinctly uncomfortable and awkward in this overbearing woman's presence. She knew it was silly, but she had no desire to involve herself in any way with her.

"Well, perhaps it would be better if you were to tell me a little about Ayudalo," said Leslie. She was hedging for time as she searched frantically for a graceful way to extricate herself from this situation.

"Well, very simply," said Philomena in her heavy husky accent as she switched to English in a condescending manner, "*ayudalo* means 'help.' It's a nonprofit organization designed to create employment opportunities with a future for deserving people who have not had the resources to acquire a formal higher education."

She went on to give a rather toneless dissertation on the details of the program in a canned, dispassionate voice. Leslie had real difficulty imagining this woman as a guiding force in such an idealistic, worthwhile venture.

"Of course," Philomena went on, "this is one of Augustine's pet projects and everyone who is anyone in this town wants to be involved."

Leslie was more discomfited than ever. She knew Philomena really had very little personal interest in this program. This was just another of her ways to secure her acquisition of Augustine. Leslie couldn't believe he could be so blind. He seemed to be almost impervious to the dark vibrations surrounding this woman.

As these thoughts transpired she could feel herself inwardly tightening. She was being slowly and ominously backed into a corner. It was bad enough having Augustine interfering in her affairs. She definitely didn't need the influence of Philomena as well. A chill accompanied this thought and she rubbed her arms in tense frustration. She attempted to smile brightly, searching for an appropriate comment that would not commit her to anything.

Augustine had been listening quietly. His gaze never left Leslie and she could feel herself growing warmly uncomfortable as she made an effort to ignore his perusal. It was an exercise not lost on Philomena, as her eyes narrowed into a hard glitter.

"Really, this is a marvelous program," said Augustine before Leslie could speak. "It has proven to be highly successful in the garment industries. I really think with those special new machines you're bringing in this would be a wonderful opportunity."

"Yes, it would seem so," said Leslie, "especially in view of the fact that I've already established my business on many of the same premises, including shareholding privileges, but I think the location of my factory so far from Ponce would present a real problem."

"Not at all," said Philomena, for the first time indicating a real interest in this conversation. "Our people come from all over the island. The base office just happens to be in Ponce, right next door, as a matter of fact, in the room adjoining this one."

Her words were stretched with a special sly twist as she puffed her cigarette, providing a fitting hazy frame for her demeanor.

"I'm sure we can work something out," she ended as her gaze pierced through Leslie. "It's just a question of a few forms actually."

Leslie was really anxious now about her apparent inability to defend herself from this woman's obvious malice.

"Tell me a little more about this shareholding program," said Augustine, effectively breaking the uneasy silence that had followed Philomena's last remarks.

"Oh, well, it's really very simple," said Leslie, rallying at last. "When we incorporated the company, we issued stock through a reputable broker."

"And just how much stock did you issue publicly?" Augustine suddenly seemed to be keenly interested.

"Forty percent," said Leslie. "Then we reserved fifteen percent for the employee shareholding program and I kept the controlling interest of the remaining shares."

"I see," said Augustine. "Don't you think, though, that that might be a little too ambitious? Many of our people barely understand the basics of budgeting their weekly paychecks. You're not even requiring that they have a vested interest. How can you expect them to recognize this as a legitimate opportunity when in effect it reduces their take-home pay and offers no real return for years?"

Leslie was annoyed and she met his gaze squarely.

"It's all been very well explained to them," she said with a patience she didn't feel. "The program is voluntary and I believe it's working very well. Such a concept has long been a proved success in many large corporations."

"Yes, I can see where this all sounds very commendable, but you know there is a point where one must be practical. Have you honestly considered the consequences should the public and shareholding shares of your company be consolidated? It seems to me that your position could be very precarious."

"I really think," said Leslie pointedly, "you don't give your people credit for common sense." She willed her rising temper to recede. "We are like a family at Los Tejidos. I truly can't imagine such a thing happening, but in any event the public shares are being purchased by multiple investors. Under those circumstances the problems you propose should be nonexistent."

As Leslie spoke she realized she had not yet studied

the broker's report with reference to these transactions. For a moment she considered asking Augustine openly about his own participation, but thought better of it. It really was an awkward question, but more importantly would indicate her ignorance in this area and leave her even more vulnerable to his spiteful inquisitions. Nevertheless she must not forget to check that report carefully. It would have all of this information.

Realizing she was more than a little tired now, Leslie decided, in resignation, to conclude this discussion as soon as possible. After all, she did not have to choose all of her workers from this program. What harm could one or two of them do?

"Very well," said Leslie as she made motions to leave, "I see no reason why we can't look into this. I'll have Juanita get in touch with you tomorrow, Philomena."

"Marvelous," said Philomena in smoldering complacency. She had listened quietly and attentively to the conversation between Leslie and Augustine, her eyes snapping back and forth between the two of them.

When Augustine arose to see her to the door, Leslie was very much aware of the other woman's penetrating eyes while she mouthed the traditional phrases of departure. Leslie realized in deflation that now not only did she have Augustine to contend with but Philomena as well. It was an unsettling turn of events to say the least and she felt powerless to prevent it.

Chapter Nine

Leslie drove home from Augustine's office in pensive silence. She relived over and over the events since her return home that afternoon and was more than a little annoyed with the results of her mercurial emotions. In just a short time she had made errors in judgment and behavior that would have been inconceivable just a few weeks ago.

It was clearly linked to that first emotional and stormy meeting with Augustine beginning with her initial fear and unease in the museum and progressing on to this almost paranoid fear of his admittedly charismatic power. Actually in retrospect she was amazed. Really, what did she have to fear from this man? Was she not secure and competent enough to handle a few probing questions about her business? Why should she immediately attach a paranoid connotation to everything he asked about or suggested? How could she have such a good time one moment with him and hate him the next?

How? she asked.

Because....

Finally she forced herself to admit it.

It was really very simple. She was physically attracted to him and the truth of the matter was that in acting in such emotional, irrational ways she had probably fueled his initial doubts about her abilities.

With this truthful admission she suddenly felt as though some terrible restrictive bonds had been removed. Miraculously she was cleansed of all embarrassment and uncertainty. She was driven by an almost insatiable desire to work as ideas tumbled through her mind and cried for expression. She was a woman, a whole woman, and her body cried for its fulfillment too. There was absolutely nothing wrong with that.

A warm shiver went through her as once again she recalled the warm softness of the child in her arms and the soft caress of her tiny lips. Simultaneously she also remembered the warm glow of Augustine's eyes and the rhythmic motion of his overpowering embraces. She savored the feeling and decreed the fantasy to continue.

In another truthful insight Leslie also realized that she had no wish to be owned by Augustine or bound to him in any way. His strength and arrogance were far too threatening, yet it was this very strength that attracted her. It was the source of her yearning, as instinctively she realized this very trait combined with her own strong resources was what she intuitively sought to produce a strong and independent child, the one she yearned for now, just as she was reaching the peak of her feminine regenerative power.

It was a heady fantasy that Leslie freely allowed herself to indulge in. She understood that she was answering some inner need, which resulted in a wonderful sense of euphoria and renewed zest. The very brazenness of candidly admitting she was attracted to a man who had forcefully triggered her emerging biological need to have a child gave her a feeling of awesome superiority.

Not for one moment did she consider the scandalous consequences should she actually consider the fulfillment of her thoughts. On the contrary the relief she felt as a result of this truthful expression of her physical needs far outweighed any such restrictions.

She knew she was fully capable of nurturing and providing for a child. Motherhood did not necessarily mean marriage or sitting idly at home. Women had for centuries taken care of their children while going about their normal tasks. Should she so desire she could do the same thing. Her career was amenable to such a situation.

More importantly she had identified the source of her unrest and now she could handle it in whatever way she pleased. A fantasy was the least of her desires, but by all means appropriate if she wished to express herself in that way.

Moments later she was home, a picture of radiance. "Mama," she cried as she danced around the kitchen and sampled the piñon prepared earlier, "I'm so happy. Everything is perfect! You were right about the pool."

"Then you and Augustine had a good talk?"

"Yes, Mama, and I know exactly how I'm going to handle these situations from now on."

"I'm so glad," her mother said in obvious relief. "Augustine is really a wonderful man. We are lucky that he thinks so highly of us."

"Yes, Mama," said Leslie as a little of her earlier wariness returned, but then she refused to allow anything to mar her newfound euphoria. "I think I really understand him now."

"*Gracias Dios*," her mother breathed. Her face was wreathed in a happy smile. "Come, let's have dinner."

"In a while," cried Leslie as she dashed up the stairs and pulled on a slim one-piece bathing suit. She skipped onto the patio and dove into the pool in one graceful motion. She felt a very sublime satisfaction as the water cooled and lulled her into a sweet tranquillity while her mother watched in delight.

Later they dined next to the pool on the terrace and Leslie felt wonderful as the supreme mistress of her home. No longer did she feel threatened by the gift of the pool. Truthfully it now seemed more like a fitting homage to her power.

Later the high tension of an almost expectant excitement would not allow her to sleep. She reached for the sketch pad, which was always near at hand. The pencil seemed to have a mind of its own as ideas continued to tumble through her mind. Slowly a slim, sensuous silhouette began to emerge. It was a floor-length, smooth, shiny sheath with spaghetti straps and low-cut cleavage designed to hug the body. She could see it in shimmery white yarn as her hand began to swish, in great sweeping motions, penciling in fleur-de-lis scroll designs emanating from a long slim center line, bursting into blossom in and around the bosom like wild wisps of flame. She reached for a shiny gold pencil and saw the design come to life as a headdress, exotic and perfect for a princess, emerged. She drew in aqualine chiseled features and felt the spirit of Aloíza come to life as smoldering great round eyes gave the face its identification.

She gazed at the sketch and realized she must make this dress for herself. It was a magnificent embodiment of her spirit. Quickly she also sketched a robe and a skimpy bikini using the same flowing design. Then, at last, she could feel her eyes growing heavier as the pencil slowly slipped from her hand and she fell into a deep restful sleep.

The next few weeks were more than a little hectic. The new knitting machines were on the way and Leslie had delegated Juanita to handle the dealings with Philomena and Ayudalo to secure the new workers. She was totally engrossed with the designs for the ski sweaters. Her spirit was restored and she was happy, easily handling the now routine visits of Augustine. Somehow in the hubbub the broker's report was completely forgotten as she grew more comfortable with Augustine and began to think her initial paranoia was childish. Augustine was listed on the report, but she had finally discussed it with Harold and while the R.B.R. Juarez Ltd. seemed to have purchased a large block of stock, prompting the SEC report, so long as she kept her majority Harold saw no problem—in fact in his eyes it was a most encouraging sign indicating professional confidence in her operation. Yet for some reason when Leslie saw that conglomerate name some sort of nagging suspicion coupled with the memory of her angry outburst over her pool seemed to persist. She couldn't quite put her finger on it, but it seemed to grip her when she remembered walking through the door of Augustine's offices.

Then in disgust she'd put it out of her mind as she now began to carefully cultivate her relationship with him. Lunches together were not that unusual especially as Doña María became more involved with the factory operation. Purposely but subconsciously Leslie seemed to avoid Magna during this time. There was usually a pretense of business, but her discussions with Augustine often became very personal.

"María," Augustine said as they lunched together in a local restaurant not long after their volatile meeting in his office. "I really think you work too hard."

"I like my work," she said as she evaded his marauding eyes.

"I know," he said, his voice dropping to his familiar growl, "but you should go out more."

He reached across the table for her hand.

"I never see you at parties or the Club Deportivo. You know you could be missing some important business contacts."

"Oh, you know better than that," she said. Leslie

met his eyes in obvious amusement. "I have plenty of social contacts. I play tennis and golf whenever I can—"

"You play golf!" he said. "I didn't know that."

"Well, I'm not very good," she said, suddenly wary of his obvious enthusiasm.

"Well, I am!" he said firmly. "And I'm an excellent teacher."

"Oh, but I'm not that interested," she said as she struggled to stall his advance.

"Nonsense," he said in his inimitable way. "Finish your lunch. The golf course is just down the road. Remember what I said about taking a day off."

"But, Augustine," she sputtered.

"No, I've made up my mind," he said. "We're going to play golf this afternoon."

"This is absurd," she said.

"Call Juanita," he said imperiously. "I won't take no for an answer."

For just a second their eyes locked in mutual defiance. Then she pursed her lips in an expression of sheer calculation.

"All right," Leslie said. "You're on."

Actually the thought of a balmy day on the wide fairways of the Ponce Country Club was rather inviting and she had a feeling that this could prove to be very interesting.

Within moments Augustine was pulling into the Villaronga drive and his strong hands were helping her from the car.

"Go and change," he said as he perused her body openly. "I have everything I need in my locker at the club."

"All right." She laughed as she acknowledged a now familiar flush that warmed her. She intuitively knew his thoughts would be mentally picturing the entire process even though she'd be behind a closed door.

"Come in and get my clubs. They're in the closet. I'll just be a second."

"Take your time," he said, barely hiding his lascivious thoughts as a suggestive smile played over his lips.

Leslie went to her room and hurriedly began to undress. As she dropped her clothes on the bed she could almost sense the vibrations of Augustine's thoughts. Her skin prickled into goose bumps of anticipation and she acquiesced to the presence of her own desires. She quickly pulled on a short culotte and a comfortable knitted golf shirt and went out to meet him with a glowing smile.

"You look marvelous," Augustine said in real appreciation as she expertly pulled her hair back at the nape and snapped a large barrette into place. His eyes played over her entire body and Leslie honestly gloried in teasing him this way now.

"I'm ready," she said with a touch of coyness. Her face shone with excitement augmented by the continued hint of challenge the afternoon promised. She grabbed her golf shoes and skipped with him down the stairs as he easily shouldered her golf clubs and heaved them expertly into the car. A half an hour later they pulled up to the clubhouse.

"Here, let me take your clubs," he said. "I'll get mine from my locker and rent the cart."

"Oh, no," she said. "No cart!"

"No cart?" His expression was almost comical.

"No cart! You said you wanted to play golf. Well, let's play the proper way. Besides, the exercise won't hurt you!"

There was a mischievous twinkle in her eyes and his surprise readily conceded to her challenge.

"I see. Then you are familiar with this course?"

"I come often," she said, "but like I said, I'm not very good. I really come more for the walking and to be alone."

"Ah," he said in amused expansiveness. "Have I stepped into the—how do you say it—house of the spider?"

"'Come into my house, said the spider to the fly,'" she laughingly corrected him. "No, no, not at all. It's just that you were so laughably pompous."

"Me pompous?" he said, actually affronted.

"Oh, forget it. Go on and get your cart."

"No, no," he said, his ample pride more than evident. "You prefer to walk, then we will walk."

She smiled and shook her head as he walked off, his pique just barely concealed.

Soon they were walking out through the broad plains and hills heading for the first hole. It really was a wonderful diversion.

As she stepped up to tee off Augustine practically had a spasm as she planted her feet, situated her arms, and prepared to swing.

"Oh, no, no, no," he said in near agony.

"No, María. Here let me show you," he said as he stepped up and soon enveloped her in his strong arms while he leisurely instructed her in the finer points of the game.

"Really, Augustine," she said as she felt her color rising and the familiar response that she now fully understood began to betray her. "This isn't necessary."

"Sure it is," he said, now obviously enjoying himself. "Anything worth doing is worth doing well."

The mischief in his words was mirrored in his eyes as he stepped around and motioned for her to swing. His eyes were glued to her trim figure as her strong arms rippled with the effort of the swing and he watched the action of her breasts.

As the ball sliced far to the right he grimaced and shook his head.

"I think we have a lot of work to do," he said.

"No, we don't," she said as thoughts of his arms embracing her at every hole, through every drive and every putt was more than a little unnerving. "You play and I'll walk."

"Oh, no," he said. "It might take the rest of the day, but we will play together."

He stepped to the tee and sent a perfect shot out through the fairway. He was magnificent and awesome and again Leslie was reminded of her earlier admissions as his attractions were more than apparent.

As they played on he finally capitulated to her rationale and actually began to enjoy her comedy of errors as she made little effort to stick to form.

"Where did you learn to play this game?" he finally asked in exasperation.

"Right here," she said. "I go by here all of the time and one day I just decided to give it a try. Taught myself," she said proudly.

"I can tell," he said. "Look, *niña*, actually you have a very good potential. Now just listen for a moment."

Again his arms went around her and she could feel his lips close to her ear.

"Relax and then concentrate," he said as his body molded to hers. "Now, very carefully, just a light tap. Fantastic!" he said as she sank a perfect putt.

Leslie barely knew what was happening. His touch had left her quivering.

"You see," he said boisterously, "you could be wonderful!"

He held her away from him and then kissed her resoundingly on the lips.

"Augustine, for heaven's sake," she said, but she was laughing too. "Behave now!"

"You know," he said, ignoring her protests, "this would be a wonderful setting for those marvelous little summer sweaters you've designed."

She watched in amazement as the wheels began to

click in his head and knew that he was about to take over again just as he had when he arranged the showing.

"Yes," he said, a definite note of calculation in his voice. "I have a friend who is a fashion photographer."

Leslie was about to protest, but then thought better of it. She had to admit that he had done nothing but help her so far.

"We will need some models, of course. You would make a lovely model yourself," he said as his voice lowered ominously.

She remembered the showing and pursed her lips threateningly.

"Oh, well," he went on, "then I'm sure we can arrange a layout in the tourist magazine, *¿Qué Pasa?*"

"But that would cost a fortune," said Leslie, a little alarmed now.

"Oh, no, there are ways," he said meaningfully. "Remember you are a part of the Fomento program."

Again she felt a rising uneasiness. She could just see herself plunging into debt and him coming in to sweep up the pieces.

Seeing her long face, Augustine nudged her chin playfully.

"Hey," he said. "I told you the photographer is a friend of mine and the rest is just connections. You will see. What little it will cost will be well worth it!"

She gave a little grimace and knew it would do no good to argue with him. Actually it was a good idea and would provide her fashions with a great deal of promotion stateside as well as here. Already she was filling orders for local speciality shops thanks to the showing. There was no doubt: He did know what he was doing.

The wind was whipping her hair and giving her an innocent, tousled appearance. Suddenly Augustine stopped his enthusiastic chatter about the layout and looked at her. His eyes were soft with passion and yearning.

"Oh, *niña*," he said as he took her into his arms, "you are so lovely. You *do* belong in a picture."

He began to kiss her lovingly, nibbling her ears as he melded his body to hers.

"Augustine," she said menacingly as she drew away. "What will people think?"

"Whatever they want to think, *niña*, but we are alone here," he said as he swept his arm over the empty vista. "Perhaps soon we won't need to worry about what they think. You know," he went on, his passion more than evident now, "as soon as you have made the final arrangements with Ayudalo I will have a talk with Philomena."

Her face froze as she realized the full implications of his words. For a while there she had almost forgotten his potential for treachery. As her distrust emerged in full bloom her icy reserve came to her rescue and effectively mantled her rampant responses of just moments ago.

They played on in controlled restraint. Augustine seemed a bit puzzled by the change in her demeanor, but he was obviously perceptive enough not to challenge her. For a while she made a pretense of enjoying herself, but the spontaneity was no longer there.

As they continued to walk Leslie slowly loosened up again and by the time the afternoon was through they had once again relaxed into amiable polite company and she had to admit that she had enjoyed herself.

Actually once she had identified her feelings toward Augustine she had placed him in the proper perspective. On the whole she found her relationship with him much more relaxed so that encounters such as this one were a careful part of her overall scheme. At the same time she was competent and businesslike, never allowing him to ruffle her with his myriad questions and suggestions while inwardly she indulged in her fantasies. She welcomed him into her dreams and used him in any way she pleased.

Augustine, in turn, was openly admiring, even solicitous, readily bantering with her through their mutual challenges while Philomena hovered in the background. She was a dark question mark that Leslie chose to ignore.

Gerald called often and the factory was a busy buzz as the orders for baby clothes began to pour in. In lighter moments Leslie remembered her special dress design and decided finally to make it herself some evening after the plant had shut down. It would only take an hour or so to run the pieces through the machine. She could put it together at home while relaxing next to the pool. She sat there often in the evening listening to her mother enthusiastically describing her gardening projects on the patio.

She was not at all surprised when a few nights later her mother announced that she was going to spend a few days in the garden center of the island, Aibonito, a town nestled in the central mountains of the island during its *Fiesta de Patronales*.

"Why, that's a wonderful idea," said Leslie. "Will Tía Isabel be going too?"

"Yes," Doña María, said. "You know Isabel and I have always loved the fiestas. They make us feel like young girls again."

Leslie laughed.

"Not only do they make you feel like one, you look like one too, Mama. I'm so happy to see you so peaceful and content now. I'm sure this is the way Papa would have wanted it too."

"Yes, I know he would," she said.

More and more it seemed to comfort her to speak of him now.

"You know, not too many people have the experi-

ence of such a wonderful marriage such as the one your
father and I had. You know when I married your father,
at first my parents were very unhappy, but then when
they saw how happy we were, how good he was to me,
they loved him like a son. They didn't see him often—
for a few years we had some very hard times until he
finished his education and established the business."

Leslie smiled as she remembered the frequent visits
of relatives from the islands over the years, their pre-
cise English and warm hearts as they fawned over her
and teased her about coming to live with them in their
sunny island home. Even better was the memory of the
few times they had gone to Puerto Rico when she was
very young. It was always more of a fantasy than real
life, and even then she always felt herself drawn to it in
her dreams.

"Then when we could have traveled more," her
mother went on in her soft voice, "he was always so
busy. He used to say, 'Maria, go on, take Leslie and
visit your family,' but you know, we were so close, as
much as I missed my family I just couldn't bear to be
away from him."

Leslie could feel tears at the back of her eyes and she
swallowed to keep them from overflowing. It must
have been wonderful to have had such a wonderful
love, she thought, but such relationships were rare, especially today.

Leslie knew that by the track record of her friends,
many of whom had already made more than one trip to
the divorce court. She was glad her mother had had
such a great marriage and that the memories of it were
sustaining her now, but at the same time Leslie also
recalled how utterly dependent her mother had been
on her father and she knew she didn't want that for
herself.

Inexplicably she thought of Augustine's unspoken
patronizing, yet reverent, assessment of marriage and

motherhood. She realized just how impossible such a role would be for her. It was a startling thought, almost an intrusion, and she shook her head impatiently as she ordered him back into his appropriate place—in her thoughts, subjugated and useful.

Chapter Ten

A few days later Leslie was once again enjoying the freedom of having the house and estate all to herself. She had seen her mother and Tía Isabel off early in the morning and then managed to leave work early in the afternoon. The sunlight was warm and just beginning to soften as she walked into the old house, feeling very much in the mood for an evening of sheer relaxation.

She realized it had been days since she had just let herself go. Perhaps influenced by her innermost thoughts, which were often preoccupied with the child she yearned for, she suddenly felt an overwhelming urge to just play. To run and frolic and give herself over to sheer abandonment. In a joyous, almost outrageous display she raced up the stairs, pulled on some shorts and a T-shirt, and ran out toward the mountain behind the house.

Leslie raced and listened to the wind until she was breathless and then she looked around among the leaves for several straight reed sticks. Finding them, she ran quickly back to the house for a brown paper bag. Her hair was flying in wisps from the haphazard ponytail she had secured earlier, and to any observer she could easily have been mistaken for a mischievous, pubescent child. Quickly she searched for some glue, old strips of cloth, and string. She worked busily and

Enter a uniquely American world of romance with

Harlequin American Romance.™

Harlequin American Romances are the first romances to explore today's new love relationships. These compelling romance novels reach into the hearts and minds of women across America…probing into the most intimate moments of romance, love and desire.

You'll follow romantic heroines and irresistible men as they boldy face confusing choices. Career first, love later? Love without marriage? Long-distance relationships? All the experiences that make love real are captured in the tender, loving pages of *Harlequin American Romance*.

What makes American women so different when it comes to love? Find out with *Harlequin American Romance!*

Send for your introductory FREE book now.

intently at the table on the terrace until at last she held up her handiwork, a marvelously designed small kite in the traditional shape followed by all of the island's children. It was something her mother had taught her many years ago, but she had never had a chance to fly her kites in the crowded city. Now she would do it and she knew it would fly higher than any kite had ever flown.

With a great shout of joy Leslie ran to the top of the mountain and stood in the shadow of the flamboyant tree as her tiny square kite, not more than eight inches in diameter, met the wind and spiraled aloft in dizzying speed until at last it came to the end of its string and became a distant dot in the clear blue sky. As she stood there alone, tenuously connected to such a seemingly fragile symbol that was in reality strong enough to ride the strongest wind, she felt wonderful and free. With a sudden sense of joy she impetuously let the string go and felt a great sense of euphoria as the kite continued upward untethered and on its own.

When she turned at last and walked down the path Leslie noticed the sunny yellow of wild canaries and *reinitas* as well as other dainty tropical birds chattering and fluttering about. She stooped to examine a plant that seemed familiar and recognized an herb her mother often mixed with others she bought from the *botánica*, an old-fashioned type of drug store that still dealt in home remedies and local witchcraft items as well as modern pharmaceuticals. Doña María made a fragrant tea from them that was marvelously soothing when served with sprigs of mint and lots of ice.

Soon Leslie was fascinated as she searched through the foliage, seeking ripe leaves and tender twiglets. She was surrounded by an intriguing world as she lay back in the setting sunlight and plucked a great blossom from a hibiscus and placed it in her hair. She picked up a fallen mango and began to leisurely peel it with her teeth, savoring its tartness. She loved it here and planned to live here forever. It was the perfect place to achieve total fulfillment.

She finally meandered back to the house accompanied by the brief evening twilight and a brilliant orange setting sun, and wandered leisurely out onto the terrace. She flipped a switch bringing the pool to life as the underwater light went on. It was a peaceful silver-blue setting warmed by the tiki lamps she lit to keep the *mimis* away. She went into the kitchen and found the other herbs neccessary to blend the tea and added her own cache. She quickly heated water after turning on soft restful music and brewed the tea, savoring its wonderful aroma as she set it aside to cool before pouring over ice. She lit several rose-scented candles and walked slowly toward the stairs in rhythm with the wafting, lulling strains of the music.

Dirty and rumpled from her romp, she quickly shed her clothes and stepped briskly beneath the shower to remove the physical signs of her outing. Then she walked nude to her room and reveled in the coolness there. Realizing she was totally alone and free to do as she pleased, she dropped the swimsuit she had reached for and slipped into the shimmering robe she had finished just the night before.

When she saw herself, brown and primitive, highlighted by the flickering flames of the golden scroll design, she felt wonderful. On impulse she grabbed the amulet she had bought before leaving Loíza Aldea and hung it around her neck so that it rested majestically and naturally between her firm nubile breasts. Slowly she swirled the robe about her naked body and delighted in its soft silkiness as she pirouetted leisurely toward the door.

As a regal princess she came down the steps and walked to the pool, where slowly she dropped the robe and allowed the moonlight to caress her body as she stood in silhouette feeling wonderfully alive and excited. She stepped into the warm water and felt the mingling of her spirit with another presence, a familiar, insistent presence that was somehow comforting as she took great gliding strokes to the end of the pool before turning to float on her back. Unaware of the sensuous silhouette created by the lapping water as it caressed her body, she floated in enchantment to the end of the pool until her toes trailed down and touched bottom. She pulled herself around in a graceful ballet motion and then she stopped abruptly.

She heard something strange.

Leslie gasped and came out of her reverie in shock when her eyes collided with the smoldering gaze of Augustine.

"You are enchantingly beautiful, María," he said softly. "A goddess beyond description."

Two tall glasses of chilled tea sat on the table as he added generous amounts of rum to them.

"I see you are acquainted with our wonderful herb teas."

He had an air of easy nonchalance.

"Do you mind if I join you? In as much as the door was, as usual, left open, I felt more than welcome."

There was a smoldering aura about him and an insistent low growl to his voice that hinted that the patience of weeks gone by was stretched to the limit. His eyes were luminous pools of desire challenging her and bidding her to submit.

Quelling her instant discomfiture, Leslie called upon all of the strength of her ancestors as her eyes narrowed into slits of seething determination. He had no doubt been there for some time and was amused by her disadvantage. She saw him glance at the robe thrown casually on the floor.

Throwing all caution to the wind, she arose from the pool, gleaming and majestic, as rivulets of water cascaded down the generous contours of her body accentuating every breathless curve. She was supremely satisfied when she heard him gasp. She came slowly up the stairs, never once taking her eyes from his as she mentally commanded him to stand where he was in homage to her power.

Leslie moved toward him seductively as he stood mesmerized watching the rhythm of the amulet as it moved between her tantalizing breasts. Her nipples were inviting as they grew taut with excitement. She advanced on him steadily, never once diverting her gaze as she saw his flame of desire rise to her challenge. He began to respond in haste and she moderated his reply as she continued to exercise her woman's prerogative.

"Dance with me," she said softly as she gracefully retrieved her robe and then moved to embrace him. The robe swirled around her as her arms slid easily into the great kimono sleeves and embodied the regalness of her eyes. Slowly she moved into his arms in gentle rhythm with the soft dreamy music and they began to dance gracefully around the patio.

Augustine's response had quickly turned to tender anticipation as he enveloped her in a soft, reverent embrace.

"You know why I'm here, then?" he asked softly as his eyes probed hers deeply.

"Of course," she replied huskily in a whispering titillation as her lips pressed close to his ear. She moved her body closer to his and felt a gratifying response, silky and sensuous through the gossamer fabric of the swaying robe.

"You're the man I've chosen to give me what I want."

"María, María," he breathed, "you are the woman of my dreams. There will never be another for me."

He held her away and gazed at her in sweet tenderness and then crushed her to him in an overwhelmingly powerful embrace that enveloped all her senses and sent tingling urgency throughout her body.

Gasping, Leslie pulled away in coyness. Acting solely on instinct, she slowly kissed him in tiny soft caresses outlining his chiseled features and nuzzling his nose and mustache before once again melting into a deep probing kiss as her tongue searched hungrily for his and met its thrusting delight in rhythm with the heat of their bodies.

"Come on," she said, twisting away from him gently. "Swim with me. Let's swim in the pool you made for our pleasure." She took his hand gently but insistently as she moved toward the inviting blue water.

"Here, let me help you," she continued as her robe swung open displaying the perfect beauty of her body in the flickering light of the tiki lamps.

Again his eyes were riveted to the amulet and the invitation of her perfect breasts, round and nubile. His tongue moistened his lips as he stood in speechless wonderment, perhaps questioning whether or not he was dreaming.

Insistently her beautifully tapered fingers reached up and began to loosen buttons as they trailed tantalizingly through the thick curly hair on his chest. They left a heated track of anticipation that transcended the reality of the situation. She pulled his shirt away, then his trousers as her hands moved down over him softly stroking, reveling in his throbbing promise as she lay his skin bare next to her own.

"You know I'm a woman with a mind of my own. Perhaps not quite what you had in mind," she teased as her eyes continued to mesmerize him.

"No, perhaps not quite," he said softly, "but then this is the age of freedom and you've always known what I wanted and needed from you."

Her hands continued to play over his torso, motioning him urgently but gently to a luxurious giant hammock filled with pillows. She slid gracefully into his lap, allowing the robe to slip again to the patio floor, and her breasts moved tantalizingly close to his waiting lips.

He sighed and his lips hungrily enveloped her breasts, going from one to the other as she gasped in delight and moved in unison with the motion of his tongue. It circled her nipples, bringing them to pulsing, rapturous peaks while his hands began to move insistently over her entire body.

"We must have an understanding," Leslie said softly as the heat of his passion drew her ever closer, insisting upon the response of her willing body.

The moon outlined their glistening entwined bodies as they swayed gently in the evening breeze. Slowly Augustine's kisses became softer, coated with wonderment as though purposely abating, falling slowly from one peak only to bring her to yet another, higher than before. They loved and touched in tender exploring ways as their lips met again and again in longer more rapturous interludes growing more ecstatic as the insistence began to build again in perfect rhythm. Deliberately Leslie stretched her body full length next to his and his hard muscular strength melded ever closer.

He whispered sweet Spanish endearments to her over and over again as the wonder of the experience began to truly enslave him.

"Oh, María, my love, we must never be apart again. You must be mine. We must agree immed—"

Her lips sought his out and silenced him in sweet ecstasy as she moved to claim the needs of both her spirit and her body. The shifting urgency of their mutual need was not congenial with the hammock although more than ample for their initial encounter. Suddenly they went tumbling among the scattered pillows as they grasped the folds of the strongly woven fabric and then fell, laughing outrageously, into each other's arms to the floor.

"Oh, come on," she cried. "Let's swim! We have the whole night ahead of us." Her voice was joyous and triumphant. In her mind she at last sealed, irrevocably, her decision to have this man in the way of her choosing.

In amused, although somewhat disconcerted, wonderment Augustine reached for her beckoning hand. She gasped as she stood in sheer awe of his magnificent, pulsating body silhouetted grandly in the light further illumining the primitive desire in his eyes.

Turning, Leslie gave a little push and dove cleanly into the water. As she came up shimmering and wet he joined her and brought his body sensuously up to hers, touching and titillating every nerve ending. The feeling was further enhanced by the lapping motion of the water as they lay back in each other's arms and floated to the shallow end of the pool.

"I want a child," said Leslie, not really believing she was voicing her thoughts but suddenly glad that she had. Forthrightness had always been one of her virtues and she had never gone wrong with it in the past.

"But of course," said Augustine, truly tender now as he turned to meet her gaze. "You can have one every year if you like. You can have anything you wish, but most assuredly you will have children!"

"No, you don't understand," she said, searching for words to clarify, but before she could finish, his lips moved sensuously over her face and down her neck in unison with her own. Once again she was swept with an overwhelming desire that, now awakened, had to be satisfied.

It was an experience far beyond her wildest dreams and she knew she would never be happy again without it, but she gave that little thought as they reached the steps and he began moving toward her room.

"*Niña*, are you sure?"

He stopped for only a second's hesitation, not really capable of stopping himself as he paused to assure her assent.

"Yes, yes," Leslie gasped.

He crushed her to him and kissed her more urgently than before as they reached the top of the steps. Augustine moved assuredly toward the half-closed door of her room and kicked the door away as he strode across the expanse and dropped with her to the antique bed. Leisurely he delighted in her beauty as the moon continued to outline their bodies. Once again he moved to bring her to a peak of ecstasy, wanting now to prolong the moment as again her hands began instinctively to touch and stroke him.

"Ah, yes, *niña*," he said as he moved above her. He grasped the amulet necklace and pulled it over her head, then his hands moved down over her body and his lips once again suckled her breasts.

Slowly, gasping with hot, smoldering need, Leslie guided him to her and slowly and gently arched her body in total abandon. His body came firmly down on hers and he moved in magnificent strength to cover her body with caresses, mouthing endearments while his mustache sensuously tickled her ear. She gasped in monumental all-encompassing delight as her body urged his on crying for more and more as at last he thrust deeply and tightly ending in a great shuddering crescendo.

She knew unequivocally as her pulsating response met his and held him in loving grasping imprisonment she had received what her body desired.

At last he moved from her and began in wondering enchantment to stroke and pet her gleaming satiated body. They lay in silence, savoring the wonder of the experience, not speaking, but never taking their eyes from each other. Finally they fell into each other's arms and rested happily and sweetly.

Then Leslie allowed her fingers to trail leisurely over him to explore and memorize the lines that would be a part of her from this day on. She felt his skin begin to prickle as her fingers wound through his curly hair. Languidly Augustine joined her in a like exploration of her body. Within moments they had reached a new peak of desire as over and over again through the rest of the night they discovered and practiced every possible delight imaginable, until finally they lay together in utter satiated exhaustion.

Leslie awoke a few hours later feeling wonderfully alive as she gazed around her room. Augustine was dressed and sitting across from her in her large comfortable reading chair. He was bent forward, hands on knees, watching her intently. He looked like a man who had just come in from the worst night of his life.

"María, mija."

He looked to the floor.

"What have I done?" he asked in despair. "I'm sorry.... I did not mean—" He broke off, searching for words.

"I came to tell you last night that I love you and we could be married soon. I've broken the engagement with Philomena, but I have done a disgraceful thing. You were a virgin and I've taken advantage of you...."

It took Leslie several moments to realize that he was really serious. This was the last response she would have expected from him. In her mind it had seemed patently clear that he looked upon her as a candidate for a mistress from the beginning. She had never once considered that he actually had "honorable" intentions toward her, which was really of little consequence to her anyway. She had no wish or desire to marry. She had gotten what she wanted and most assuredly vanquished this man who had thought to own her. Now she was disgusted by him as he sat weak and apologetic before her.

"Marry you!" she said in derision. "I've never had any intentions of marrying you and I never will! I wanted you to fulfill my own needs. I chose you for that purpose, but never, never, would I allow you to own me or use me. I used you!"

As she sat there haughty and naked, casting aspersions on him, his worried, apologetic demeanor vanished instantly and was replaced with a fuming bull-like rage.

"You used me!" he shouted in seething, growling rage. "You used me. Never! You are mine. You *will* marry me! I will not allow you to have my child without claiming it. This is my island, my people, and I make the rules when I so desire."

"Get out," said Leslie through gritted teeth. "I have no further use for you at least for the moment. But you will come back," she said softening into seductiveness, "when I want you to."

"I will come back when I please," he said in a deadly growl. "You are mine now. You will marry me and we will have lots of children. Yes, lots of children. No other man will ever touch you. I won't allow it!"

Leslie blanched, but her resolve remained firm as she glared at him wordlessly.

"You will need me, *niña*," he said as his voice softened somewhat. "You will see, and you will come to me."

Augustine came across the room and held her chin firmly in his hands as he spoke to her, willing her to meet his gaze.

"I will leave now, because it is the proper thing to do and I have arrangements to make. Please try to keep the door locked. Someday your carelessness is going to cause you problems."

He turned and walked through the door, leaving Leslie seething in the bed as she stared after him. She grabbed a vase from the nightstand and threw it at the door.

"Don't tell me what to do!" she shouted as she heard him go out the front door.

In an absolute rage she jumped from the bed and pulled off all of the rumpled bedclothes not wanting any reminder of him to remain. She stomped down the hallway to the bathroom and stood beneath the shower, enjoying the hard pounding of the water on her body. Slowly calmness overtook her and the wonder of the evening before began to once again emerge. Her hands moved over her body to massage and explore as over and over again she felt the magic in her womb, wondering if she had received the gift of life.

Her anger dissipated as she reveled in her conquest. She rubbed herself briskly dry with a colorful bath sheet and then wrapped herself in its luxury as she padded down the stairs. She saw the crumpled robe and hammock twisted in comical disarray. The two tall glasses of tea sat with ingredients separated into layers in dismal melted neglect surrounded by puddles of water.

Suddenly as she once again recalled the firm, but soft closing of the front door she felt just the tiniest prickle of regret. She wondered then just what Augustine was talking about when he said he had arrangements to make.

Chapter Eleven

Leslie glanced at the clock and realized it had grown very late. Usually she was at work by this time. She was just stepping to the phone to call her office when it began ringing with a strange sense of urgency. When she picked up the receiver Juanita was on the other end of the line.

"Doña Leslie?"

"Yes."

"I'm sorry to bother you at home, but Philomena is here and she's having a fit!"

Juanita was speaking in a frantic whisper and Leslie could feel a small round knot beginning to form in the pit of her stomach.

"Of course, Juanita. I'll be right there. Ask her to wait in my office."

"She won't do that," said Juanita. "She insists upon being in the workroom and she's causing trouble among the workers. Please hurry. I can't handle her!"

Leslie tried to reassure Juanita, but her own emotions were anything but calm as she hurriedly pulled on clothes and set out for the factory. When she arrived she could hear Philomena's voice before she even entered the building. She took a deep breath and put on a gracious smile as she entered the lobby. Juanita was instantly calmed when she saw her employer's confident and nonchalant manner.

"Good morning, Philomena," Leslie said with just the slightest nod of her head in a cool clear voice. "Is there anything I can do for you?"

The other woman turned around, a dark cloud of animosity.

"Well, I see you have arrived just in time for coffee, something I understand your workers rarely have." She was snarling and her tone was cutting.

"I beg your pardon," said Leslie in an authoritative, deadpan voice, "but I believe that is a management concern."

"Precisely!" said Philomena as she flew across the room giving a fair imitation of a hawk swooping in for the kill. "Ayudalo has provided you with workers who among other things are packing boxes and not learning a thing about running the knitting machines. Now I've learned that there are no organized coffee breaks or lunch hours in this factory!"

"Most assuredly there are not," said Leslie, standing her ground. "The workers help themselves to coffee and eat whenever they want. Most plants couldn't follow such procedures because the workers would abuse them, but most of our people own a part of this plant so they want to ensure its success."

The workroom had grown exceedingly quiet during this fiery altercation, but Leslie could feel the pride and support of her people as they, one by one, went back to work ignoring Philomena.

"Now, if you would just step into my office," Leslie continued, "I'll be happy to discuss this with you."

She had begun moving toward her office, giving the other woman no alternative but to follow.

"First of all," said Leslie, refusing to acknowledge to Philomena that she was in any way disturbing or troublesome, "I didn't know that your workers were unhappy here. If your people are dissatisfied, perhaps you would do better to place them with some other company."

"Oh, no," said Philomena, "that's precisely what you want me to do. Ayudalo takes care of its people. You won't find it so easy to hoodwink my people with empty promises and reduced paychecks when they are already being paid the lowest wages possible!"

"Philomena, I really don't see why you're bringing all of this up now. After all, you came to me and suggested that I participate in your program."

"I did not!" she said, quite angry now. "It was Augustine's idea completely. While you may have been able to delude him with your wide-eyed idealistic garbage you can be sure that I will have none of it. I'm here to protect my people and you can be sure that I will do so!"

A calculating look came into her eyes.

"I think an audit of your books to see exactly how much the workers should be receiving in this so-called shareholding program would be in order."

"I think not," said Leslie. "Your workers have elected not to participate in the program and my other workers are of no concern to you."

"That may well be," said Philomena as she arose in agitation, "but that could change. Most of our workers are protected by unions. I've already seen a number of improprieties here that are not consistent with our usual work standards."

"As you wish," said Leslie levelly. "It's been nice chatting with you."

She moved to escort the fuming woman to the door.

"You are, of course, welcome to visit at any time."

"You may be sure I will," Philomena said as she swished out of the room theatrically.

When Leslie at last heard the other woman's car zooming away she retreated behind her desk and called upon all of her inner strength to calm her churning emotions. It was extremely important that her workers not see that she was in any way affected by this stormy, unreasonable challenge.

"Juanita," she called as she flipped on the intercom and continued in a bright and cheerful voice. "Do you think it would be possible to bring me a cup of coffee?"

"*Sí*, Doña Leslie," said Juanita.

The relief in her voice was obvious.

"I'll be happy to, and..." she continued with just a hint of teasing in her voice, "may I have a cup also?"

"You bet," laughed Leslie. "You can have anything you want!"

The dark cloud brought in by Philomena dissipated completely with her laughter and Leslie arose to go out among her people. The machines clattered happily and the wild riot of yarn colors was cheerful and uplifting, but nevertheless Leslie was deeply shaken on the inside.

She knew Philomena meant to cause trouble. She had felt it from the time of that first meeting at the party and now that Augustine had broken their engagement there was no question about it. These were extremely unsettling thoughts and Leslie gave an outward sigh of relief when Juanita suddenly appeared not only with coffee but with a message that Gerald was on the line from New York.

"Gerald, darling," she cried just seconds later. "You don't know how wonderful it is to hear your voice!"

"Ah-ha! I knew you'd finally get around to really missing me," he said with a laugh. "What's the matter? Has the bogeyman come around and you need old Gerald to protect you?"

Although he continued to laugh there was a note of seriousness in his voice. Leslie marveled at his ability to be so perceptive where she was concerned.

Inexplicably the sound of his deep masculine voice abruptly brought Augustine to mind and she was instantly reminded of the night before. For the first time she began to feel the pricklings of concern as she comprehended stark reality and compared it to the fancifulness of her secret fantasies.

"Oh, no," she said in jocular response as she forced herself to clear these thoughts from her mind. "I've just had my first set-to with Philomena. We hired some workers, you know, at Augustine's suggestion from the charity that she heads, Augustine has apparently just broken his engagement with her and she has been here trying to stir up problems among my people and just in general—"

"Don't say anymore," said Gerald in mock dismay. "I get the whole picture. I told you, you'd better stay out of the way of that man."

"Well, it's really not all that serious," said Leslie. "Nothing I can't handle," she continued with false confidence. "Now, tell me what's on your mind."

"Oh, nothing much, except to tell you that your ski sweater designs are a smash hit and you're going to have orders coming out of your ears. I'm promising seven-day delivery. Do you think you can handle that?"

"With the new machines, no problem," said Leslie. "They're arriving today and we can be in production in a week. You know, I can't thank you enough for going out of your way to help me like this."

"Not at all, but everything does have its price, you know. I'll be down again in a few weeks and I'm expecting the usual red carpet treatment."

"You've got it," said Leslie. "How about Juanita as your personal guide?"

"Right on," he said as they both laughed.

They set a firm date for his visit and then Leslie thoughtfully turned him over to Juanita to continue the arrangements. She smiled to herself. It was obvious that Gerald was more than a little smitten and she was sure this was turning into a serious relationship for both him and Juanita. She had to admit, she approved of it completely.

The machines arrived later and in the ensuing hub-bub Leslie had little time to reflect on the evening before, but by midafternoon her body was physically reminding her of her ardent activity. She realized at last she was really very tired and she needed some time alone to think.

As she drove slowly down the drive to her stately old family home, for the first time it looked lonely. She realized then that she hadn't heard one word from Augustine, but then their parting had been rather volatile and final, to say the least. As she ambled into the house she touched the table and straightened the hammock. She went upstairs and retrieved the bed clothes for the laundry and found the amulet tossed casually to the floor. She crossed her arms and held herself as she realized how foolish her actions of the evening before had been especially if Augustine chose not to be discreet.

It was one thing to be a barefoot primitive running through the hills and yet another to be a self-sufficient career woman in a big city where one's personal life was strictly his own business, but *quite* another in a city such as Ponce.

A wave of depression began to sweep over Leslie as she forced herself to drink a glass of juice, reaching almost instinctively for something that would be nutritionally good for her. Slowly she moved her hands over her body and realized she still very much wanted a child of her own—not just *a* child or *any* child, but *Augustine's* child.

In sickening despair she relived the events of the evening before, reveling again in the glory of their lovemaking. She remembered Augustine's gentleness and strength. It was a moment of truth and she knew she wasn't just attracted to Augustine, she loved him. In spite of his arrogance he was also a sweet man, a natural leader deeply committed to his people. In her paranoia she had been too blind to see his honorable affection and intentions. In brazen foolishness she had been derisive of his declaration of love for her and yet, in all truthfulness she still had to admit she could not accept the role of the submissive, dominated wife. He was still the conquering conquistador who wished only to place her among his other acquisitions as a receptacle for his children and nothing more.

These thoughts collided and sparked her already short temper. Why after all should she not live her life as she pleased? If she wished to have a child she would have one. There was no need to marry or worry, she thought. Perhaps her wish would come true.

Leslie refused to think of her mother's reaction should this come to pass, and as the days went by it seemed more and more that her thoughts had been exceedingly fanciful. The entire episode between her and Augustine took on the tinge of unreality.

For all intents and purposes as far as Augustine was concerned their night together had never happened. At least that was how it looked outwardly. He continued to pay periodic visits to both the factory and their home. In the presence of others he was as solicitous and polite as he had always been, but on the few occasions when he and Leslie were alone, his eyes were icy as he looked her over knowingly. Never, though, did he make an advance.

It was patently clear that he was deeply and irrevocably offended by her refusal to marry him and her derision of his love. His manner was almost cruel and cynical as he made low, deadly comments while also carefully and astutely watching her for signs of physical change. When it happened she could always sense his eyes first. One day she was working alone at her drafting board when the tension in the room signaled his presence.

"I see you are, as always, very busy," he said with a little smile.

It quickly turned to a wry, noncommittal look. His eyes dwelled purposely on her breasts before traveling carefully downward to note the smock she wore to protect her clothes from the inks she was using.

"And I see you need to take greater pains with your appearance now."

There was an ominous question that hung in the air as he continued out into the studio before she could reply. His visit was all the more infuriating because he apparently had no reason for coming other than to remind her of his bad humor. She heard Tía Isabel greet him and noted the return of warmth and concern in his voice.

She couldn't deny that she was hurt by his actions. She had been sure he would have second thoughts and want to resume their affair and she had coached herself in preparation for that. She was not prepared for this cold derision but was almost blessedly so preoccupied with problems at Los Tejidos de María that she had little time to think about it.

The news of the broken engagement between Augustine and Philomena had kept the town buzzing for weeks due primarily to the erratic actions of Philomena as she openly libeled Leslie with accusatory remarks about the factory's operation. She had managed to instigate a government inquiry, which was unsettling to Leslie's workers and hampering her efforts to get out the first big orders of ski sweaters.

The most disconcerting thing, however, was Augustine standing on the sidelines watching, making no effort to quell Philomena's outrageous charges. It was almost as if he were challenging Leslie to handle this situation properly. It hurt and left her deeply scarred as she continued to contend with her twin emotions of love and hate. There were times when she was close to him, when she thought she would die just from wanting to touch him, and then he would turn on her like a viper and cut her to the quick with his arrogance and derision.

She remembered the day she was sitting at her desk looking wearily over her efficiency reports and a number of employee suggestions, which were now more strident and demanding than any heretofore slipped into the box for that purpose.

The intercom buzzed.

"Doña Leslie?"

"Don Augustine is here," he said as he came through the door with a warm smile and a twinkle in his eyes.

Leslie responded immediately with a like demeanor.

"How nice to see you," she said sincerely. "You're certainly looking chipper today."

"Yes, well, of course I have reason to," he said with an air of nonchalance. "I've been conducting some very interesting business."

Although she was instinctively wary of his deceptive humor of recent weeks, Leslie suddenly felt a yearning she could not totally conceal. He had an almost mischievous, childlike aura about him that at the same time filled the room with his magnetism. Before she could conceal her thoughts their eyes met and he quickly noted her emotions. His expression registered disinterested smugness as his eyes began a blatant physical perusal of her body that left nothing to the imagination concerning his thoughts.

The growl of his voice took on an extra degree of emphasis. "Having problems?" he asked, noting the disarray of the papers on her desk.

"Well, yes," she said a little hesitantly, "but nothing I can't handle."

She could feel the familiar warmth of the flush that his presence had consistently inspired and cursed her body for its constant betrayal.

"There seems to be a little discontent with—"

"As you said," he broke in with an arrogant wave of his hand, indicating his lack of interest, "I'm sure you can handle it. You are, after all, a very strong woman. Your forte is absolute power. In any event it can't be too bad. Philomena tells me that even the Ayudalo employees are now participating in the shareholding program."

Leslie stared at him and realized he was baiting her in a particularly snide way. The blow to his machismo was never more evident as he came around the desk.

"You'll have no trouble," he said, "in making insects and other weaklings grovel at your feet."

He lifted her chin and forced her eyes to meet his snapping gaze while the silence stretched tautly between them. Leslie's heart was both anxious and angry as it pounded against her chest. She was speechless, powerless, to answer him.

"You want to be a man," he continued harshly, "well then, act like one and handle your problems like one. This is no time for sniveling and sighs."

Augustine released her chin roughly and then turned shakily away. It was obvious that he had come close to a dangerous loss of control as rage emanated from his still thoroughly insulted body. He left the room with long strides, never looking back.

Leslie was beginning to feel that this was all more than she could handle as the end of the month rapidly approached and her sweater orders were falling behind. The enthusiasm of her workers had been irreparably damaged when Philomena made a big issue of their take-home pay on the last payday. The last straw was when Juanita had come in and told her there was serious talk of unionizing.

Almost as if her car had a mind of its own Leslie drove to Magna's house. She hadn't seen her friend in weeks, but now she knew she had to talk to someone who might understand, woman to woman. This was one time Gerald couldn't fill the gap.

"I don't know what it really is," said Leslie as she sat drinking chilled wine on her friend's sunny flower-filled patio after making all of the time-worn excuses for the long interval since they had visited.

The whisper of the ceiling fans throughout Magna's house seemed a fitting accompaniment for her friend's calculated calm, which nevertheless had a little edge to it. "You're depressed, *niña*, and well you should be. We've been worrying about Los Tejidos at my office."

"Oh, I know," cried Leslie. "It just seems that since Augustine showed up I've had nothing but trouble."

"I warned you about Latin men," said Magna, unable to keep a hint of stridency from her voice.

"But this has nothing to do with anything like that," said Leslie weakly.

Suddenly she felt threatened by the tone in Magna's voice and realized this woman was not only a friend, but a professional who could influence her business. Her intent to be candid and seek her friend's sympathy and advice had totally disappeared as paranoia reared its ugly head.

"Actually Philomena is the problem," Leslie went on warily. "Augustine owns a few shares of stock in Los Tejidos and of course Mama is very taken with him—you know all about that—but I made a terrible mistake when I became involved with Ayudalo."

"I don't understand Augustine," said Magna, her dark eyes snapping. "I mean I haven't heard from you in weeks, but I know he has vast interests, his family holdings are gargantuan. I just can't conceive of his taking such an interest in a company where he holds just a few shares. There has to be more to this."

Now Leslie was acutely uncomfortable. She had come here expecting warmth and laughter and suddenly she was surrounded by a well of censure. Her inborn independence shaped her next words. "I think I'm capable of handling my own affairs," she said in stilted tones.

Magna looked at her, immediately contrite and sympathetic. *"Mija,"* she said in the island's traditional familiarity between close women friends too, "I'm sorry. It's just that I've been a little hurt by your avoidance of me lately. Now, tell me, what's the real problem?"

Leslie looked at her for a long moment and felt the beginning of tears behind her eyes. She reached out and touched her friend's hand. "Thank you, Magna. You really are a good friend to me and I love you dearly, but I think you've made me see this is really one thing I have to handle and figure out for myself."

"If you say so," said Magna, a reservoir of sympathy now, "but remember I'm always here and usually I'm not such a harpie with friends I love so much. *Ten cuidado, mi amiga.* You are in my prayers."

After her visit with Magna, Leslie was truly tired and beaten. She knew she was beginning to experience some of the telltale signs of burnout as she began to grow more distant not only from Magna, but also her mother, Tía Isabel, and others who had been close to her. She could feel herself growing cynical and negative as her usual good spirits were rapidly becoming things of the past. Now she was beginning to feel physically ill. She had begun to have backaches and for a while she was nauseated and tense. She had at first felt great excitement over these symptoms, but nature had summarily assured her that the child of her heart was also not to be.

It was a deeply depressing blow. With each day of Augustine's continued rejection the subconscious thought of this child had been in many ways her anchor and hope. It made everything else bearable. Now that hope was gone along with everything else.

In reality she should have been greatly relieved. Common sense had eventually told her that she was really not being very fair to the other people in her life, yet her yearning had not in any way abated. It was all the more poignant because she knew beyond a shadow of a doubt how much she wanted a child and how much she wanted it to be Augustine's—and they, in their demonic quest for supremacy over each other, had nothing left but mutual contempt.

With each passing day Gerald had grown more concerned as Leslie relayed the problems. He finally decided to come down early and was troubled when he arrived at the house late in the evening and Doña María told him Leslie was at the plant.

Actually Leslie had finally begun to pull herself together. Using all of her fortitude and resources, she had finally grown tired of this sinking, defeated feeling. She had decided to remedy it by returning to the source of her greatest satisfaction. She was busily working over one of her machines when Gerald appeared.

"You worry over that machine as though it were a child," he said. "You must know every part and each needle must have a name."

Leslie laughed as she looked up at him in the dim light.

"You're early," she cried. "I didn't expect you until next week."

As she talked she finished removing a small garment from the machine.

"I see you're still preoccupied with little things."

He began his comment as a joke, but suddenly grew serious as he became aware of the soft aura that seemed to surround Leslie as she examined the tiny sweater lovingly.

"My God, Leslie, you look as though you had made that for your own child."

Leslie felt herself beginning to blush and looked

quickly away and forced herself to assume a business-like expression.

"Oh, it's just another little design. I was inspired by a fern leaf and I was anxious to see if it would work. I guess it would be almost unnatural not to think of babies when you're working with their clothes. They're such fun."

"Leslie, you are absolutely glowing. If I didn't know better— I mean, honestly, you've always been like a madonna on a pedestal—so small and exquisite, but... untouchable."

Leslie looked at him suddenly, alarmed and confused. Gerald was her rock, a foundation of friendship that she clung to. His voice had just taken on an intimate quality, which distressed and frightened her. The introduction of such an element would most certainly ruin their friendship and she frankly was just not up to that at the moment. She was just beginning to put her feelings and emotions into perspective again.

"I suddenly have the very distinct feeling," Gerald went on, "that you want very much to have a child. If I didn't know you better I'd think you were already pregnant."

Greatly distressed now, Leslie sought to quickly change his thinking.

"Oh, Gerald, be serious," she said with a contrived laugh. "You know this is all a job to me. My baby has always been my work."

"That's what I've always thought," he said, still not totally convinced. "You've always been so straight and narrow. Why, if I'd ever once thought you really wanted to be domestic—"

"Gerald, don't!" Leslie said sharply. "We have a wonderful friendship," she said, consciously softening her words. "I've always thought of it as one of those very special ones—you know, uncomplicated—"

"Maybe for you," he laughed, "but let me tell you,

you're one sweet little thing and it wouldn't take much encouragement to warm up this old man's blood!''

There was a grin on his face as he came across the room to her. Slowly he raised her from the chair and turned her to meet his gaze.

''Maybe it's time we started to really examine our relationship and companionship we find so congenial,'' he said tenderly. ''Maybe we're both trying to tell each other something.''

''No, Gerald, no, please,'' Leslie cried as tears sprang to her eyes. ''Maybe things about me are changing. You know at my age it's only natural for a woman to reexamine her priorities, but my feelings about you haven't changed. You're my friend and I beg you not to take that friendship from me just the way it is. We've known each other too long and...anyway, I can see you're very attracted to Juanita. That's a feeling that is much more legitimate romantically than what you feel for me. You know that as well as I do.''

He gazed at her a moment longer and then nodded in assent.

''You have changed though, Leslie. You're involved in some way with someone and I think it's serious.''

She turned away, unable to meet his probing eyes squarely.

''It's that basic Cro-Magnon type Rivera,'' he said, suddenly aghast as he grasped her shoulders and forced her to meet his gaze. ''It *is*, isn't it?'' he demanded in astonishment. ''Leslie, for God's sake you can't be serious! He's completely wrong for you!''

''Good evening, María, I see you are working late again.''

Leslie and Gerald whirled around as Augustine stepped into the room, his eyes glowing, his voice harsh.

''How many times have I told you, you really should be careful about locking doors, María? You know how very dangerous it is for a woman alone in the evening, but then I see you have the protection of Senor Masters.''

His eyes had appraised the situation, and Leslie could sense a well-concealed possessive rage as Augustine walked toward her.

"Perhaps the two of you would be so kind as to have dinner with me. There is a wonderful native barbecue just up the way. I'm sure Senor Masters would find it interesting.''

Acting almost as if they were two naughty children caught in an act of mischief, Leslie and Gerald quickly acquiesced, glad that they had somehow avoided punishment from this bear of a man who had managed to instantly intimidate both of them. Leslie never thought to ask Augustine about the real nature of his visit as they quickly followed the direction of his arm and gathered their things to leave.

She struggled to silence the pounding of her heart as her fingers traced the throbbing vein coursing wildly up her blushing neck. She flung a light shawl over her shoulders, a silky shimmering garment that was another of her own creations, and Augustine stepped quickly to help her adjust it. He grasped her arms firmly and sent tremors through her as he gallantly led her through the door. She sensed Gerald's acute and perceptive interest as they all continued out the door to Augustine's luxurious car.

Moments later Augustine bantered good-naturedly with the owner of the roadside barbecue, Tío Tom's. It hung precariously on the mountain with platforms propped by stilts creating the floor. An array of picnic tables and benches for seating were scattered around. The smell of seasoned chickens skewered over the coals, along with corn, plantains, *pasteles*, rice and beans, and other native dishes, was delicious in the smoky atmosphere, but within moments Leslie felt the

results of her stress as her stomach began to grow
queasy and her complexion paled. Through her sheer
act of will she managed to calm her momentary discomfort, but not before two very astute pairs of eyes
had examined her thoroughly and noted her distress.

"You really must not work so hard," said Augustine,
concern and questions evident in his voice, which was
soft and intimate as they seated themselves on the edge
of the bench.

Leslie reached out and touched the smooth texture
of the giant elephant-leaved plants and other foliage
surrounding them, which dripped with rain-forest humidity. She was momentarily and therapeutically distracted by the ever present and persistent *mimis*. She
swatted at them viciously in a somewhat overreactive
motion.

"We really ought to have the red oil from the *achiote*
seeds on our skin instead of in our food," said Augustine in amicable chitchat. "The Tainos used it as an
insecticide."

He was smiling in gracious amazement, obviously responding to Leslie's discomfort, but Leslie also sensed
a general softening about his demeanor that had not
been evident in weeks—actually not since their night of
passionate lovemaking. Inexplicably she felt a flash of
hope as she looked at him intently.

"I have something of great importance to discuss
with you, María," he said as he broke into her reverie.
"It is of a rather private nature, so I wonder, Senor
Masters, if I might prevail on your good graces to retrieve Doña Leslie's car after we have finished dinner? It has to do with the factory and I'm sure she
would wish this to be a private conversation."

Gerald looked toward Leslie, obviously somewhat
discomfited by Augustine's presumption.

"Is that what you want, Leslie?" Gerald asked,
pointedly making no effort to hide his bristling.

Augustine's eyes never left her face as he puffed a slim cigar, arrogant and assured, yet Leslie sensed something. Something had changed and whatever it was, it was better than the impasse they had been in. She realized she very much wanted to talk with him, if only to clear the air.

"Yes, I think that possibly might be the wise thing to do," she said hesitantly. "If you don't mind, Gerald...."

She reached out to pat his arm in reassurance and again she sensed an imperceptible tension as Augustine continued to glower at her lazily.

"Fine!" said Augustine heartily. "That settles it!"

As platters of steaming food began arriving at the table Leslie suddenly felt a terrible sinking sensation firmly anchored in some intuitive foreboding that she could not accurately identify.

They all continued to laugh gaily in an obviously contrived atmosphere until at last Gerald was dispatched with her car and Leslie was ensconced in the sumptuous luxury of Augustine's car heading toward the bright lights of Ponce.

Chapter Twelve

"I understand, María, that you haven't been feeling well," he said, breaking the silence in a low but very controlled voice, "and that there is talk of unionizing at your plant."

Leslie was silent as the car raced through the darkness. It was almost as if she were in another world. Although Augustine looked at her appraisingly he did not press her for a comment. As they neared the plaza Leslie realized they were going to his office. For a moment she panicked and then realized it really didn't matter where they went. Nothing mattered so long as they were able to somehow resolve their differences.

Augustine maneuvered the car smoothly through the wrought-iron gate, which he opened with a touch control from his car. They drove slowly around the back of the old building, where he stopped. He moved around to open her door and his strong hands guided her insistently toward the rear door of his office. Throughout all of this Leslie had continued to remain silent.

When they entered the masculine room she turned her back to him and wandered about. Finally she selected a luxurious chair and sank into it, allowing her shawl to trail carelessly to the floor. The silence was growing awkward as Augustine moved about the room turning on a few soft lights. He went behind his desk and reached for a cigar from an ornate cigar box.

"Would you care for some wine?" he asked.

Her voice was quiet and polite and his eyes searched hers, probing and questioning.

Leslie could feel herself beginning to melt and suddenly her independence and pride overwhelmed her.

"What happend to Doña Leslie?" she asked heatedly. "The woman you addressed a few moments ago at Tío Tom's?"

The seconds of silence before he answered were piercingly taut in the heavy dramatic atmosphere of the nineteenth-century room. He looked at her distastefully.

"You call her a woman?"

His words were tinged with instant lip-curling arrogance although he spoke softly in the modulated sounds of Spanish. He handed her a glass of wine and she set it untouched on a nearby table as his eyes glittered and openly ravished her body.

"That name," he continued in his low growl. He shook his head in derision. "It means nothing when a man looks at you."

Augustine took a sip of wine and savored it slowly behind suggestive, arrogant lips. He set his chin firmly, but his voice was soft.

"It says nothing of your kiss or the promise of your soft body."

He gestured with his cigar as he moved a step closer.

"María," he said, almost whispering, "María is a name, a beautiful name, the name of a woman meant to be loved and respected as only a woman can be."

His body burned with fire and Leslie could feel her own igniting as she rose and moved away from him unsteadily.

"And this María," Leslie said sarcastically with a

toss of her head, "she would be meek and humble and stupid. I suppose her *only* mission in life would be to have children and lie in submission at her man's feet!"

Her body was stiff with defiance as she dared him to answer her.

There was a note of satisfied supremacy in his voice as he chuckled deeply. He openly savored the heaving of her breasts as he quietly relinquished his glass of wine and moved leisurely toward her. In the dimness of the room his strong hand reached behind her neck and deliberately twined through her satin hair until his fingers gained purchase at the back of her head and pulled her strongly and urgently to him.

"Yes, she would have children," he said. "My children. And they will have a father and they will have my name, but such a woman," his lips whispered huskily next to hers, "would be there solely for the pleasure of the man and to be pleasured from a love so hot it would sear the gates of heaven." His voice rose in supremacy. "A love, María, that we already have," he said softly, "that we've already experienced, and that we must have again."

His mouth came crushing down on hers and Leslie was consumed as a passion wilder than anything she had ever imagined again answered his urgent demand. She could feel her body clinging to his as Augustine slowly released her in an act that had its origins in millennia past.

"You are María," he said as he treasured every vivid detail of her vanquished image. "In my heart you are María and you are mine—only mine."

He held her away and firmly met her bewildered eyes.

"And now you must be the woman that you are, that you were meant to be. You will leave the things of men to men."

With that he released her and strode away leaving

Leslie completely disoriented. When she slowly realized what had transpired in that tempestuous scene her anger was lethal. His satisfaction and elementary dismissal of the entire incident was more than apparent as he retrieved his wine and cigar.

"Now that that's settled," he said matter-of-factly, "tomorrow you will see a doctor and begin to take proper care of yourself and your condition. I will take care of the union and the strike it threatens."

"You will do no such thing," she spit out. "Los Tejidos de María is mine. It's my company and *I* will run it. You have nothing to do with management. You are only a shareholder!"

"Ah, but I do," he said in self-satisfaction, "for you see initially I bought only a few of your shares for myself as a little side venture and possible tax write-off, but then when I met you and saw the promise of the business I arranged for my family enterprise, Rivera, Bonilla, Ruben & Juarez, Limited which I control, to purchase all of the remaining public shares. Surely you received a notice from the SEC?"

Leslie felt herself sinking bodily. The sign near the entry door of Augustine's offices on the day when she had been so angry flew past her eyes again. She remembered seeing only the Rivera as she rushed in unannounced, but the bottom name Juarez had been subconsciously noted and had been haunting her all this time. Obviously the computer could not print all of the letters in the name.

The low growl of his voice caressed her ear insidiously as she returned to the present and he continued on. "I've systematically been buying the rest of the public shares in my own name to keep the price reasonable—forty percent of the whole as I understand it. That means, my darling, with other arrangements I've recently made we are, in effect, equal partners!"

Leslie stared at him speechless.

"You can't mean that," she said at last, her eyes wide with astonishment. "My broker assured me that I would have the controlling interest and there are other investors. I've seen the report. In any event, though," she said as relief washed over her, "I own forty-five percent. We are not equal. We provided that safeguard from the very beginning."

Her bluster and bravado died though as the full impact of his words sunk in and she realized she had not yet received the latest report.

"And so it would ordinarily have been," she heard Augustine saying expansively on the outer edges of her consciousness, "but the wise business*man*, *querida*, would have kept not only forty-five percent of his stock, but to be absolutely sure *he* would also have kept the first option to repurchase the shareholding stocks from his employees—especially under such an ambitious program that requires no vested interest."

Leslie stumbled blindly toward the chair and reached for the glass of wine she had ignored moments before as she realized what he must have done. She remembered the Ayudalo employees' sudden interest in the shareholding program during the past few weeks and felt a bitter bile rising in her throat. It was all a game. He had been playing with her from the beginning. He had waited cynically in the wings knowing the ultimate triumph was his.

The option was a small detail she honestly hadn't thought of. She had wanted the program to be simple and unencumbered to encourage significant participation. In her naiveté and idealism she had never thought of the employees selling their stock once they were convinced of its value, let alone the entire public block being in one person's hands at such an early stage of development. She was merciless in her own chastisement as she realized she had failed to see all of the warning signals, but even in the face of her instinctive distrust of Philomena she still had trouble comprehending such an obviously devious, underhanded maneuver from either her or Augustine.

"Now, I have some papers here," she heard him saying, "which need to be signed in the presence of my lawyer tomorrow, that I want you to look over and then we need to go over the arrangements I've made for our marriage agreement."

"Our what?" exclaimed Leslie.

The shock of this announcement was the exact catalyst needed to bring her back to objective, rational reason. "I'm signing no papers," she said vehemently, "especially if they have anything to do with my company and I'm certainly not making any marriage agreement with you. You do *not* have a controlling interest — you said yourself we are equal and I have no intention of giving up the management of my company!"

"You will do as I say," he said quietly, "or I will simply transfer my stock into the shareholding program and gain controlling interest in any event. I've done this because I can't allow this factory to be ruined. I've waited and watched carefully. You're a wonderful designer, but you're obviously a poor manager otherwise you wouldn't be having the troubles you're having now."

"How dare you!" she said in total outrage now. "You deliberately allowed that conniving woman, Philomena to create chaos among my workers and you have the audacity to question my abilities?"

"Sooner or later it would have happened anyway." He shrugged her anger away. "Oh, I admit that Philomena has been a bit of a pain, but there are always people like her around ready to cause problems. Now, I have copies of the official government inquiry report that I plan to go over as soon as possible. I'm going to return you home and then I will be at the plant tomorrow to take care of these problems."

Moments later they were once again on the way to the Villaronga estate. Leslie had refused to speak to Augustine again, but he ignored her silence as he continued to quietly address her.

"I had hoped, my darling, you would come to me after you realized how much you love me and how silly these games are that you play. I've known many women and only a woman in love could love the way you do. The only thing between us is the management of this factory and your ridiculous independence. When this obstacle is removed, then we can be happy together. I know you want this as much as I do, you just need a little time to get used to it. Unfortunately the state of your health and the events at the factory will not allow me any further patience. There is no alternative but to act now."

His voice was soothing and cajoling, but each syllable he uttered served only to enrage her more as Leslie continued to glare at him in the dark silence.

When the car finally pulled up to her home Leslie slid quickly from the seat of the car and left Augustine to fend for himself. As she rushed past her startled mother and on up to her room she heard Gerald in the background speaking with Juanita on the phone.

She could picture Augustine making his polite social amenities as the sound of low voices followed her progress. She sat down angry and shaken, waiting to hear the retreat of his big car. She heard heavy steps coming down the hall and thought for a second he had followed her to her room. She was greatly relieved when Gerald stuck his head in the door.

"What's going on, *paesana*?" he asked in feigned comedy, but there was no doubt about the seriousness of his concern.

"Oh, Gerald," she cried as she fell into his arms, "Augustine's found a way to take over the factory and he's insisting that I marry him too."

"Wait, wait, just a minute," said Gerald. "All of this sounds a little fishy to me. What's really going on between you two?"

"Oh, you're just as bad as he is," she said suddenly angry with him too. His very masculinity antagonized her. "All of you are the same," she said in disgust.

"Mija!"

Her mother came gushing through the door.

"Augustine has just told me of your plans. I had no idea."

Her demeanor changed to instant concern when she saw Leslie's distress.

"Mija, what's wrong?"

"There are no plans, Mama. None. Don't believe anything that man says! Please. I just want to be alone."

"Listen, doña," said Gerald, "I don't know what's going on here and Leslie is obviously too upset to make any sense right now. Juanita is on the way to pick me up and I'll see if she knows anything about this. Tomorrow I'll see Augustine and get to the bottom of this. In the meantime why don't we just leave Leslie alone for a while."

He motioned the older woman toward the door as he ended.

Leslie now turned to her with tears in her eyes.

"Oh, Mama, I'm sorry. I didn't mean to snap at you. It's just that I have a terrible headache and sometimes Augustine can be so difficult. I'll talk to you about it tomorrow, Mama, I promise."

"Well, if you say so," her mother responded hesitantly, "but I'm going to get you some aspirin and a cool drink and then I want you to take a cool shower so you can rest well."

Gerald and Doña María left the room as Leslie began to follow her mother's instructions.

Early the next morning, unable to sleep after a fitful

night, Leslie got up and crept out of the house. She drove down through the mountain road, aimlessly at first and then found herself confronting the convergence of Salud and Marina streets in Ponce. The resulting V-shaped sliver of land between them held an outdoor conch shell-shaped auditorium and a tall, slender obelisk monument.

Feeling almost as if fate were drawing her, she stopped the car. In the early morning the normally crowded narrow streets were deserted and she parked easily. She could smell the aroma of fresh baked bread as some hearty souls ambled out with their bags to retrieve their favorite breakfast. Leslie stepped gingerly to the park, which had a carpet of red flamboyant petals all around. She looked up at the needle-sharp monument commemorating the abolition of slavery in Puerto Rico and read the plaque designating this as Plaza Abolición.

She felt a sense of poignancy as she saw the face of Augustine through her bitter tears. He was right. She did love him, but for all of his talk of emancipation and freedom he had never once considered hers. There was no question but that marriage to him would be subservient and unequal. She could not possibly be happy in such a situation.

As she looked down to the ground the red flamboyant blossoms took on the tinge of blood and she thought of their many ancestors who had died so cruelly under the hands of tyrants. She wondered how a man could have such a combined diabolical—saint nature. Why couldn't he treat her as an equal? Why couldn't he recognize all of her talents? Why couldn't they just talk as partners with respect for one another? Why?

As she continued to touch the smoothness of the monument her pain and confusion were almost unbearable. Her feelings were so strong, surely there must be some way of resolving their differences on an equitable basis. She knew she had to try.

She walked back to the car and headed instinctively down Avenida Salud toward the plaza. Again she easily parked in front of Augustine's office. She was just about to leave her car when she saw Philomena emerging from the high porch on the side of the building. She was obviously leaving from the back door, which Leslie had been through only hours before. Leslie edged her car forward. A minute later the gate responded to a touch control and as the other woman's car zoomed away Leslie was sure she saw the edge of Augustine's big car parked in the back.

She could feel a blind rage overtaking her as the knife of jealousy stabbed straight to her heart. How ridiculous that she should think there could be a common ground of any kind between her and this obnoxious man. He had left her and gone straight to Philomena. That was obvious. His office was a perfect place for a rendezvous. Philomena would never have come to her office so early otherwise.

Slowly she drove on while angrily chastising herself. Augustine had only one thing on his mind—to maneuver her, through brute force if neccessary, into an impossible position so that he could take over her plant. He was acting out of pure vengeance. His machismo demanded that he destroy her. His pride could not sustain her seduction and blatant use of his body. She had invaded the unique purview of men. Now he must make her crawl and he had cunningly devised his strategy so everyone would think his intentions were noble and honorable while he continued to conduct his life in any way he pleased. It was all very clear now. Magna was right. Latin men could never be trusted.

As these revelations came crashing down on her, Leslie realized she had to do something. In just a few hours Augustine would be at the plant ready to assume command. She had to find a way to stop him.

The papers.

He had papers he knew she must sign to effect the transition in leadership otherwise they continued to control the factory on an equal basis—unless, of course, he transferred his stock to the shareholding program, and now in the glare of the morning light Leslie suddenly knew that was more of a bluff than a threat.

No.

She needed to stall at least for a few hours until she could get her strategy worked out. Quickly she put her little car into gear. Soon she was in La Rambla. Thinking little about where she was going, she zoomed across Calle Guadalupe, and headed out into the country and realized she was headed in the general direction of the Taino dig near Tibes. She came to a well-kept service station where the road forked in two directions. She stopped to fill her tank with gasoline and ask for specific directions. It was a perfect solution to her immediate problem. No one would think of looking for her there.

The drive was beautiful, but the road was very narrow and twisty, requiring all of her concentration. She drove carefully while also looking for signs of the museum housed near three thatched huts that the gas station attendant had indicated as the way to identify the site. Finally just as the sun was beginning to blaze at its hottest she thought she saw it. She drove down a small road and parked her car some distance away. The road was rutted and she didn't think she should subject her car to such a rough passage. She elected to follow the path by foot instead.

Leslie walked slowly and allowed her thoughts a free rein. She once again acknowledged her longing for motherhood, but at the same time her career and business were also equally important to her and a real source of sincere satisfaction. At the same time she was in love with part of a man. Yes, as bad as he obviously was, she could not deny it. She still loved Augustine and that love made her extremely vulnerable. The only way she could possibly be happy with him was if he effected a great change in attitude and only an utter fool would become involved with a man such as Augustine thinking she could change him.

No, it was an impossible situation and now that she had seen that he was definitely afflicted with the Latin penchant for many lovers, not to mention vengeance, Leslie knew her innate pride and intelligence would not allow her to enter into such a ridiculous arrangement and he was not going to blackmail her into it either. Power or no power, she had equal rights to legal representation and she would fight him to her last breath.

With that resolution she stepped into an open field much like the one near Loíza. Within moments someone came from the museum and began to tell her about the park, which was still officially an archaeological dig.

The now familiar story of Agueybana was again related to her. In spite of herself, as she heard again how this valiant male chieftain had fought to end the enslavement of his people, Augustine again invaded her thoughts. It was his spirit that was compatible with the spirits here and suddenly she realized it was this alliance of spirits, hers with Aloíza and his with Agueybana, that had brought them together in the first place. They were really two very similar people and had not these other foreign influences with insistence upon domination been introduced they would have had a magnificent communion of the spirit as well as the flesh.

It was such an introspective, hopeful sensation that Leslie momentarily thought she was going to faint.

"Senorita, please," she heard the young guide exclaim. "Sit down over here. You've been out in the sun too long."

His voice was kind and Leslie smiled as he assisted her to a mammoth mango tree, where she sank gratefully to the ground. He rushed away and returned quickly with a cool drink and a small snack, which he insisted she eat. Within seconds she felt much better.

"Tell me more about the Tainos who lived here," she said conversationally as the young man joined her in the shady spot.

"Well, the women comprised most of the labor force and the men were the hunters and protectors—"

"But," Leslie broke in, "I thought these were primarily matriarchal societies."

"Oh, they were in the beginning, but somewhere along the line the dual roles of mother and hunter seemed to become incompatible. Probably when early agriculture began it just seemed natural that the roles became delineated. One of the things, though, that never seemed to change," he said brightly, "was an important social event that may have also been a religious ceremony. It was a party they called *Areyto*."

At the mention of a party Augustine entering her mother's party flashed into Leslie's mind. She could remember him enjoying himself with the oysters and crabs. Surely these primitive people must have had the same good times and Augustine was by his own admission as much of a *jibaro* and therefore ultimately a Taino as every other native of this island. Again this was a charming thought that she knew was self-defeating.

At the thought of the party Leslie also realized guiltily that when she had made her hasty plans for the day she had forgotten entirely about her mother. Doña María would probably be worried about her. She really must find a phone and call her.

As she finally wound down the road again after

thanking her young guide profusely for his kindness, some of his last words began to echo through her mind. Had she with her wishful thinking managed to unrealistically glamorize the dual roles of motherhood and career? Had he not just said that even this original nonsexist culture eventually evolved into delineated roles due to sheer expediency and convenience? Was she, along with so many other so-called "modern" women, ultimately giving up her freedom and very uniqueness by insisting upon assuming a traditionally male role? Did it ultimately mean, at the bottom line, she thought, one really had to make a choice? Both roles were truly not possible?

"I don't believe that," Leslie said out loud to herself in a firm voice. "I just don't believe that."

At any rate even in those primitive societies women and men seemed to have chosen tasks that they specifically enjoyed doing, and while they worked in some fulfilling satisfying way, their children were right next to them. No, women had often had a diversity of choices, but in most cases their satisfactory fulfillment had always depended entirely upon their personal understanding of this and a suitable choice of mate— something she obviously was not managing very well.

Finally, she concluded, an intelligent man who loved her would recognize and encourage all of her talents. Her problem was a very simple one: She had fallen in love with a man who was simply not compatible with her except on a physical basis.

Then the thought of her night of lovemaking with Augustine triggered the thought of the child. Blindingly she realized how wonderful it really would be to have a loving, understanding mate who would not only work next to her, but also stand bravely in front of her protecting both her and the child.

Fleetingly she touched her face and gazed straight ahead. *Yes*, she thought, *what I need is someone who would cherish me.* Something that was definitely not possible with a man such as Augustine. He understood only two words: *conquer* and *submission.*

It was clearly up to her to end this charade once and for all and she wasn't about to allow herself to use the excuse of her mother's feelings again either.

That had also, she told herself sternly, been a rather convenient copout to continue this silly love–hate farce so she could indulge in rather juvenile, overembellished fantasies.

Yet she couldn't stifle a small uncertainty as she remembered her mother's joy and miraculous recovery since Augustine's introduction. She knew in her heart Doña María was pleased with the thought of her marriage to Augustine, but then her mother would be the last person on earth who would want her to marry a man who would make her unhappy and surely she would help Leslie in her fight to keep control of her factory once she understood the entire situation.

As she came to the gas station she stopped to call Doña María. There was no answer so she called the factory. Juanita answered.

"Doña Leslie," she cried. "Where have you been? Everything is a mess here!" Her voice was strident with a tinge of censure.

"Juanita, what are you talking about?" Leslie asked with a sinking feeling.

"It's Philomena," she answered. "She's been here all day with Don Fernando Aguila and Don Augustine. Everyone's gone crazy!"

"Leslie," said Gerald, coming onto the line in his most conciliatory voice, "you really must come in. I think everything can be worked out, but we need your help. Augustine has just—"

Leslie held the receiver from her ear, purposely not wanting to hear what Gerald had to say, then slowly hung it up. She felt for sure that she had been the vic-

tim of deception and disloyalty. She didn't know how
he had done it, but Augustine must have won over not
only her mother, but Gerald and Juanita as well. She
grimaced as she remembered speaking to Gerald with
unreasonably angry words the night before. Then she
also recalled Juanita's hidden looks of late. She probably welcomed the news of Augustine's takeover and
Leslie's possible engagement to him. It was a stagger-
ing thought as the enormous success of Augustine's
cunning strategy began to penetrate and she like a fool
had played right into his hands, doing nothing to stop
him.

It wasn't long before the events of the day were clari-
fied for her graphically. When she stumbled back to her
car she had thought to distract herself with the radio.
She turned it on as an announcer was just ending a local
news roundup. In short terse sentences she heard that
the workers in her factory had announced a special
meeting; Philomena, as the head of Ayudalo, was sup-
porting the organization of a union at Los Tejidos: marriage plans had been announced between Leslie and
Augustine; and he was acting corporate head of Los
Tejidos de María in her absence.

Chapter Thirteen

For one very long moment Leslie was completely demoralized and then all of the fire of her temper raged forth and consumed her as she stepped on the accelerator and headed toward the plant.

"The nerve, the insufferable nerve," she seethed as she drove with a vengeance. He would dare to assert himself in such a blatant way, putting it on the radio! She had been gone for only a few hours.

Her car screeched to a halt as she stormed into the factory and walked straight to her office. "Get the hell out of my office!" she shouted as Augustine and Gerald both looked up at her in astonishment.

She looked out the window as the noise of congregating people came to her attention. She saw workers leaving by a side entrance. Some were stopping to listen to the strident voice of Philomena as she urged flyers into their hands and announced the time of a meeting to be held that night.

"María," said Augustine in his most conciliatory voice, "you must talk with them."

"Talk with them! Yesterday I left a plant with people who were working. What have you done in just a few short hours?"

"They are working," Augustine said as he looked at his watch and gave her a glance of censure. "It's afternoon break time."

Leslie looked at him sharply.

"I'm afraid," he went on, "Philomena has decided to be a little more than a pain."

"Oh, she has?" said Leslie in a low voice. "Well, then handle her! I'm sure the great chieftain Augustine Rivera can put her into her place."

"Leslie, please," said Gerald breaking in. "Augustine has the best of—"

"Don't tell me about this man, this snake in the grass," she spit out in her most guttural tones. "There's nothing I don't know or understand about this man and he's not going to take over this plant with or without your help!"

Her innards were scalding with rage and it took all of her strength to control the shakiness that threatened to send her completely out of control.

"I want all of you out of this office immediately," she said with a forced calmness.

"I'm afraid that's not possible," said Augustine. "You see, whether you like it or not we *are* partners now and I insist upon investigating every aspect of this business."

She looked at him with daggers of fire and then as the events of the past twenty-four hours began to take their toll, she slumped in momentary discouragement.

"All right," Leslie said as she refused to meet his eyes. "It seems that you will not rest until you have destroyed or changed everything I've tried to achieve and all because you are not man enough to acknowledge my business expertise."

She spoke the last words with a flicker of her earlier spirit as she drew herself to her full height and challenged him to answer.

"You call this business expertise?" he said. "Your employees are practically out of control and they think so little of your shareholding program that they sell their stock to buy rum for their parties."

Leslie looked at him with the utmost in contempt. "And who gave them the money?" she sneered. "Who undermined a chance they had to have something more, all because of his own greed?"

She hated him for making her feel so ugly, but she meant every word of it.

"The great benefactor," she said levelly, "who deliberately took advantage of his people's naiveté."

"Are you quite through?" Augustine asked in a deadly voice.

"No, I'm not through," she shouted. "I won't ever be through until you are out of here and out of my life!"

"You are through," he said as he walked around and carefully took her arm. "Now I want you to go out there and talk with your people. Reassure them."

"You go straight to hell," she said as she pulled herself away roughly. "I don't need directions from you."

There was a light tapping on the door. Leslie turned around as Juanita came into the room.

"Pardon me," she said as she looked uneasily from Augustine to Leslie, "but there are some people here who wish to deliver a desk for Don Augustine."

"Yes, yes," said Augustine with exaggerated enthusiasm. "Have them bring it in here. Place it on the other side of Doña Leslie's. I want to be able to look at her."

Leslie looked at him with open-eyed outrage, everything about her totally aghast. "I don't believe you," she said in a low voice.

"Believe it," he said in a clipped voice. "We are going to be working together from this day on. Tomorrow we will talk about our marriage plans."

"Now that's enough!" said Leslie, all of her patience finally exhausted. "Gerald, how can you stand here and listen to this?"

"Really, Leslie," said Gerald hastily, "I honestly think you should try—"

"Get out," said Leslie as she turned her total wrath on him. Something just seemed to snap. "Get out and take Juanita with you! As far as I'm concerned you're all traitors and I don't want anything to do with you."

"Leslie, for God's sake get a hold of yourself," said Gerald. "Be reasonable! I've never seen you like this. You sound like a maniac."

"Maniac?" she said, then she made another attempt to calm herself. "There is your maniac." She pointed to Augustine. "And his mate is outside the window there!"

She flinched away from the anxiety in Gerald's eyes. Augustine went about placing the desk in the room as though she weren't there.

"Leslie," said Gerald as he came to her and held her at arm's length, "look, I know you're tired and you're overwrought, but you need to get control of yourself. You've got to sit down and talk with Augustine. You really don't have any choice."

She looked at him and tried to comprehend what this old and dear friend was trying to say to her. He gauged her reaction and then went on.

"Now, I've spent most of today talking with Augustine and I honestly think the two of you just need to sit down and communicate. You both have some preconceived notions—"

"I can't," said Leslie in absolute weariness. "I just can't, not right now."

The workmen finished placing the desk and Augustine looked at it in satisfaction as he turned around and brushed his clothes with a dismissing motion. "Thank you, Senor Masters," he said graciously, "but I really think you have done enough for today. "I'm sure Leslie will talk to me." He turned to look at her. "You see, it was he, my dear, who convinced me to reexamine my conclusions about your business acumen. As a result I've decided rather than to just take over, I will work with you side by side for a time and I will not make an effort to purchase more stock from your employees, but we must come to some satisfactory agreement."

Leslie thought she had reached the limits of her outrage, but this arrogant man who only hours before she had agonized over was more than she could stand. Yet her years of keen business experience finally came to her rescue and she realized there was truth in what Gerald had said.

"All right," she finally said in resignation. "All right, but not right now. Perhaps a little later or first thing tomorrow."

Both men looked at her, one with deep concern and the other with smugness.

"Later then," said Augustine. "That will be fine."

"Very well," said Leslie as she turned to leave. "I'm rather tired and exhausted. I'll call you in a while."

"Take all of the time you need," Augustine said softly as he came up behind her. "You must take care of yourself."

In spite of the emotions they had just exchanged, Leslie's heart began to beat faster and she felt a rush of blood. His voice was sweet and sensuous. She met his eyes and saw again genuine concern and probing questions. She wrenched herself away defiantly and knew she was in the presence of treachery.

A moment later when she got in her car to leave she remembered Philomena coming from Augustine's office that morning. Suddenly she was more than just tired and weary. She had no desire to return to her home or to see her mother—not just yet. She drove with a weary purpose toward Magna's office. She needed some advice and it had to come from an experienced person.

When she arrived at Magna's office her secretary told Leslie that her friend had gone to see Sister Margarita at the Centro de Orientation in the Playa. It was one of Magna's favorite charities, responsible for turning around one of the more notorious areas of the city. Leslie arrived there a few moments later and was greeted by dozens of happy children, many of whom were carrying cameras.

"Do you want your picture taken?" asked the cheerful voice of her friend as Magna came to greet her.

"Oh, not today," said Leslie with a sigh. "I'm afraid I'd break the camera."

"Trouble?" queried Magna.

"Yes," said Leslie nodding her head with a grimace.

"Come on," said Magna as she took her arm. "I'll buy you a coffee at the Club Nautico. We can talk there."

"Thanks," said Leslie as she felt the beginning pricklings of tears again. She reached out to tousle the head of one of the children and felt a pang of longing and remorse so deep she thought she would surely die. She knew now any hopes she had ever had of having a family of her own were dead. She could never marry the man she wanted and loved, and any other arrangement just to have a child would be a sham. Augustine's treachery had transcended her wildest imaginings and she knew now she could never compromise herself just to satisfy a physical need. On the contrary, she had to concentrate on refuting his announcement of their impending marriage.

As they walked toward their cars, they were greeted by the kind, warmhearted Sister Margarita who worked tirelessly in this successful and innovative community program after retiring from years of stateside service. She smiled broadly as she gave Leslie the traditional kiss of greeting.

"Congratulations, Leslie, I just heard the news about you and Don Augustine. You know, he is one of the finest men in this town, always generous with us. He helped with the grant for this photography program and you know last year some of our children's photos won awards at the Metropolitian Museum of Art.''

Leslie sensed her friend's small intake of breath although Magna artfully hid the sound of her surprise.

"Thank you," said Leslie hesitantly as she avoided Magna's eyes, "but actually I think that announcement may have been a little premature."

"Well, he is a fine man and should make you very happy," said Margarita. "I'll pray for your happiness."

Leslie nodded numbly as she climbed into her car and gave thanks for the few moments of grace she would have before facing the puzzled expression of Magna as they both drove the short distance to the private yacht club.

"So what's going on?" asked Magna a few moments later.

Leslie looked at her friend and finally made no effort to check the tears as fragrant coffee wafted around heightening all of her senses.

"I love him and he's impossible," said Leslie as she finally met Magna's eyes squarely.

"That bad," said Magna as she looked her over astutely.

For the next half hour the emotional story poured from Leslie in jumbled sentences. Magna listened carefully and asked guiding questions to clarify the sequence of the tale, while also making appropriate sympathetic comments when merited.

"I've done everything you warned me not to do," Leslie finally said as she dabbed at the persistent tears. "I just can't seem to help myself."

"You know, sometimes I talk too much," said Magna compassionately. "No one can control whom they fall in love with and when it happens it is in many ways the most magical thing in the universe, but also the most miserable when we feel trapped by it."

"I can't cope," said Leslie in defeat. "I'm going to lose my factory and everything that means anything to me. I have such a feeling of rage and I feel so ugly, yet when I think of him when he's tender and introspective...."

"I think you *have* seen the real Augustine and you love him," said Magna with a sigh. "Gerald is right. The two of you need to communicate."

"But you said—"

"I know what I said," said Magna. "But I also know how empty life is without love. To live happily with the one you love must truly be the greatest miracle on earth. Just loving someone with all your heart is a miracle and if there's any possibility of putting it together I think you should at least try."

"How can you say that after everything I've told you?" sputtered Leslie. Yet she couldn't deny the warmth she began to feel as the hope of Magna's words spread over her. "The way he has carried on with Philomena and God knows how many other women and now this tacky way of undermining my business...."

"I see a desperate man," said Magna levelly. "In my bones I'm sure he loves you. Augustine has always been a man of honor. Everyone knew his alliance with Philomena was more political than romantic, but then neither of them had ever been serious about anyone else. Philomena was once a warm and happy woman until she was jilted in an early love. Since then she has looked on men as mere acquisitions, but surely you know she and Don Fernando Aguila are an item now."

"No, I didn't," said Leslie in surprise. Then she remembered the night of the party. "Well, then, why is she causing me so much trouble at the plant?"

"Pride, silly pride," said Magna with a sigh. "We all have it and it never fails to cause trouble when we react to it badly. Augustine should have allowed her to break the engagement.''

''Did I hear my name?'' asked a familiar voice.

Leslie turned and looked straight into the troubled eyes of Augustine.

''Your mother is worried about you, María. I promised her I would find you.''

With a pang Leslie realized she had forgotten her mother completely and she had not touched base with her all day. She met Magna's eyes and sensed her friend's support.

''It's been a long and tiring day, María,'' he went on softly. ''Why don't you come with me for a few hours on my boat? Perhaps there we could talk.''

Leslie gasped. ''It's nearly evening,'' she said, unable to hide the fluster in her voice.

''The Phosphorescent Bay should only be sailed at night,'' said Augustine. ''Come, I'll call your mother and then I think we should talk.''

''There's nothing to talk about,'' said Leslie as she glanced around to see if anyone were watching them. ''We can take care of our business in my office tomorrow.''

Magna gave her a serious look and managed a nearly imperceptible shake of her head, as her eyes told Leslie to listen to her heart and not her head. ''The Phosphorescent Bay is lovely at night,'' she said. ''It's intriguing to see everything in the sea outlined like Christmas ornaments. Such a diversion might be just what you need.''

''Are you sure?'' asked Leslie a little hesitantly. Her eyes were slowly drawn to Augustine's.

''I'm very sure,'' said Magna softly as she noted the mutual anguish and uncertainties so shallowly concealed by both of them. ''Go.'' Magna rose and gave Leslie a little push in Augustine's direction.

"I have no clothes, I'm not dressed properly," said Leslie still a bit hesitant.

"Don't worry about that," said Augustine as his hand gripped her arm firmly and took up the impetus of Magna's encouragement. "I always have spares on board."

For just a second Leslie felt a familiar pang of alarm as she wondered how many women Augustine must entertain in this way to be so well equipped.

"The first rule of any good sailor is to always have spares," said Magna hurriedly. "Go on. I'll call Doña María," she ended.

Leslie looked back for one last fleeting glance as Augustine hustled her toward the door, then they started down the steps. Magna gave Leslie a big smile and nodded affirmatively as she walked on with Augustine to the dock where his small cabin cruiser was berthed.

The silence between them was uneasy as Augustine moved around to ready the boat for sailing. Finally, out of neccessity, he enlisted her aid with the ropes and other paraphernalia he quickly assembled. As Leslie helped him with the anchor after the engine roared to life, she felt a peculiar numbness that made her feel as if this were a dream rather than reality. The aura of vengeance she had earlier envisioned around him seemed to have disappeared in the wake of gentle words and genuine concern.

The boat moved out into the crystal blue water as Augustine traveled west, giving a wide berth to the smelly refineries that bordered Ponce on the southwest. Soon, though, the breeze was wonderful as the peace of the calm ocean settled around them.

Actually Leslie was dressed fairly appropriately since she still had on the clothes she had worn to Tibes, but Augustine shouted and pointed to the cabin a few moments later. "There's swimsuits in there," he said.

"I'm sure something will fit you." There was a hint of a leer in his eyes that made Leslie uncomfortable in more ways than one.

"No thanks," said Leslie, who marveled at his ability to act so nonchalant after the events of the past twenty-four hours.

"Okay, then hold the wheel for a few moments while I change," he said.

Leslie felt an immediate wariness. She didn't know that much about boats.

"Come on," he said. "Put on this life jacket while you're at it."

She moved hesitantly toward him.

"Here," he said as he handed her the wheel. His arms went around her as he positioned her and she felt the easy play of the wheel in her hands. "Just hold her steady," he said, his lips just a hair's breadth from her ear. "There's nothing to it when the sea is so calm."

She flushed as her body responded wildly to his touch and realized what a ridiculous position she had unwittingly placed herself in. Why had she listened to Magna? What had gotten into her coming out here alone with a man who just hours before had vowed to take over not only her factory, but her life and family as well?

"Be back in a minute," he said as he ducked into the cabin below.

Leslie knew she had to stand her ground and gathered her emotional resources to handle this situation. Then for the second time in twenty-four hours she decided that since she was there she may as well make the most of her situation and try to straighten this mess out.

Augustine reappeared just moments later and Leslie was immediately reminded of their night of wild and tender love. He was magnificent in his loose trunks and terry jacket, which revealed the wide expanse of his hairy teak chest. He trod silently around in his deck shoes as he checked out the boat once again. Leslie realized at last that he too was just a tad uncomfortable. He was obviously looking for things to occupy himself.

As they traveled west they were enshrouded in the red blaze of a magnificent setting sun. In the distance Leslie saw dolphins silhouetted in the glorious light and suddenly longed for the freedom of spirit they must enjoy.

"Look," she cried as she pointed toward them. The wind carried her word like a tinkling chime. Augustine came toward her and smiled in appreciation.

"Let's swim with them," he said. Leslie couldn't ignore the infectious excitement in his voice. "Go on." He took the wheel from her and brushed his hand over her arms. "Go down and change into a suit and we'll go out to them."

"Do you think we can?" asked Leslie.

"Sure," he said as his eyes grew warm with tenderness and excitement. "I do it all of the time and there's nothing in the world like the experience of swimming with them."

It seemed like the obvious thing to do—something they had planned for years as Leslie suddenly relaxed and went to find a swimsuit.

"Of course you don't have to put on anything at all," Augustine called after her with a lewd twinkle in his eyes as he saw her instant change in demeanor, "but then again you know I'm not that kind of guy."

She laughed in spite of herself and bounced down into the cabin, which was small but comfortably appointed. She saw a small closet filled with women's apparel and saw the suit Augustine had admired many weeks before at the factory when they had given the showing to his friends. She sucked in her breath in a quick reflex and then decided to ignore the obvious implications its presence there produced. Quickly she stepped into it after throwing her rumpled clothes into a heap.

"I knew I'd like it," Augustine said as she stepped up onto the deck a few moments later.

"A little presumptuous, aren't you?" Leslie stated levelly.

"A little," he said after a calculated pause. A hint of a mischievous smile played around his lips and suddenly the well of longing in Leslie that cried for expression willed all of the anger and animosity of the past twenty-four hours away.

Augustine noted her response and she noted his satisfaction, but somehow none of that mattered now. She was here now and she wanted whatever was offered. The poignant words of Magna echoed in her brain and left her feeling very mellow and receptive.

"Where are they?" asked Leslie as she scanned the calm waters with just a hint of whitecaps here and there.

"There!" he shouted as a dolphin rose from the water followed by another in perfect twin circles not more than twenty feet away.

"They're beautiful."

"Well, here, give me a hand with the anchor," said Augustine. "We can both go in. It's safe."

"You're sure?" she said excitedly as she helped him anchor the boat. "Won't they go away?"

"No. They can tell when you mean them no harm. Just go easy," he advised as he took her hand. They walked to the edge of the boat and dove off together.

The water was warm and exhilarating as Leslie surfaced in a wonderful floating euphoria. Augustine came up beside her and then began to glide with strong, easy strokes. Leslie soon matched him and felt a wonderful peace as they traveled around the bobbing boat and suddenly felt the thrill of the nearness of the dolphins as two of them arced out of the water again, just feet away.

Augustine went toward them and submerged himself so he could surface close enough to touch them. Leslie followed and soon felt the wonderful silkiness and energy of the dolphins' bodies as they swam easily among them. They must have played for nearly a half hour, alternately swimming, floating, and diving back into the water from the boat until the sun nearly finished its descent and just a red haze was left on the horizon of the ocean.

"That was wonderful," said Leslie as she sat on the boat, struggling for breath while lazily drying her hair with a towel Augustine had thrown to her. She was aware of his eyes as he stood and watched her from his position at the wheel.

"Lovely."

Leslie stopped in midmotion and purposely met his eyes. "You know, Augustine when you're like this, you're wonderful. If only you could just—"

"Shh," he said as if he didn't wish to be distracted. "Enjoy the last of the sun. We're coming into the bay now and I'll stop and get us some empanadas to eat. I think there's some wine in the little fridge."

She gave him a little look of annoyance.

"There's plenty of time to talk," he said hastily, noting her impatience with his evasion. "I want very much for us to talk out our problems, but moments like this do not happen every day. I want to remember you like this—in the wind, your hair blowing, the sun setting behind you while the bay below comes to life...."

The introspective gentle man whom Leslie loved most was in full control now and she felt his strength and magnetism reach out to her. She couldn't resist and for some uncanny reason, in spite of all her earlier feelings, she no longer wanted to, at least not here in the middle of the ocean. That could wait until she returned to the real world.

They glided into the small port at Playa la Parguera

and Leslie noted the old-fashioned buildings from an earlier era, particularly Hotel Villa Parguera, as sight-seers clamored aboard glass-bottom boats to view the mysteries of the bay. The evening was softened by the moon and stars with only a tiny hint of stridency as notes of the tinny island music bounced jauntily out over the water.

Within moments Augustine had secured several of the steaming pastries filled with meat along with a small portion of the traditional rice and beans. As they headed out over the magical waters and the breeze turned a little cooler, he brought Leslie the matching wrap to her suit. He anchored the boat and turned on soft music from his small radio while they ate in a rather extraordinary communion.

"This is the way life should be lived," said Augustine as he lay back and took in his surroundings with great satisfaction.

Leslie waited to see where he was going with this before she attempted a response.

"I hope you're beginning to feel the peace of it," he said as he gazed into her eyes. "We have so much to talk about, perhaps now is the time?"

"I don't think so," said Leslie, suddenly obstinate. She had wanted to talk earlier. Why should he set the time and place? All at once, as fast as it had left, she felt all of her earlier antagonism returning. She realized sinkingly she had once again put herself in this man's power, thanks to his insidious gentleness, which he used in such a devastating way.

"As you wish," he said completely unperturbed. "I'm perfectly content to just enjoy the stars and the ocean. We'll have plenty of time to talk in the office.

She noted him looking her over carefully and realized he was examining the contours of her bathing suit with a new fascination.

"Your health seems to be very good, María. You

swam like a fish and your appetite is restored too. I'm very pleased, but we must still make arrangements for a complete checkup. Your mother is very worried about you too. That swimsuit is also very flattering, perfect for—"

"Really, I don't want to discuss any of my personal business with you," said Leslie with a decided edge to her voice. "I think maybe we should be returning to Ponce."

"You're probably right," Augustine said with a smile, "but I'm glad we did this. I think everything will be a little easier now."

"Don't count on it," she said. "This has been nice and I guess it won't hurt if we try to act like civilized human beings, but nothing has changed. I will not be your—"

"Leave it, María," he said hastily in a commanding, albeit soft, voice. "We'll return now and tomorrow we will talk."

He stepped up to the wheel and started the motor with a roar. Soon the boat was traveling at a high rate of speed and Leslie had no idea where they were as the darkness enveloped them. The boat seemed to zig and zag and she felt the spray of the salt water in her face as they raced on like demons. The lights on the boat were the only thing that sharply countered the darkness, although the moon and stars followed them with a deep midnight glow.

Suddenly there was a loud noise and Leslie felt herself being pitched forward. The rush of water accompanied a crunching, ripping sound as the boat came to a sudden violent halt.

"What was that?" she screamed as she rubbed her head where it had been bruised when she tumbled.

"I don't know," said Augustine. "Are you all right?"

"Yes." She tried to crawl toward him, but realized the boat was listing in a funny direction.

"Caraho!" he shouted. "We've hit a coral reef and we're totally hung up. I shouldn't have been going so fast at night."

"Well, what are we going to do?" asked Leslie, unable to keep the panic from her voice. "Are we going to sink?"

"No, no, I don't think so," he said, his annoyance more than obvious. "It looks like we hit it and then bounced on top. We're completely grounded. I'll have to call for help, but I'm not exactly sure where we are so it may be morning before anyone can find us. Whatever you do, don't try to leave the boat. The coral is poisonous and will cut you to pieces."

"But didn't you know this was out here?" she asked angry now.

"Well, yes and no," he said noncommittally as he fiddled with the radio. "These reefs are all over the place just below the water. They can usually be seen during the day, but in the dark I just didn't realize I was so close to them."

"Well, do something," said Leslie as she watched him adjusting the radio.

"I will, *niña*," he said with a calculated calmness, "but whether you like it or not, my sweet Doña Leslie, I think we are going to spend another night together. It's a good thing everyone already knows I'm your fiancé."

Chapter Fourteen

In the next few minutes the ship-to-shore radio emitted a series of high-pitched sounds and finally connected with the Coast Guard station. Leslie refused to acknowledge the full intent of Augustine's earlier words as she gazed away and did her best to calm her acute agitation. Just as he had expected, the Coast Guard advised Augustine that it would probably take some time due to the darkness.

Miraculously the boat was still, and, for the most part, upright with just a slight list to the side, but it was nevertheless awkward to move around and Augustine prudently cautioned against any unnecessary motion as he came to her side and pulled her close to him.

"I think if we're quiet," he said, "the boat will remain as it is. I'll leave the lights on, but with the Phosphorescent Bay so near it may be hard to differentiate us from the air."

"Is this an indication of your fine management skills?" Leslie asked sarcastically as the ramifications of this situation began to fully dawn on her and she pulled away from him.

"Now, this is no time to get temperamental," he cautioned. "I'm as annoyed and sorry as you are, but we must work together now. We can't take the chance of being cut by the coral and there might be the danger of sharks too."

Leslie gasped as yet another danger was added to the list, not the least of which was this proximity to Augustine. In spite of her fear and anger she could feel her body radiating to his as the warmth of her longing reached out to him. She shivered as the breeze grew cold and moist.

"Here, *niña*, don't be so stubborn," Augustine said gently as he put his arm around her again. The familiar growl of his voice titillated her and sent chills from the tip of her ear to her toes. "We need to be close to each other to keep warm. Perhaps if we're still for a while I can sense the amount of shifting. I think maybe we might be able to move into the cabin without too much danger, but it's better to wait and be sure." He snuggled in close to her and began the comforting motions of tucking her jacket around her.

"You sound as though this were an everyday situation for you," Leslie said acidly as she tried to avoid the results of his ministrations. Again she was fighting the twin emotions of anger and love as her body instinctively responded to the promise of being in his arms for the next few hours. She looked away, fearful of meeting his eyes.

"No, not really," he said with a hint of humor, "but the waters are so shallow around here that it's not unusual for the novice sailor to be grounded. This happened once a very long time ago to me, but then we were on an island."

"We?" asked Leslie unable to hide her instant suspicion tinged with a jealousy she simply couldn't control.

Augustine smiled with a ready retort on his lips, but before he could utter a sound there was a loud bump against the part of the boat extended above the coral reef that was more deeply submerged. The bow shuddered and they both froze.

"What was that?" asked Leslie tremulously as she burrowed deeper into his arms.

The boat wavered in the water but managed to maintain its tentative equilibrium as the waves lapped around it in a washing motion.

"I hope not what I think," said Augustine as he pulled her closer and looked warily out over the water.

"What?"

"Don't worry about it."

"Tell me," Leslie persisted. A note of stridency had come into her voice.

"Cálmate, cálmate," he soothed. "It's nothing. The boat probably just shifted."

"Something hit us!"

"Must you always have the last word? Could you not trust me, just once?"

"It was a shark, wasn't it?" said Leslie, unable to quell her rising hysteria.

"And if it was?" he said with just a hint of an edge to his voice. "Does it make you feel better to know that?"

"I prefer the truth no matter what," she said as she immediately regained her full composure and realized he still very much fit the mold of the old-fashioned Latin male with his built-in arrogance and protective assumptions. "I'm not a child who needs to be protected from the truth. Now, just how much danger are we in?"

Even in the dark her eyes were beacons, which met his equally. He gazed at her reflectively for several seconds and then gave her a nod of understanding. She responded with a sense of warmth and camaraderie that melded with the instinctive passions of her body into a new, more binding emotion.

"Not very much, I think," he said slowly as he sensed a new acceptance from her. "So long as the boat holds together, I don't think we can sink here. That may or may not have been a shark. Actually there is nothing to attract them to us and it's dark.... If it were, it was probably just a chance accident. I doubt if it will be back.''

As he talked the moon came out in breathtaking beauty and also silhouetted the remainder of their dinner leavings, which had vaulted into the water and was now floating about. The oily wrapper around the empanadas was clearly visible and near it an ominous fin circled, sending chills through both of them as the wrapper disappeared beneath the water in one gulp.

"Stay quiet," said Augustine into her ear. "Just don't move. I'm sure it will go away."

Leslie's body stiffened and broke out in goose bumps from both her fear and the titillation of his mustache so close to her ear. Augustine held her close and turned her head into his shoulder as he watched the water for further signs of the sharks.

Within a few moments there were several fins making a wide arc around the reef in obvious reconnaissance. Leslie and Augustine sat motionless, bound together by both their fear and love as their bodies molded into one. The sea was still calm and the only sounds were of lapping waves as the dark points sliced through the water in deadly silence.

Suddenly there was a wild commotion in the water as the water splashed and rose in volcanic motion. The body of a shark went hurtling sideways followed by the arcing body of the bottle-nosed dolphin that had swum under it at a high rate of speed and then butted its natural enemy with the force of a huge battering ram. Quickly it was joined by others and soon the sharks were all scattered as the dolphins pirouetted around them in what could have easily been called a dance of joy by Leslie and Augustine.

"Our friends," said Augustine in honest admiration. The boat was swaying dangerously in the melee of waves caused by the battle, but Augustine paid it no mind. "They're one of the few creatures in the sea who can battle the sharks."

Leslie's heart was beating so fast she had trouble finding her voice. "Do you mean those were the gentle creatures we were swimming with earlier?"

"I don't know if they're the same ones," said Augustine, the relief obvious in his voice, "but I do know I'm grateful that they were near. The sharks actually meant no harm either. They're only fulfilling their role as scavengers in the ocean."

"That's easy for you to say," said Leslie tartly. "I don't particularly relish being thought of as a piece of trash they need to clean up!"

"You have a point," said Augustine with a smile, "but you know, *niña*, after all of that wild commotion the boat is still stable. We can probably move safely to the cabin. I think the reef has simply anchored and grounded the boat at an odd angle and there is enough water to keep it upright while the bottom rests on the coral. It's probably going to have to be removed by a helicopter, but for the moment until help arrives I think we are fairly secure."

He rose carefully and tested his footing, watching carefully to see if the boat shifted. He made it to the cabin door and back. "Come on," he said as he reached for her hand. "Let's get inside where it's a little warmer."

Leslie grasped his hand gratefully and inched with him to the cabin where she immediately felt snug and secure. The spotlights of the boat beamed out across the water as Augustine once again radioed to check the progress of the search. He advised of sharks in the area and was assured that several boats and helicopters were out but hadn't sighted them yet. To complicate matters a low fog was closing in.

"Caramba," said Augustine beneath his breath as he

looked out and saw the mist rapidly closing in. "I think there is nothing to do but try and rest," he said as he pulled Leslie to him in reassurance, "and wait."

Carefully he dropped the bunks, which made a double bed across one end of the cruiser, and quickly arranged blankets and pillows.

Leslie was drained of all emotion now as the events of the past two days finally took their toll in the form of complete emotional and physical exhaustion. She no longer had the ability to be angry, fearful, or suspicious. She wanted only to crawl into Augustine's arms and wait for the inevitable, whatever it was.

"Come," said Augustine gently as he pulled her close to him on the bed. "We are safe," he murmured as his lips caressed her brow. "Our friends the dolphins are with us and the Coast Guard will find us in the early light."

She folded snugly into his arms and reached for a blanket as the soothing comfort of his protective voice carried her away.

"You're damp." His fingers felt the edges of her swimsuit. "You must get out of that or you'll end up with the *munga*."

"Never mind," she said groggily. Now that her body had felt the promise of rest she could no longer avoid the drowsiness it offered to succor her ravaged emotions.

"No, *niña*, here I'll help you. Get beneath the blanket. I'll find something dry for you."

His fingers began to nimbly undress her as she struggled against him.

"No, no, leave me alone," she insisted. "I just want to sleep."

"You can't sleep in something wet." With one motion he stripped the suit from her and pulled it over her legs in an awkward motion.

"Stop," said Leslie, but her voice died into a murmur. "Just leave me be. I want to sleep...."

"And so you shall," said Augustine in honest amazement as she drifted off in front of his eyes. He expertly tucked the blanket around her and outlined her form with his hands as he looked at her tenderly and kissed her brow once again. "I don't think I'm ever going to understand you," he finally said in resignation. He stretched his body the length of hers and lay quietly beside her, then turned and kissed the nape of her neck while pulling her in closer and melding his body along her spine.

Hours went by and finally Augustine too gave in to his fatigue. The two of them were gently lulled by the soft waves slapping on the side of the boat, which began to list more and rolled their bodies more tightly against one another.

Leslie awoke with a wonderful feeling of warmth. It was still dark and she didn't readily recognize her surroundings. She felt her body instinctively responding to Augustine as he lay beside her and without thinking she began to trace the planes of his face. She turned and felt the rough rasp of the blanket on her naked body and suddenly felt the need to hold him as the hair from his legs titillated the smoothness of her thigh when she moved. As he moaned and turned from her she could see he had removed his swimsuit too and she marveled at the perfection of his body.

Without thinking she bent to kiss the lips she had dreamed about and yearned for during days and hours of agony. It seemed right. The man she had communed with only a few hours before was the man she loved and now in this place it seemed that they should be together.

Again Augustine moved and slowly began to waken. Leslie could see just the beginning peeps of the rising sun's rays as her fingers traveled over his rough beard and felt the thrill of wanting him. The blanket dropped from her and she felt the resiliency of the hair on his chest as it brushed her nipples and sent waves of desire through her. Slowly his eyes opened and he looked at her in wonder as he instinctively reached for her and devoured her lips with his own. He pulled her down and covered her body as the blanket went flying and she felt his hardness against her thigh. His hands began a steady marauding as he moved over her body with his tongue and brought her quickly to a peak of gasping desire.

"*Niña María,*" he breathed, his voice still shadowed with sleep.

His hair was tousled and they were a rumpled couple locked in a moment of natural desire. Slowly his lips moved down over her neck and hungrily found her breasts as she ran the tips of her fingers over his spine and then reached to stroke the promise she wanted so much.

"I want you," she breathed. "Now."

"You're a dream," he whispered. "I never thought you could be so real."

"I am real. We're together now."

"No, *niña*, no," he said, suddenly wide awake. He pulled away from her. "We must be married first! I cannot allow—"

"You can't resist me," Leslie said with a sudden supremacy as she met his eyes in an open challenge. "You want me; you know you want me," she said as all thoughts of their situation were forgotten and her fingers continued their stroking magic. He moaned in passion. "Love me now, Augustine."

"No, *niña*, no!" he gasped, but she could see that he was beyond the point of turning back as his lips came down on hers once again and he moved to cover her body and take her as his own. Their murmurs of passion filled the small space as he fought the last vestiges of his resistance.

Suddenly the boat shifted, slamming them against the wall. There was a wave of noise surrounding them. The giant blades of a helicopter roared above them and they heard the trolling motor of a boat close by. Quickly they sprang apart, grabbing blankets to cover themselves. Leslie scrambled wildly for her clothes, but knew it was too late when they heard a wild knock on the door.

"Anyone home?" a jaunty voice called out.

"Yes, yes," Augustine called hastily as he too looked wildly about for his clothes.

"Ready to go? Ooops," said the smiling face of a young Coast Guardsman as he stuck his head through the door. "Sorry," he said as he quickly retreated. "We'll get you off as soon as you're ready to go."

Leslie's heart sank in mortification and she colored from head to toe as she looked away from Augustine.

"There's no question about it now, *niña*," said Augustine in a low voice. There was an air of supreme satisfaction about him. "You have no alternative now, but to marry me as quickly as possible. Your mother and Tía Isabel could never live this down and neither, my sweet, could you! Unless, of course, we are the wildly in love betrothed about to be married."

"You wouldn't," she said in instant outrage.

"Not me, my pretty," he said with a practically non-concealed glee. "You are the one who wanted this and now there is no way to keep it from getting out."

"I hate you."

"I hardly think so," he said as he handed her the dry swimsuit and adjusted his own clothes. There was a satisfied twinkle in his eye combined with an insufferable arrogance as he leisurely appraised her body, which sent Leslie over the edge in a silent ineffectual rage. "Shall we go and meet our rescuers, my future Senora Rivera?"

"Don't touch me," she hissed as he moved to hand her through the door.

"Now, now, now," he cautioned. "A little maidenly modesty is advised, but remember you are really radiantly happy."

Leslie looked up into the eyes of the rescue commander and realized she did have to conduct herself with a worldly sophistication if she were to survive with her pride intact.

"Are we glad to see you," she gushed as she covertly shrugged Augustine's arm away.

"I'll bet you are," the commander said a little tongue-in-cheek.

Leslie was greeted with other knowing smiles from all aboard, but when Augustine emerged there was instant respect and she was genuinely glad for his protection. She raised her head and stepped smartly to the plank that had been laid across to their boat and then watched as the helicopter dropped a rope and maneuvered Augustine's damaged vessel away from the reef so that it could be secured to the Coast Guard ship.

An hour later they were greeted by an anxious troop as Magna, Gerald, Doña Maria, and all of the others who loved them dearly cried in thanks for their rescue.

"Everything is fine, fine," said Augustine exuberantly over and over again.

Leslie looked at him with mixed emotions. After the initial chagrin of their compromising position had lessened she couldn't deny the desire and need that had created it. Something had happened between her and Augustine during the night and she knew it was good, but his obvious display of dominance and arrogance in front of both the Coast Guard and their family and friends was rankling. In the glare of the morning sun she remembered his position at Los Tejidos and how he had acquired it, and all of her earlier emotions returned.

"Doña María and Tía Isabel," she heard him calling as his arm went around her robustly, "do you think you can plan a wedding, a really wonderful wedding in thirty days? After our experience last night María and I realized we want to be married as soon as possible."

"Leslie," the two women cried in unison. "How wonderful. Of course we can!"

Leslie did her best to give them all a bright smile as she noted the Coast Guard men talking animatedly among themselves, their gestures punctuated by big grins as they secured Augustine's damaged boat to the dock. Her eyes met those of Magna, which just for a second had a question in them, and then she saw her friend's happy acceptance of the situation too.

"It's wonderful," Magna whispered as she gave Leslie a hug. "All night I hated myself for pushing you to go on that boat with him, but now I'm glad. I know this is right for you."

"I think she's right, cupcake," said Gerald as he gave her a hug too. "After talking with him yesterday I think I read Augustine all wrong right from the beginning."

Leslie nodded in polite understanding and accepted their sincere congratulations, while her emotions screamed on the inside. She had only herself and her uncontrollable emotions to blame for this. Now she would be Augustine's slave forever. How could she have been so stupid? Every chance she had ever had to be his equal was gone. She walked wearily away, a captive of his embrace as everyone followed along clucking over them and insisted that they go home to rest.

Six hours later Leslie wearily entered her office and found Augustine already there. "María darling," he said. "What are you doing here? You should rest. I was going to come to you a little later."

"I had to come," she said wearily. "I remembered Philomena was having some kind of meeting last night."

"Yes, I know," he said, "and I'll handle it. I'm going to talk with her, but in the meantime I have something for you. I'm so happy now that I know how much you want me."

Leslie blanched a little as he pulled a small velvet box from his pocket. He snapped it open to a small exquisite ring set with diamonds, which was obviously only half of a wedding set.

"Augustine, please, you really are rushing this."

"You *will* wear it, my darling," he said with a hint of steel in his voice. "It's absolutely necessary that it be on your finger immediately. Already we are the talk of the town, but fortunately most *Ponceños* pride themselves with being in the twentieth century. I'm doing this for you. If we are not betrothed and married immediately, you will never again be respected in the way that you should be in this city. There are witnesses to our passion."

Leslie looked at him in chagrin and felt the beginnings of tears. "I was asleep.... You took advantage of me while I was asleep."

"I took advantage of *you*? Really, María, I only hope your passion never dies."

His eyes sparkled with a satisfied smugness and Leslie hated him. Just once, once more, she'd like to see and touch the man she had discovered on that long ago day in her parlor: the same man she had known last night, who had swum with the dolphins: the man who had shown her compassion and understanding, who earlier wooed her with a gentle caution: the man who had actually for a moment acknowledged her as an equal and discussed their situation candidly. Now in his supremacy, which he obviously loved, that was all gone. She knew she'd lost him and she would never see him again.

The ring was beautiful and in any other circumstances she had a feeling that she would have cherished this moment, for she knew that she truly loved him with all her heart. But even that was to be denied her. The ring was being forced on her. It was an order, a command.

She trembled as he forcefully slid it on her finger while his strong hand grasped hers firmly to quell any resistance. "I love you, María, can't you see that?" he asked as a touch of tenderness finally entered his voice and he forced her to meet his eyes. "This is truly the right thing to do." He brushed her lips with his own and held her close. "I mustn't ever allow anyone to say anything against you. You are too perfect for that."

Leslie felt an acute sense of unease with those words and she had the sinking feeling that her battles for individuality, not to mention independence, had only just begun.

"Now, please, I really think you should be home resting. I've arranged for Doctor Cassava to examine you."

"I'm going nowhere," Leslie said firmly as she met his eyes with all her wrath. "I have work to do here. My business is in danger."

"As you wish," said Augustine with his now infuriating sense of confident patience. "Then we will work together."

He stepped around to his desk, which faced hers, and met her eyes squarely as she took her place and began to examine the mail. The intercom on her desk buzzed.

"Sorry to bother you, Doña Leslie," Juanita said hesitantly, "but your broker is on the phone from New York."

Leslie reached for the phone. "Yes, Harold," she said, instantly alert.

"Listen," he said, his voice a little strange over the pinging line, "I hate to tell you this, but I think there is a move to take over your company."

"Tell me about it," said Leslie wearily. She looked into Augustine's inquiring eyes and could have killed him with the daggers she sent his way. The memory of his underhanded scheme to take over Los Tejidos de María washed over her anew as she talked with the broker. She was left with an acute feeling of defeat as she finished the call.

As if to echo her feelings and give emphasis to her worst fears she heard the workroom grow ominously quiet. Then the machines came slowly back to life. A few moments later Philomena strode into the office unannounced, followed closely by Don Fernando Aguila.

"Well, I see the two lovebirds have finally decided to come to work," Philomena said haughtily. Her eyes scanned Leslie and immediately took in the ring sparkling on her finger. Leslie tightened and prepared for the worst.

"I hardly think that is of any concern to you," said Augustine blandly.

"Perhaps not," she said as she glanced over the new furniture arrangements in the office, "but I just wanted, out of respect for our past relationship, to let you know, Augustine, that I'm thinking seriously of filing a class action suit against this company."

"On what basis?" asked Augustine impatiently.

"Actually," said Don Fernando, breaking in hastily, "Philomena really wishes to discuss the meeting held last night. She also has other personal concerns to be thinking of right now so we need to get this cleared up."

Leslie had witnessed this entire exchange in numb silence, but now she was newly amazed as Philomena turned to her handsome escort. An obvious look of calculation passed over her face and then when she met Don Fernando's eyes she actually visibly softened.

"I hope," said Augustine, apparently impervious to the phenomenon taking place between Philomena and Don Fernando, "you are not thinking of doing something very foolish, Philomena. I told you yesterday morning when you came to my office your actions were premature."

Leslie's head snapped as she looked at him and realized that must have been why she saw Philomena leaving his office just before her anguished trip to Tibes. She colored as she remembered her jealous assumptions and her tortured reaction to them.

"As I was saying," she heard Augustine say through the haze of her confused reverie, "until we have thoroughly examined this government report, you are not working in the best interests of Ayudalo or yourself." There was a hard look on his face as he said the last words.

"What do you mean by that?" asked Philomena.

"Translate it any way you wish."

"It's obvious your allegiance has changed. You no longer care about Ayudalo. Money and power and—" She sniffed as she looked in Leslie's direction.

"Cuidado!" Augustine said in his first show of temper. "Be careful with what you are saying, Philomena. I am and always have been on the side of what's best for my people and this island. Nothing can change that!"

Philomena looked hastily away and turned unconsciously to Don Fernando for comfort. "Obviously it will do no good to discuss this with you," said Philomena. "I guess we will simply have to let this situation run its natural course."

"I'm warning you, Philomena," said Augustine in a deadly voice.

"I hardly think you are in any position to threaten

me," said Philomena as she prepared to exit. "You no longer could vote or influence the board of Ayudalo without incurring a serious conflict-of-interest charge."

Leslie watched in utter amazement as this charade continued to unfold in front of her eyes. It was a serious situation involving the future of her business, yet she was being treated as if she were little more than a disinterested bystander. Augustine was handling the situation remarkably well as he astutely ignored Philomena's last comment and immediately turned on his charm while politely escorting them to the door. But Leslie was newly appalled as she realized his easy words of justice and equality were actually little more than glib comments, especially where she was concerned. With every second, every word, every action, she could feel the bonds of servitude tightening around her. She wondered fleetingly if she would ever again have anything to say about her own business, let alone her personal desires.

"Really, I'm sure," she heard Don Fernando saying in a conciliatory voice as she came out of her web of troubled thoughts again. "I'm sure everything can be worked out. Remember that I sit on the board of Ayudalo too."

"Of course it can," said Philomena in her own inimitable style as she followed Don Fernando's lead. "I'm sure when Augustine fully discovers all of the problems here they will be easily corrected."

Leslie looked at the conniving, simpering woman and felt an instant derision, which finally turned to real anger as she realized how her business acumen was being insulted.

"I hardly think you can count on that," said Leslie. "I am still the controlling executive of this company!"

"Well, then we shall see to it that that is changed!" Philomena walked out in a huff, allowing the door to slam behind her.

"Now why in the world did you do that?" exclaimed Augustine. "I had her calmed down."

"You're deluding yourself and I am sick and tired of this entire situation," said Leslie as she felt the heat of her emotions enveloping her. Now was the time to have this out and get it over with. The words were barely out of her mouth when Gerald came through the door.

"Whooeee," he said with an exaggerated grin. "I just passed Philomena and she looks like she's about to cook someone alive."

"That just may be the case," said Augustine with an impatient sigh as he looked at Leslie with a barely concealed annoyance.

"Well, listen, guys," he said with his usual exuberance, "I just wanted to wish you both the best. It's time for me to make it to the airport. Remember I'm counting on those ski sweater orders. We've got a lot of new clients and they'll want to know that you're reliable."

"Got you," said Leslie as she met his friendly eyes. "Don't worry, we won't have any problems. I'm sure Augustine will see to that."

She threw a petulant look in Augustine's direction, which Gerald failed to notice along with the snideness in her voice as his attention was drawn to Juanita entering the room. She was obviously preparing to take him to the airport.

"I assumed it would be all right to take Senor Masters to his plane," she said a little hesitantly.

Juanita looked away and seemed to be just a bit flustered. Her eyes came to rest on the ring Augustine had just forced on Leslie's finger. Juanita grew visibly more flustered and seemed to unconsciously massage the same finger on her own hand as she looked into Gerald's eyes.

"Well, of course it's all right," said Leslie as she puzzled anew at her secretary's actions. Surely by now Juanita and Gerald had come to some comfortable understanding that should have provided her with a better sense of security than she obviously had so far as he was concerned.

"I'll be seeing you at the end of the month," Gerald said as he came to give Leslie a good-bye hug and kiss. "I wouldn't want to miss the wedding. Be happy," he said then in a low voice as he nudged her chin. "I'm sure you're doing the right thing. Just remember though if you ever need me, I'm always there."

Leslie felt the eyes of both Augustine and Juanita boring into them as she responded with a wan smile. For just a few seconds she'd almost forgotten the final touch to this charade. She fought valiantly to conceal her true feelings from this, her very closest friend and confidant. Never, never, could she let even Gerald know what a botch she had made of this, her actual seduction of Augustine. If he knew her real fears about her relationship with Augustine— No, no, she thought hastily. If she never handled another thing in her life, this she must face and handle herself."

"Take care," said Gerald as he took Juanita's arm. For just a second his eyes flickered as they met Leslie's again and she sensed the hint of a question. "Leslie . . . ?"

"Yes!" she said a little too quickly.

"Everything *is* all right? You are happy?"

"Yes," she said emphatically as she wreathed her face in her brightest smile and stilled her wringing hands. "Everything's fine."

Gerald looked at her for a few seconds more and then seemed to be satisfied. "Take good care of her," he said as he shook hands with Augustine, who was silently accompanying them to the door.

"You can be sure of that," said Augustine in a low voice. He squared his chin and met Gerald's eyes. "I love her very much."

Leslie looked away and brought her hand to her

mouth as the door closed and she stepped to the window and followed the rest of Gerald's exit from there. She knew she was totally and completely alone now. In a final moment of truth she wondered if she really could handle it.

When Augustine came up behind her seconds later and placed his hands on her shoulders and brushed her brow with his lips she looked straight ahead as tears blinded her, yet even now she couldn't deny her response to his touch as her blood raced madly to her brain.

"We will be happy," whispered Augustine as he turned her around to face him. "I know I am handling this somewhat badly, but really it will not seem so once you have rested and thought this through. We have to think of the time. You love me and I love you." He kissed her tenderly and traced her face with soft caresses. "Nothing can ever be wrong about that."

"So be it," said Leslie in final resignation. "I won't fight you anymore, but I must insist upon a role in Los Tejidos."

"But of course," said Augustine tenderly. "I've always said that you're a wonderful designer. Now I want you to go home and rest. As soon as I've had a chance to get through that report we will talk."

Leslie looked over to his desk and saw the voluminous stack of papers bound in a blue cover. It would take hours to get through those tedious pages. The phone rang and Leslie answered hastily.

"Leslie, darling," said Tía Isabel in her best matriarch voice, "I have wonderful news. We've found your grandmother's wedding dress and I'm sure it will be perfect for you."

Leslie met the eyes of Augustine as she realized he had heard her aunt's words.

He smiled radiantly. "How wonderful. Your mother is really going to love this."

In final acceptance as Leslie responded to her aunt, she fully understood the stark reality of her situation and all of the ramifications it might produce and she knew there was no turning back now.

Chapter Fifteen

Over the next few days Augustine began to read the government report in earnest and the attitude of the workers at Los Tejidos de María seemed to grow increasingly tense with each mention of the grievances that Philomena felt supported her class action suit. The friendly faces of some of her closest, most loyal employees, such as Juan Pacheco and finally even Juanita, seemed to take on a tinge of suspicion.

Conflicting commands by both Augustine and Leslie only added to the confusion as their differences flamed forth time and time again. In every case, however, Augustine always managed to make it seem as though Leslie were just momentarily confused or preoccupied with their marriage plans. Always he defended her eloquently while quietly wielding absolute power over all of the business decisions. His patronizing smugness embellished by his overly demonstrative declarations of love and respect were sending Leslie quietly mad.

It should have been easy to simply say "Enough! I've had enough and won't endure more!" But with each passing day as she warred with her own desires both physical and emotional she was more deeply embroiled in the hoopla as the entire family pitched in to create a happy wedding for them while aristocratically and imperiously feinting away all snatches of scandal concerning their intimate night together on the boat.

Leslie simply could not let them down in the face of all that and in the deepest pocket of her most secret soul she wasn't at all sure she wanted to.

If only Augustine could just be the man who truly appealed to her instead of this domineering tyrant with his belittling patronization, she was sure this could have been a very happy time for her.

"Have you been to the doctor yet?" asked Augustine. He had obviously been gazing at Leslie for some time as she looked up and met his eyes directly across from her own desk.

"I'm fine," she said evasively.

"But you must—" he began with a touch of sternness in his voice.

The buzzer on her intercom rang.

"Doña Isabel needs you," said Juanita in a flat voice.

A pang went through Leslie as she realized how lifeless her secretary seemed to have become in the past week. Astutely Leslie realized she hadn't heard from Gerald in that time either. She hoped yet another heart was not to be broken before this melee was over. She got up without further acknowledgment of Augustine's rather personal inquiry and went to find her aunt.

She walked out to the showroom and remembered again that seemingly long ago day when she had given the showing for Augustine. Everything had grown so complicated since then. She gave a little gasp as she saw her aunt kneeling in front of a gorgeous heirloom wedding gown that was fitted to a mannequin. Tía Isabel's mouth was full of pins as she gestured Leslie into the room.

"It's beautiful," said Leslie as she let her breath out softly.

"Yes," said Isabel, "and I think you will be especially lovely in it. It's never had blue eyes to set it off before. Now come, you must try it on. I'm sure it's going to fit."

In spite of her best efforts to control them Leslie felt the threat of tears as she looked hastily away while her aunt busied herself removing the dress from the form.

"Here," said Tía Isabel a few moments later as she carefully handed the dress to Leslie. Her words stopped as she looked at Leslie astutely.

"Mija," she said, suddenly perceptive and wise as only she could be. "What's wrong? I do not sense happiness about you."

"Oh, nothing, nothing," said Leslie a little nervously as she reached for the dress.

"Leslie Marie, I have been a part of too many weddings in this family—nieces, nephews, my own children, as well as many cousins. I know when something is not right."

Leslie looked away, unable to face her aunt.

"Tell me," her aunt insisted. She lifted Leslie's chin and forced her to look at her.

"It's silly. I—I don't really know."

"No," said Isabel, unconvinced as she reached for her niece's hand, it's more than just jitters and you've had plenty of time to rest up from your recent ordeal."

Leslie realized almost gratefully that she was in the presence of the final power in this family. Tía Isabel would not release her until she was satisfied that all was well. If there was a problem, she sincerely wanted to help.

"It's Augustine," said Leslie a little hesitantly as she shifted the dress in her arms. "Sometimes he just shows so little consideration of my talents—the way he's just taking over Los Tejidos."

"But you love him, don't you?" she asked softly.

Leslie looked her in the eye and felt that her heart would break. "Yes," she said after a long moment, "but our spirits are not together. We are not communicating."

Isabel looked at her for a long moment. "You know,

Leslie, the women in our family have always been strong and free. Your mother can attest to that. And we love our men with great devotion, but if you are not really sure...."

"I have no choice," said Leslie. "I've made some dreadful mistakes and I can't allow you and Mama and the others, all of my workers here who depend on me, to suffer."

"Surely you are more intelligent than that," said Isabel with a hint of impatience. "You are strong enough to do anything you wish. No, *niña*, whatever this is, it is within you yourself. You don't have to try that dress on. You don't have to wear it."

Leslie looked at the soft dress layered with antique lace as it lay crumpled in her arms. She thought of her many hours of longing and visualized the child of her dreams. The clatter of her factory went on around her and sketches of her latest designs lay haphazardly on the drafting table across the room. She met her aunt's eyes again through a mist of tears.

"Is the love strong enough to find a way?" Tía Isabel asked as she patted Leslie's hand. "Augustine truly seems to worship you. He guards and protects you."

"He does," cried Leslie, "but somehow it seems to be in all the wrong ways."

"You're sure of that? You know this factory is not a family. You must think this through carefully, *mija*, but in the end you must consult only with yourself."

Leslie realized sinkingly she could not after all articulate her feelings to her aunt and expect a real understanding. Her problems had really transcended Tía Isabel's generation and this was still a culture in which the family and all of its traditions came first.

"There are times when it's good to have a strong man by your side," Tía Isabel went on, "but remember, *niña*, you must allow him to be a man. Now, I can't believe you would have allowed this to come so far if in your heart you did not really wish it. Shall we try on the dress or not?"

Leslie pursed her lips in emotional indecision.

"Try it on," said her aunt with a gentle firmness. "Perhaps it will help you to know your own mind."

Leslie's hands were shaking as she slipped the lovely old dress over her head. It fit her perfectly and transformed her into a dream. All the while her aunt's words echoed through her mind. "The women in our family have always been strong and free...." She thought fleetingly of Aloíza.

She stepped out of the dressing room and met the admiring reverent eyes of Augustine. "María," he breathed. "I have never seen such a beautiful bride."

"And you should not have seen this one," said Tía Isabel firmly.

"Oh, don't worry about all of those old wives' tales," he said as he came to Leslie and took her into his arms. "María and I have already broken all of the traditions, but I know we will have a perfect marriage anyway."

Leslie's heart sank as she realized there was no rational way to combat the insidious servitude he created with his reverent definition of womanhood.

"I was just coming to find you," he said as he continued to admire her. "I wanted to discuss some of the points in the government report, which by the way is very good, but I think such trivia can wait in the wake of something so much more important."

"No," said Leslie hastily as she felt a tiny glimmer of hope. "Wait. I want to discuss it with you."

"No, *niña*, really it's not important. I want to hear from Tía Isabel how the rest of the wedding plans are progressing."

In final despair Leslie tried to comprehend how a woman as intelligent as she was had gotten into such a ridiculous situation. She was deeply in love with a man she simply couldn't talk to. He wouldn't listen! How could this be? And yet, here she stood in a traditional wedding dress about to sell herself into servitude.

"No, Augustine," she heard herself saying in a loud voice as she broke into the soft conversation between her aunt and him. "I don't want to discuss the wedding. I want to discuss our business and for once you are going to listen to what I have to say!"

"Really, María," he said quietly, "I knew you were straining yourself. You need to see a doctor."

"I do not," said Leslie vehemently. "Either we talk now and really communicate or there will be no wedding! I am not your slave."

Tía Isabel's face was impassive as Leslie's eyes blazed into Augustine's. She knew her aunt was watching her carefully and Leslie sensed an intuitive support and understanding from her. In that moment Leslie truly knew what it meant to be a Villaronga woman.

"You are blowing this all out of proportion," said Augustine reasonably. "Surely if you wish to talk about this we can. I only wished to ease your burdens. A wedding should be a very special thing for a woman."

"Allow me to decide what's special and what isn't," said Leslie. "If we don't get this mess in the plant straightened out I'm going to be ruined, but then you really don't care about that, do you? You have dozens of other businesses, but this one is mine. I created it. I introduced new ideas and it was working until you and Philomena came along to destroy it. You make all of these noble sounds, but I'm beginning to think that would make you happy!"

"You are wrong, María. I want to save this business. I want to save it for you and for the good of the island, but you must understand that you have certain limitations."

"I refuse to listen to this from you," said Leslie as she finally gave full vent to her anger, which had been damned for weeks. "You are deliberately refusing to recognize what that report really says."

"María, I think we should discuss this in a calmer way."

"When you have read the report through I will discuss it with you, but until then you will not make any more executive decisions or countermand mine. *I* am in charge. Do you understand that?"

"No, María," he said. "I was afraid it would come to this. You are *not* in charge. I've just acquired letters of assignment from your mother. I have control of the majority of stock now."

"You did what?" Leslie shouted in outrage. "You promised— You told Gerald—"

"I kept my word. I didn't buy stock from the employees. Your mother is honestly worried about the strain you're under. She did this for your benefit. You know you've been more than a little distraught lately and it was the only way I could get Philomena to stop her class action suit, which while not really legitimate would have created very bad publicity. Even so the employees are still talking of unionizing."

"You are even worse than I had already imagined," said Leslie in low guttural tones. The wedding dress was now a macabre foil to her demonic face. "I could not possibly ever think of having anything to do with someone so low and underhanded."

She raised her hand to rip the dress from her body but was stopped by Augustine's swift motions as he grabbed her and forced her hand away from the cloth.

"No, María, no," he said. "We mustn't allow this to kill our love. You came to me. You loved me. We cannot give up something so perfect for such a senseless thing as this factory."

"Don't ever touch me again," she said as her eyes bore into his in absolute hatred. "This factory means everything to me and to think that you would use my mother in such a way...."

Tía Isabel had moved outside the room when she saw the emotional nature of their conversation. The room looked bare and empty now as Leslie felt her heart beating in uncontrollable rage while yet her insidious body warmed to the touch of this reprehensible man who refused to keep even a gentleman's agreement.

"Leave me," she said. "I cannot bear to look at you."

"You are lying," said Augustine. "You will always want me. No other man will ever satisfy you."

"You are dead," she said venomously. "The man I loved never lived and I will not allow you to use me in his place."

"Think about it. Think very carefully, my Doña Leslie...." He dropped his hands as she stepped toward the dressing room and began to remove the wedding dress derisively.

"Remember," she heard his soft voice insisting as she pushed the dress from her body, "the way you loved me, how our lips met and our bodies fulfilled one another."

"Viper!" she swore as her body began to betray her. He calculatingly recalled detail after vivid detail of their lovemaking in a smooth, sensuous voice.

"I don't want to hear this." She pulled her clothes on rapidly and tried to push past him after leaving the wedding dress in a heap.

"You *will* listen," Augustine said as he pulled her close and forced her into his embrace. His lips came scalding down on hers and she fought her instant rampant response. "This and only this, matters, María."

"No," she said as she pushed him forcefully away. "No!" She pulled the engagement ring from her finger and threw it at him. "Take this! I don't ever want to see it again." She rushed blindly from the room and hoped fervently the clatter of the machines had drowned their angry words. Tía Isabel stopped her as she raced for the exit.

"Don't run, *niña*," she said sternly. "If this is your plant and it is truly what matters to you, don't quit now. Stand and fight. This may be your only chance for happiness."

"I can't," she sobbed. "Can't you see? It's hopeless now."

"No, my Leslie, no. You really have all of the power. Stop and think about it and then use it. Go to your office. Make him come to you there."

"I can't, I really can't," said Leslie. "At least not right now. Later."

"Later, then, but don't take too long," Isabel said firmly. "Remember you are a Villaronga."

"I know," said Leslie. "Just give me a little time. But really," she went on in exasperation, "there's nothing I can do. Augustine won't listen to me."

"He will," said Isabel. "He can't bear the thought of actually losing you. You have only to calm yourself and think this through."

Leslie visibly willed her wild emotions into submission as she looked at her wise aunt for a long moment. "All right," Leslie said hesitantly. "There's nothing more I can lose. I only hope you're right."

Her aunt gave her a staunch nod of understanding as she propelled Leslie toward the workroom. *"Vaya con Dios,"* Isabel said sagely. "Just put yourself in God's hands."

Leslie gave her aunt one last look and quickly headed toward the exit. Juan Pacheco almost ran head-on into Leslie.

"Doña Leslie," he said hesitantly. He wrung his hands unconsciously and looked to the floor before meeting her eyes again. *"Perdónemie*, but I really must have a short word with you."

"Certainly, Juan," she said as she cleared away the last vestiges of her emotions, "but could it wait for just awhile?"

"No, really, I think not," he said as he set his chin in an obvious demonstration of strength and bravery on his part. "I am deeply concerned about the future of this factory and I think you really owe us some sort of explanation."

"What do you mean, Juan? It is you, the workers, who are talking of the union and strike, which you know would be disastrous to us right now."

"Only because we no longer know if we can trust you," he said sadly. "You know that is not what I want, but if it is neccessary then all of us, even Juanita, will have to participate."

Leslie blanched as the total gravity of the situation finally enveloped her. She suddenly realized why Juanita, who had always been so warm and supportive, had suddenly changed.

"Theoretically even your Tía Isabel and Doña María would have to participate if they are to work here on any basis."

"But I really don't understand why you are even thinking of this," Leslie said. "I have done nothing except to try to build something for all of us and I've been generous in offering you opportunity. It is the workers themselves who have sold the opportunity away."

"Only because we no longer know where your allegiance lies. We do not really understand what is taking place. We were happy with things the way they were."

"But surely you understand that I've had no choice about this," said Leslie. "I am the real victim."

"No, we don't, Doña Leslie. That's what I'm trying to tell you. If something is not explained soon we will have no choice but to strike. Another meeting is being planned for this afternoon and I'm sure the union will be formed then.''

"Look, Juan," said Leslie in her most serious voice, "I have never had anything but the highest aspirations for all of us and there was nothing wrong with the operation of this plant. There is a government report that states this clearly and in fact commends our operation. It's available to anyone who wishes to read it, but I think you should speak to Don Augustine. He is the one who truly does not understand."

"But I thought— We all thought—"

"What?" demanded Leslie.

"Well, that you were taking all of your direction from him now."

"You are wrong," said Leslie with her usual spirit. "On the contrary! I'm doing everything I can to salvage our original operation but I must have your help."

"But, forgive me," he said shyly, "if you are to be married to Don Augustine...?"

"Trust me," said Leslie. "I'm going to the museum to think some things through, but I can tell you absolutely that as it stands now there will be no wedding and I will go to court to restore our original management concept if I have to."

"*Segura?*"

"*Segura,*" said Leslie firmly. "You can count on it."

"I *will* speak to Don Augustine, Doña Leslie. You can count on my support."

She paused for another second as Juan walked staunchly toward her office. She waited and then stuck her head back into the reception office.

"Juanita?"

"Yes," the secretary said listlessly.

"Listen, I'm going to the museum," Leslie said brightly, "but there were a few details about the last ski sweater orders that I needed to discuss with Gerald and

I really don't have time to do it now. They're in on my desk. Would you mind giving him a call?''

"No, not at all," said Juanita.

Leslie saw her visibly brighten, but her eyes were still a little hesitant. "Oh, and would you also tell him to expect a visitor." Before she could finish, she saw Juanita's expression plummet. "I'm going to send you up there next week," said Leslie. "I want to be sure those first big deliveries are absolutely perfect."

"Do you mean that?" said Juanita excitedly.

"I certainly do," said Leslie smiling. "It was Gerald's idea in the first place and how could I turn down the only brother I've ever had? You should be able to reach him now. I just remembered he had an emergency and he's been traveling all this week."

"Oh, yes," said Juanita in obvious relief. "You know I had forgotten that too. I've been so worried." She looked away a little sheepishly as her eyes grew bright.

"Well, don't worry about anything," said Leslie firmly. "Everything is going to be all right. I promise you."

She could hear the soft sounds from her office as she walked away. Juan was apparently talking with Augustine, but in spite of her bravado in front of her employees she still needed time to think. She had no idea how she could possibly put everything back together, but she knew now she had to try.

Twenty minutes later she was walking up the winding stairs in the entry foyer of the museum. As she reached the second-floor galleries she was immediately challenged by the bizarre, almost brooding, art of the Middle Ages. It seemed flat and lifeless, heavily influenced by religious themes. Yet in a way it seemed fitting for her mood as she carefully examined her own actions over the past few months.

Had she, in her quest to overpower Augustine, actually created the key for her own defeat? "No," she said impatiently. She had already been through all of that during the trip to Tibes. What was done was done, right or wrong and she couldn't change it, but there had to be a way. Since their outing on his boat neither she nor Augustine was operating in a very rational manner. That was patently clear after their last scene together. She knew she had made a terrible mistake in responding to him in such an ardent manner, but then again she could not deny the honesty of her actions. Their emotions were so deeply embedded in a wild savage love that they ignored all reason. There was no hope so long as they were locked in this unending power struggle. She had to solve this herself. This couldn't be solved by her mother, or Gerald, or Tía Isabel, or Magna. She must simply stand by her honest feelings and hope in doing so she would find a way to appeal to Augustine's as well. Most of all she had to be strong, secure in the fact that he really did love her and wouldn't want to lose her.

Leslie walked around the entire museum allowing the peace of the place to invade her soul. She quickly exited the gloomy Middle Ages exhibits and allowed only the most positive of thoughts and feelings to impregnate her mind as she walked again past the portraits and pastoral scenes of the Great Masters. She went to the garden where she had first seen Augustine and remembered the almost instant chemistry between them.

She left the museum and went to the Santa María church where she sat quietly for a few moments. Then she drove down to the Plaza Degateaú and remembered the evening she and Augustine had strolled the paths there. She went past his office and knew the time for the final stand was near. She glanced at her left hand and poignantly felt the bareness of her ring finger as she gripped the steering wheel, yet there was a satisfied sense of freedom too. She wanted that ring back. She candidly admitted it, but only if it was given as a mutual symbol of sharing, understanding love. Only if it was given by the Augustine who was the embodiment of his strong, dignified *jíbaro* ancestors. She still didn't know if he really existed, but perhaps she should find out. It might take months or years, but she would try.

Leslie turned resolutely and went back to Los Tejidos de María. When she arrived, the plant was ominously quiet. She saw workers beginning to emerge and remembered Juan's words about a meeting. As she left her car she saw several signs proclaiming, "*Huelga*. Strike!" and her heart sank. Could it be that they were planning to form the union and walk out right now when they were just about to fill their largest orders? She saw Philomena's car and knew the very worst of her fears was about to be realized.

She drew on her final reservoir of courage and walked resolutely into her office. Augustine sat quietly at his desk totally engrossed in the government report. He held the engagement ring in his hands and rolled it from one finger to another.

"María," he said. His face was open and sincere. "You've come back."

"I think we're going to have real trouble this afternoon," she said as she met his eyes with a steady gaze. "Did you have a good talk with Juan?"

"I did, I did," he said as he arose to assist her to a chair, "but more importantly I've finally completed this report."

Leslie looked at him suspiciously. This was not quite the way she had expected the confrontation to progress.

"I've been wrong, María. You are, in fact, a genius. You should become a consultant for all of the garment industries in the island."

Leslie looked at him in total amazement and then realized sickeningly she was really seeing his most base side. He was deliberately pandering to her, wanting her to believe he had changed totally in just a few short hours. Her eyes glanced from the engagement ring to his face and she knew this was his final treachery. He must have realized after talking to Juan that he must have her help to prevent the strike and should they fail then the failure would be hers not his. Now he would say or do anything to save his reputation and stop this challenge to his supreme authority. All of her new-found strength and resolution drained from her as she realized she could not possibly battle such outright dishonesty and hope for a positive result.

"You are despicable," she said. "What makes you think I could possibly believe anything you have to say now after the way you've acted all this time? Can't your machismo and pride withstand the thought of failure? Be honest. You don't want this plant to succeed. What you've wanted from the very beginning is to destroy the real me, but then you still want to be able to take over as the honorable patron and you think I will come crawling to you in gratitude!"

"María, no!" he said desperately. "I am willing to make concessions. I know now you are right."

"Liar," she shouted. She could take no more. She turned and ran out the door. There was no way to get to her car. It was surrounded by people and she saw Philomena watching her with a satisfied look.

Leslie turned blindly and headed down a small overgrown ravine behind the factory. Augustine followed and his words echoed after her. "Maria, please, I'm going to tell the employees you were running a model plant. There will be no changes."

He was lying. She knew he was lying. Oh, this was really the most base of all his underhanded maneuvers. Even worse than taking control of her mother's stock.

She refused to answer as she plunged on. She could hear a stream in the distance. The abundant foliage took on a menacing cast as ferns and other plants created a dense shroud across her path and tears blurred her vision.

In bitterness she scrambled on, not wishing to hear his voice or to be near him ever again. Slowly she began to descend down a wide rocky path with the stream traversing the middle. In her struggle to keep her footing she dropped her purse, which came to rest at the bottom of a tunnel. Leslie realized there was a good chance that she could get lost and not be able to find her way back, but it didn't matter now. She was beginning to feel numb as the shock of this final debasing estrangement from Augustine effectively blocked her normal sensations. She continued down a rocky waterway that was somewhat like a long drawn out waterfall with the water babbling and gurgling in incongruous good cheer, adding an almost idiotic twist to this whole scene.

"María!"

She still heard Augustine calling. It seemed that others were calling too.

She hurried on, not at all sure where she was going. The stream finally dropped into a little lagoonlike setting that would have been lovely in any other situation. It was a rocky basin surrounded by verdant shrubs and one very curious bush filled with flowers that resembled inverted bells. She paused to catch her breath and dropped wearily beside the beautiful pool.

"María!" said Augustine breathlessly as he broke into the clearing and ran to her side. "Please! I've never been so sincere. You are brilliant and I've been a fool!"

"I don't believe you."

"Believe me, my darling, please believe me."

He gathered her to him and kissed her face softly.

The track of his lips sent an instant spark through her. For just a second she gave in to the instinctive response of her body as his lips caressed her and sent her wild with desire. He parted her lips and kissed her deeply in a wild yearning. "María, I love you, can't you understand that? We've got to work together now."

She reacted in instant disgust. "Don't touch me. I'll never believe anything you have to say, and I'll do nothing to help you deceive my employees!" She got up and brushed herself off as she turned her back on him.

"Doña Leslie?"

She looked up and saw one of the Ayudalo employees carrying her purse. "Juan Pacheco sent me to help find you. He needs you."

Leslie looked at the young man quizzically. "I'll be right there," she said as she reached for the hand he offered to help her up the ravine. Augustine followed and when they came out in the clearing of the parking lot Juan Pacheco was addressing the rest of her workers.

"My friends, I have waited a long time for an opportunity such as we have here. Stop and think about what you are doing! You *own* part of this company. Everyone here has bought shares in Los Tejidos, thanks to the generosity of our good Doña Leslie. The good Don Augustine foresees a great future for this company. There is a government report that assures this. We can all read it."

He paused as he saw Leslie and Augustine coming toward the parking lot. "Yet today, on the word of someone who cares nothing for this business and for a few pennies more an hour, you are talking about destroying a great dream and opportunity. Before you leave this plant and everything Doña Leslie has tried to do not only for herself but for us and our island, ask yourselves a simple question: Can we as part owners of this factory afford this strike? Ask yourselves very carefully.''

His eyes were hypnotic as one by one he forced his co-workers to meet his gaze. Leslie could tell that it was taking all of his stamina to maintain such a high level of strength and control, but she held her breath and watched silently as one by one the workers returned to their work, their anger apparently gone.

Tears of gratitude sprang to her eyes as she went to Juan and shook his hand. "I will be in your debt forever," she said.

"No, Doña Leslie," he said. "It is I who am in your debt." He turned and walked away from her with a universal dignity.

Augustine went to Juan too and then immediately began to shake the hands of each of the workers as they slowly returned to the plant while continuing to converse among themselves.

"So you have won again," said a husky voice at Leslie's elbow.

Leslie turned to see Philomena glaring at her. "We've all won, Philomena. Can't you see that?"

"In a way I suppose you're right," she said as Don Fernando Aguila came to her side. "I can see by the way this was handled I was making a great mistake with Augustine. He's not the man I thought he was."

Leslie couldn't hide her surprise as Philomena's lips curled derisively. "I've learned now who my real friends are," said Philomena, but a note of softness crept covertly into her voice in spite of her aggressiveness.

Don Fernando put his arm around her protectively.

"Don Fernando and I will be married soon and of course I won't have the time to spend with charity that I did before."

"I'm happy for you Philomena,' said Leslie as she extended a hand to each of them. "Congratulations."

"Thank you," said Don Fernando as he looked into Philomena's eyes.

Leslie watched as the strident woman visibly softened. It was as if a small miracle had occurred. It was true. Love could make a difference. A small pang went through her as she thought fleetingly of Augustine's last declarations. If only...she thought as she watched Augustine boisterously laughing with Juan as he accompanied him through the door into the plant.

But it was too late and she knew it. She had formed her resolutions that afternoon sure that her battles with him might last for days or weeks, even months. She hadn't been wrong. She didn't for one minute believe he could have changed so quickly. In the past weeks he had committed every conceivable ethical indiscretion showing little or no concern for his actions, as though he, and he alone, was privileged to act in that way. He had used his position in the community ruthlessly and she could never forgive him for that.

She turned to leave.

"Juanita," she called.

Her secretary looked at her for a long second and then looked to the ground. "Doña Leslie," she said as she swallowed hard, "I'm sorry I was out here."

"No need for that," said Leslie with a wan smile. "I know you were caught in the middle."

Juanita flashed her a grateful smile. "Thank you, Doña Leslie. No one could have a better boss."

"Never mind," said Leslie with a touch of confusion. "Listen. I want you to go inside and make sure everything is in order. I'm not feeling very well."

"I understand," said Juanita. "Don't worry. I'll take care of everything."

Leslie looked all around her. Just moments before the area had been filled with her employees about to strike. She should have been happy, but she felt nothing but defeat. Over and over again she heard Augustine's booming voice. She knew that in spite of all the positive rhetoric uttered just moments before her life would never be the same again. It had changed irrevocably on the day when Augustine first set foot in Los Tejidos de María and now she would never be happy again.

She touched her face where only moments before his kisses had once again tapped her rampant physical response. She could sense him now, watching and waiting for just the right moment. She knew she had to get away and gather her strength to end this charade once and for all. She went quietly to her car and was just leaving as Magna and her mother came into the drive.

"Leslie, wait," called Magna.

"No," said Leslie. "The plant's fine. I'll tell you about it later."

Before they could reply she gunned her car. She was on the road before anyone else could stop her.

Chapter Sixteen

Leslie was completely overwhelmed with her confused feelings. She was blinded by tears as she headed into the long drive of the Villaronga estate. She had only one thought—to get away for a few days. Her strength was gone and she couldn't possibly face this dilemma right now.

As she rumpled through her clothes, throwing garments and toiletries haphazardly into an overnight bag, she was choked with rage as the full implications of the afternoon's activities became clear to her. Augustine had unequivocally taken over her life, stolen her family, her friends, and her business from her. In spite of what he had said and what had happened, all of that was extremely clear now. As she packed she tried to remember the exact location of a small hostel located near Adjuntas. It was not far from here and it should be perfect for her needs at this moment.

She quickly thumbed through some tourist guides that were mixed in with other magazines. She came to it at last. Hacienda Gripiña, a restored coffee plantation with a small hostel in the original house. She stepped to the phone and quickly confirmed a reservation for herself.

She thought of leaving her mother a note, but decided not to. She regretted upsetting her, but she really didn't know what else to do. Right now she just wanted to be totally alone and isolated.

Leslie had been so proud of Los Tejidos de María, but she had allowed herself to make too many mistakes while under the influence of her volatile emotions. People dear to her, her mother, had actually begun to mistrust her. After this last ploy of Augustine's even Tía Isabel might be doubtful of Leslie's instinctive convictions. Now, while things were calmed down at the plant, she needed this buffer of time to settle her thoughts and plan an effective strategy to truly reclaim what was rightfully hers. Augustine had to be removed entirely from the picture. She admitted candidly that if she continued to resist him he would ultimately destroy the very essence of her independence. She had no doubt of that now.

Leslie was engrossed with her thoughts as her little car continued to climb the road toward Adjuntas. There was more traffic than usual and driving required more than her usual concentration as she rounded curves and sounded her horn resoundingly to warn oncoming cars of her approach. All in all, though, it was a perfect outlet for her turbulent emotions.

As she neared the area of the hostel she realized she had left the tour guide with the exact directions behind. She looked for signs to Hacienda Gripiña and was gratified when a clearly marked one finally came into sight. She turned into a curved paved drive where a huge palm stood in majestic sentry over all of the other smaller trees and bushes lining the roadway and created a twisting, colorful green tunnel.

She followed the yellow curb until at last a small brightly painted house came into view. It was surrounded by beautiful foliage. It created a bright accent and blended beautifully and cheerfully with its surroundings. As Leslie stepped from the car she was immediately impressed with the quiet country atmosphere accompanied by appropriate sounds. She could actually hear tiny drops of moisture falling from the leaves. She reached for her luggage and saw a rustic fieldstone wishing well not far from a babbling stream spanned by a small arching foot bridge. Nearby was a fresh-water swimming pool made by damming the stream. A bright yellow water wheel turned near it and young children played happily around it.

It was a wonderfully serene, beautiful place and Leslie momentarily felt a real pang of poignant regret that she was there alone. This was the perfect place for lovers who needed only the company of each other to be happy. She could picture Juanita and Gerald here, or her mother and father. A spasm went through her followed by an even greater pain as she thought of Augustine and how wonderful it would have been to spend time here with him if only things had been different.

In retrospect she really didn't know why their relationship had seemed to be on a disaster course from the beginning. For some reason there had always been this raging antagonism, yet Leslie concluded in honest indignation, had Augustine not been so chauvinistic, if he could just have communicated with her on an equal basis, she would never have felt so threatened.

Now, though, it really didn't matter. She couldn't deal with outright treachery. Inevitably her thoughts went back to the very beginning as she made her way up the walkway to the beautifully ornate front doors set inside a wide veranda. In all truthfulness Augustine had usually been polite and solicitous, but it was an insidious politeness. He had never trusted her management expertise. He had always been condescending and held rigidly regimented views of a woman's role and there was no way, in spite of what he had just claimed, that that could have changed so quickly.

Oh, yes, he had feigned friendship and love, plying all of his cajoling charms and she foolishly, instead of utilizing these very traits to her own advantage, had met him head-on in outright battle. Then he had pirated and stolen everything dear to her, pompously assumed she was carrying his child while ultimately demanding that she submit to him as his subservient chattel wife. Surely no conquistador could have been more brutally successful. Finally he had employed every conceivable means to maintain his hold over her. His declarations a few hours earlier were the final insult to her intelligence.

Leslie could feel tentacles of anger reaching out to enslave her again as she struggled awkwardly through the door with her purse and overnight case, but her emotions were immediately diverted by the curious combination of primitive, Victorian, and modern decoration that greeted her in the lobby of the hostel. It exuded a marvelous atmosphere and charm. The quiet was still present as she made her way past willowwood rockers and modern tables beneath clusters of globular lights shaded in dark plastic. Huge primitive motifs similar to those she had seen at the Taino sites decorated one narrow wall set off by twin doors that looked out over the veranda with a background of lush foliage.

She arrived at the desk and rang the small bell. Within moments she had registered and was heading for one of the small rooms. The unique decorating theme had been extended to it, preserving completely the atmosphere of the original coffee plantation house.

After dropping her bags and freshening up a bit, Leslie decided to take advantage of the house specialty, freshly ground coffee. As she entered the small dining room she discovered the quaint atmosphere was repeated there too. Small tables surrounded by dark hardwood chairs with rush seats were warmly inviting. The pale buff walls were lined with pictures depicting the activities of the plantation in earlier years.

Again Leslie felt the overwhelming wish that she could be sharing her experience and for the first time realized what it really meant to be lonely. Something deep inside her told her this was going to become a regular feeling and it was triggered all the more painfully by her continued thoughts of Augustine.

For all of her anger over his brutal, cavalier ways, it was rapidly, in this peaceful dreamy setting, taking a backseat to her longing for the sweet, gentle, idealistic, introspective man she had glimpsed on occasion. The man who could be almost like a child himself when he wished to play and a man who cared so deeply about his people that he spent every moment trying to protect them, encourage them to live up to their potential: a man proud of his heritage and deeply committed to his island.

Why, oh, why, could she not know just this man? Why did she also have to pit her strength against his arrogance and now his deceit? Why could they not have worked together? The questions replayed in her mind until the steaming coffee was brought to her and she drank it, not actually enjoying its magnificent flavor or aroma. She felt like the lonely vignette she presented and sighed knowing how deeply she loved this man who really did not exist except in her fantasies. She thought again about his last words at the plant and firmly quelled the feelings of hope they had finally begun to generate as she soaked up the peace of her surroundings.

A glance at her watch told her it was still early, yet she had no desire to sit in her room alone so she decided to take a walk and, being practical, went back to her room for her sketch pad, camera, and a light sweater. Sketching her new designs would be therapeutic.

As Leslie walked back toward her room she thought

she heard a nearby rustling noise but dismissed it thinking someone else had probably entered another room before she entered the corridor. She quickly turned the lock on the old-fashioned door and went in leaving the door ajar as she gathered the things she needed. She was just about to grab her sweater when she heard the door of her room close with a sharp click.

She turned in startled confusion realizing someone had stepped into the room.

"Running away again, *niña?*"

Leslie's heart began to race as the familiar low growl of a voice she loved in spite of its arrogance addressed her from behind. She whirled around and met the glittering eyes of the man she had chosen, the man she had challenged, the man she must conquer. She rose to her full height as he stepped toward her.

"What are you doing here? How did you find me?" she hissed as she sought to somehow protect herself from the radiations of his natural charisma.

"We found the guide book, I surmised your plan, and I called to see if you were registered here—very simple."

Very simple!

The very words were an arrogant insult as though she were some inane, transparent child. They were absolute proof that his earlier words of conciliation were totally insincere. She was instantly so angry that she felt nothing less than a physical assault would suffice, but she managed a stiff, shaky control.

"Well, you may be here, but as far as I'm concerned you can just get out! You are an impossible man! I don't ever want anything to do with you again." She was close to shouting.

The smoldering aura that seemed to constantly envelop him reached out and touched her like a silvery mist. Leslie could feel herself warming as he stepped closer, riveting her eyes to his own.

"No *niña*, no," he said softly.

"I am not a *niña*!" She was shouting now as she struggled fruitlessly against both herself and him. Hysteria enveloped her, while at the same time the rest of her turned soft with yearning. "I am not a little girl! I am a woman, equal to you!"

"Yes, yes, you are a woman," he growled as he reached out and pulled her to him. "A wonderful woman, a brilliant woman, and I love you very much."

Leslie struggled. She could feel herself melting. She beat her fists against him in double edged frustration. "You can't come around forcing yourself on me," she said breathlessly, "thinking everything will be all right after one good toss in the sack!"

"Oh, but it will, *niña*, it will," he said as he began to kiss her gently and urgently. "Surely by now you know that there has never been any question about your passion."

She gasped, struggling to quell her own responses. "You've demoralized me all of this time, refused to recognize my talent, now you degrade me. You can't come here and just think you can say you're sorry and everything will be all right. I know how you are with women. I've seen Philomena coming out of your office early in the morning only hours after you professed your love for me. I know what kind of man you are."

"Now, you know what that was all about," he said as a calculating gleam came into his eyes. "So why, María," he asked, a wonderous anticipation in his voice, "why would you bring that up now? You've spent the whole day telling me how much you hate me. Why would Philomena coming out of my office matter, even if your insinuations were true?"

Leslie stopped her struggle and stood very still as she closed her eyes. It was no good. She couldn't fight it. "Because—" she stammered, "because I—"

He lifted her chin and forced her to face him as he

swept her into his arms. "Say it, María, say you love me." His lips sent fire through her and suddenly she wanted him. Nothing else mattered. She must have him at least one more time. Then she would leave him, rid herself of him forever, but she had dreamed and yearned too long for just this moment. Her arms went around him as he carried her to the bed. His lips showered her with soft urgency. She buried her face in his neck as she courted him with her body. All of her muscles became sinewy and feline with urgency as the magnetism of their bodies melted into time-worn, natural ecstasy. The quarrels, the antagonisms, everything, was forgotten except for their mutual desires.

Gently Augustine dropped with her to the bed as they lovingly lay bare their flesh. Their eyes were like hypnotic beacons as both moaned with urgency, afraid to speak until they had once again known each other as one. With deep sensuous need Leslie stretched herself the length of him and felt his hard muscles meld into her as she opened her lips and welcomed his thrusting, probing tongue. Her hands ran over his body, traveling through the silky resilient curly hair on his chest and dancing lightly over the hard buttons of his nipples.

With a groan of desire Augustine's lips traveled down her neck in a fiery tract. He buried himself in her breasts and succored them lovingly and urgently until the nipples stood in rigid, inviting peaks. Slowly he moved down over her, caressing and touching. His fingers brought her gasping delight. As if in ultimate commitment his caresses went ever lower until finally in utter abandon his flickering tongue brought her to the precipice of a shattering crescendo.

Leslie's hands reached for his strength and stroked and massaged him, wanting to give him every possible ecstasy, until at last her lips began to reciprocate his gift. His gasp told her she was once again supreme.

She lifted herself up over his subjugated, ecstatic body and lowered herself slowly and expectantly over his strength, pausing to nuzzle in slow fluid movements the point of throbbing desire until at last he pulled her convulsively closer, ravishing her breasts. Their coming together was an explosion almost beyond their sustaining capabilities as their eyes met in mutual desire and understanding. His great body rose to meet hers while they clasped their arms in rigid strength.

They whispered to each other words of love and need, until finally they experienced the ultimate surge of satisfaction. In wondrous, happy fulfillment Leslie opened her eyes and pushed moist tendrils of hair from her face. With a soft growl Augustine pulled her down and kissed her gently as he brought her body next to his and slowly began to massage her into peace.

"You are my queen," he said, "and I will love you always."

Leslie could feel herself falling into an overwhelming drowsiness and she had no wish to think or talk. She wanted only to be next to him, near him, touching him for just a while longer. She snuggled into his great arms and allowed his lips to soothe her with their special lullabyes. Soft kisses traced her face and her eyes until at last they both lay exhausted in each other's arms. They dozed dreamily away.

With a start Leslie awoke about an hour later. She realized in shattering chagrin that she had capitulated to her carnal desires and nothing had been settled. Yet as she looked at Augustine as he lay there innocent and vulnerable and remembered the strength of their desire just moments before, she knew she loved him and there had to be a way.

Slowly she began to get dressed. "Augustine," she said softly, shaking him gently, "Augustine...."

He awoke leisurely and began unconsciously to reach for her.

"No, Augustine," she said firmly. "No. Please get dressed."

She was suddenly acutely intimidated by their intimate surroundings. She realized they needed a more neutral spot so the air could be cleared once and for all and dressed in uneasy silence, afraid to speak. Augustine watched her warily, but perceptively allowed her to set the scene although as he slowly dressed again he perused her warmly and sensuously the whole time.

"Come on," said Leslie as they stepped into the hall. She took his hand and led him toward a table in the dining room. "We need to talk—calmly and intelligently."

"Yes, we must talk," he said firmly, but affectionately, "but first I want to apologize on my word of honor. For a man who prides himself on his fairness and objectivity I've been blind in my lust for you. From the first moment that I saw you, I've wanted you. I wanted to own you and I never, in my mind, could remove you from that beautiful setting in the museum. You were so vulnerable, so classically feminine and I wanted you in just that way, imprisoned on a pedestal completely under my control."

He looked at the floor.

"I couldn't accept the strong, unattainable, independent woman I met later at Los Tejidos de María. She didn't need me and she answered to no one but herself. I deliberately refused to acknowledge all of your talents and subconsciously I did everything I could to intimidate you into becoming the woman I first envisioned. Then when I thought of you having my child and after the night on the boat it was imperative that we be married immediately. Never could I allow anyone to think you were less than perfect. I didn't care. I would do anything to make you mine, supposedly to protect you.

You are right, though. I was thinking only of myself and I was wrong," he sighed, "very wrong."

In blinding enlightenment Leslie realized how foolish some of her judgments about him had been. "I think we've both been overreacting to some erroneous assumptions," she said as she reached for his hand, "but now that we've said it and cleared the air, why don't we just go back and start all over again?"

"Unfortunately life is not like that," said Augustine, ever the philosopher. "We are here now, today, and this is the moment we have to live. What's done is done, the good and the bad. We've both been unreasonable. The question is can we accept it, understand it, and forgive it?"

Leslie looked at him for a long moment. Her eyes searched his face and probed deeply searching for the answer, the right answer. "You know," she began, "I've spent a great deal of time in the past weeks learning about our common ancestors. I've imagined myself in the role of others long since dead, looked to them for inspiration, and even likened you to an apparition or two. I think I've learned from them how the roles of people, men and women, are dependent upon their individual circumstances, their personal drives and their ability to utilize their available resources. Ultimately the choice is a personal one."

She paused, her gaze never wavering from his eyes. "I love you. I want to be with you working, fighting, loving, playing, whatever," she said with an expansive motion. "I want all of that and I want you to be the father of my children, but most of all I want to be your partner. Your equal. My life won't be complete without you, I know that now, but I *must* have the privilege of making my own choices and preserving my own uniqueness."

Leslie continued to hold his hand as he returned her gaze across the table. "We are two very strong people," he said at last. "We have a strong heritage and you must know that people come to expect a certain behavior from you especially when you have been born to certain responsibilities. I've probably been taking that image a little too seriously where you're concerned."

His eyes were hypnotic as they looked deeply into hers. "I love you too, my darling, more than any man should ever love any woman, to the point of being utterly enslaved by you. It's a very bad position for a man to be in. I went crazy thinking of you having my child and not wanting me." He pressed her hand to his lips and searched her eyes for understanding. "You forced me literally to fight for my very dignity."

"It's a bad position for anyone to be in," said Leslie softly. "You placed me in the same position. I've been fighting you from the very beginning. I too have a confession to make. I allowed you to suspect that I was with child when in reality I've known for some time it was not to be."

She saw his face register an instant note of sadness and disappointment and it was a curiously satisfying comfort to her as she went on. "That's really the whole point. Love is not a contest. When a man and a woman love each other there should be only sharing and fulfilling. We've been like children playing a silly game, living in fantasies."

She allowed a coy look to play over her face as she looked at him shyly through lowered lashes. Her lips were inviting as she went on. "I think in the past few hours you've made me realize I want very much to grow up and live the rest of my life with you starting today if possible."

"I think that is more than possible," he said a tad mischievously as he looked at her tenderly. "You're brilliant, you know. Those reports I read were beyond belief and your employees frankly insist that you continue as the chief corporate officer. After you left this afternoon, they voted resoundingly to remain non-union on that basis. Of course most of the discontent was coming from Philomena's people and they admitted that she had put them up to it threatening to put them out of the Ayudalo program if they didn't.''

Leslie paused for a long minute. ''What do you mean?''

''I mean,'' said Augustine, ''you have a wonderful career ahead of you and I would be honored to work with you on an equal basis if you'll have me, my Doña Leslie.''

He spoke the name softly, but with a special emphasis. Suddenly Leslie realized with a special pang how very blunt it sounded, how very much she had liked the soft intimate sound of María and the special way he spoke it.

''Does this mean,'' she asked in mock dismay although there was a hint of seriousness to her tone, ''that María no longer exists?''

''Not at all, *mi querida*,'' he said gently. ''María will always be in my heart as the love of my life, but Doña Leslie is the astute, brilliant businesswoman whom I will never, ever tangle with again, unless of course,'' he said with a chuckle, ''I happen to be right.''

Leslie looked at him and smiled, happy to spar with him on this loving basis. Several other couples had entered the dining room and they looked on fondly as Augustine and Leslie walked arm in arm toward the veranda. Leslie laid her head on Augustine's shoulder and reveled in the warmth of his embrace as they looked out over the valley.

''I love this island,'' she said softly, ''and I love you.'' She took a second to muster her courage. ''Do you think you could put the engagement ring on my finger again?''

She searched his face as he slowly turned her toward him. There was an amused twinkle in his eyes. ''Well now," he said as he pulled her close and nibbled softly on her ear, "I think that could be arranged, if you could give some serious consideration to just one thing."

"Oh?" She laughed, clearly pleased.

"Yes," he said, attempting to give his voice a deep and serious timbre while he fumbled through his pockets and finally found the sparkling ring. "A very important consideration."

"And what might that be?" For just a fleeting second she wondered if they were going back to square one, but his eyes were dancing pools of jest.

"Well," he said, pausing expansively, "I must insist that if our first child is a girl we shall call her Augustina."

"Oh, no!" said Leslie as she brought her hand to her head and cupped her brow in amused exasperation. "You don't mean that!"

"I do," he said as he placed the ring on her finger again and then brought her hand to his lips for a soft caress as his gaze drew suddenly serious. "Just as I mean everything this ring represents."

She met his eyes and matched the intensity of his gaze and then melted as his eyes grew soft with merriment again.

"Well, why not?" she said as they both collapsed into laughter.

"Why not, indeed."

They fell into each other's arms and headed back to the tiny room at the end of the hall.

"I think, my Doña Leslie," Augustine said as he picked her up and carried her across the threshold, "we have a wedding to attend."

"Yes," Leslie laughed, "but Doña Leslie can't go. Only María will be at that wedding."

"I doubt that,' said Augustine with a chuckle as he dropped with her to the bed and began caressing her softly. "I don't think the two of them will ever be separated again."

"Does it really matter?" she asked as she returned his kisses and pulled him closer.

"Not at all, *mi querida*," he said, "because I love both of you."

The Villaronga house was filled with gaiety as guest after guest arrived at the *fiesta de bautismo* of Leslie and Augustine's first child. Leslie was really enjoying the christening party as she looked around with a real sense of satisfaction. Her family estate had been totally restored to its earlier splendor. The antiques shone with polish, and the pool and gardens were the peaceful oasis they were intended to be. Her eyes returned again and again to the lovely bassinet where her six-month-old baby girl lay gurgling and cooing to all who passed by as they paid their eloquent respects.

"She seems to be bearing up remarkably well," said Augustine as he came up behind Leslie and nuzzled her ear with his mustache.

"But of course," said Leslie with a mischievous smile. "She is a Williams Villaronga, you know."

"Yes, of course," he teased back. "The Rivera Platos could have nothing to do with it."

Leslie smiled and gave him an affectionate squeeze. "Are you happy?" he asked as he smoothed the folds of the baby's elaborate white christening gown, which had been laid aside after the church ceremony.

"Yes, very," she said as she touched the simple white embroidered shift on her baby's round body and thrilled to the touch of the child. She looked into his eyes. "You know, though, I think I'm going to create a whole new line of christening dresses. Don't you think the idea of this two in one worked well?"

"Ah, María," he sighed affectionately, "is there ever a time when your mind is not working?"

"Oh, yes," she said with a coy glance as her arms went around him. "You should know all about those times."

"All right, lovebirds, the party can officially begin now," said Gerald as he shook Augustine's hand and gave Leslie a hug. "The godparents are here."

He turned around and pulled Juanita into his embrace. She smiled and gave Leslie a hug too. "The ceremony at the church was so beautiful," she said.

"Yes, it was," echoed Gerald. "Hopefully there will be another someday with the two of you as godparents." He gestured toward Leslie and Augustine and gave Juanita a meaningful look.

"Of course, in good time," said Juanita with a laugh, "but you know right now I'm having a wonderful time working and enjoying New York." She gave Gerald an affectionate hug.

"You know, I'm beginning to think bringing this smart little cookie to the big city was one big mistake," he said. "She's never going to be domesticated again, but then I have to admit she has a real business flair and she's burning up the town as your sales representative."

"I know," said Leslie. "We may have to expand our operation again just to keep up with the two of you."

"I love it," said Juanita as she reached out to touch the baby. The wedding ring on her left hand flashed in the light. "I really do. Every day is like a new adventure."

"I'm glad," said Leslie. "Everyone should experience the satisfaction of fulfilling all their capabilities. Then when you are ready, all of the other traditional roles are sweeter than ever." Augustine squeezed her affirmatively.

"I'm counting on that," said Juanita, "but until then we're very happy just the way we are."

"But your mama isn't," said Gerald gregariously. "I mean she takes being a grandmother very seriously and you know I have to agree. It just wouldn't be right to deny the world another magnificent rendition of the Masters line."

"Oh, I'm not so sure about that," said Juanita tartly.

"Well, at least we can put together a name I can pronounce."

"And just what is wrong," said Leslie in mock outrage, "with María Augustina Rivera Williams Platos Villaronga?"

"Stop, stop," said Gerald in defeat. "I think I liked the two of you better when you didn't get along. This constant compromise is almost disgusting!"

"Don't you believe it," said Leslie, laughing.

They all turned as new cries of greeting broke out. "Mama!" cried Leslie. "I didn't think you were going to make it."

"Yes, it's so nice to see our world traveler," said Augustine as he gave Doña Maria a big hug.

"Oh, I'm so sorry," she gushed as she went straight to the baby basket after kissing Leslie. "Our plane was hung up in Madrid and Isabel was so furious because I talked her into spending an extra day in Granada." The baby gurgled at the sound of her voice and smiled brightly. "Oh, you sweet thing, I can't believe how you've grown in only two months."

"And how long will you be home this time?" asked Magna who had also just arrived.

"Oh, maybe a month or so," Doña María answered, her face flushed with excitement. "Then I'm going to Africa." She was whisked away by friends as she began to recount tales of her travels in the past two years.

"I can't believe how your mother has changed," said Magna as she greeted Leslie.

"Nor I, you," said Leslie as she reached to shake the hand of Magna's husband. "I'm so pleased that the two of you are together again."

"I guess perhaps I decided to take a little of my own advice," she said, "especially when I saw how well you and Augustine were able to work out your differences."

"I'm happy for you," said Leslie, "and you look happy too."

"I am," said Magna, "there's a lot to be said for communication."

The music grew louder as everyone began to sing and dance while enjoying the mounds of food and drink. Juan Pacheco broke away to present his eldest son to Leslie and Augustine.

"This is Juan Junior," he said proudly. "He will begin his studies at the Catholic University this summer."

"That's marvelous," said Leslie, "and remember, Juan, you are welcome to work with us part-time while you are studying."

"Thank you," said the young man. Although he seemed a little selfconscious, his dignity and respect were unmistakable. "May I also offer my sincere congratulations to you, Don Augustine, on your being nominated as a candidate for governor."

"Thank you, thank you," said Augustine robustly. "No doubt someday I will be saying the same thing to you."

"Perhaps," said the young man with a shy smile as he turned to enjoy the rest of the party.

"And look who we have here," said Augustine as he greeted the next guest. "Philomena, I've never seen you look so lovely."

"Nor have I felt so lovely," said Philomena as she patted the mound of her round stomach.

As Leslie echoed Augustine's happy greeting, Philomena looked into Don Fernando's eyes and both seemed to grow younger as they moved away to greet the other guests.

"Now that has to be the perfect example of love conquering all," said Leslie with a sigh.

"No, my sweet Doña Leslie," said Augustine with supreme satisfaction, "*we* are the perfect example of that."

Harlequin reaches
into the hearts and minds
of women across America
to bring you

Harlequin American Romance ™·

YOURS FREE!

Enter a uniquely exciting new world with

Harlequin American Romance ^{T.M.}

Harlequin American Romances are the first romances to explore today's love relationships. These compelling novels reach into the hearts and minds of women across America... probing the most intimate moments of romance, love and desire.

You'll follow romantic heroines and irresistible men as they boldly face confusing choices. Career first, love later? Love without marriage? Long-distance relationships? All the experiences that make love real are captured in the tender, loving pages of **Harlequin American Romances.**

What makes American women so different when it comes to love? Find out with **Harlequin American Romance!**

Send for your introductory FREE book now!

Get this book FREE!

Harlequin American Romance

Twice in a Lifetime
REBECCA FLANDERS

Mail to:

Harlequin Reader Service

In the U.S.
2504 West Southern Avenue
Tempe, AZ 85282

In Canada
649 Ontario Street
Stratford, Ontario N5A 6W2

YES! I want to be one of the first to discover

Harlequin American Romance. Send me FREE and without obligation *Twice in a Lifetime.* If you do not hear from me after I have examined my FREE book, please send me the 4 new **Harlequin American Romances** each month as soon as they come off the presses. I understand that I will be billed only $2.25 for each book (total $9.00). There are no shipping or handling charges. There is no minimum number of books that I have to purchase. In fact, I may cancel this arrangement at any time. *Twice in a Lifetime* is mine to keep as a FREE gift, even if I do not buy any additional books.

Name _____ (please print)

Address _____ Apt. no. _____

City _____ State/Prov. _____ Zip/Postal Code _____

Signature (If under 18, parent or guardian must sign.)

Take these
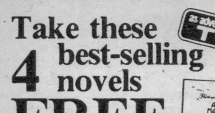

4 best-selling novels
FREE

Yes! Four sophisticated,
contemporary love stories
by four world-famous
authors of romance
FREE, as your
introduction to the Harlequin Presents
subscription plan. Thrill to **Anne Mather**'s
passionate story BORN OUT OF LOVE, set
in the Caribbean.... Travel to darkest Africa
in **Violet Winspear**'s TIME OF THE TEMPTRESS....Let
Charlotte Lamb take you to the fascinating world of London's
Fleet Street in MAN'S WORLD ....Discover beautiful Greece in
Sally Wentworth's moving romance SAY HELLO TO YESTERDAY.

 *The very finest
in romance fiction*

Join the millions of avid Harlequin readers all over the
world who delight in the magic of a really exciting novel.
EIGHT great NEW titles published EACH MONTH!
Each month you will get to know exciting, interesting,
true-to-life people . . . . You'll be swept to distant lands you've
dreamed of visiting . . . . Intrigue, adventure, romance, and
the destiny of many lives will thrill you through each
Harlequin Presents novel.

Get all the latest books before they're sold out!
As a Harlequin subscriber you actually receive your
personal copies of the latest Presents novels immediately
after they come off the press, so you're sure of getting all
8 each month.

Cancel your subscription whenever you wish!
You don't have to buy any minimum number of books.
Whenever you decide to stop your subscription just let us
know and we'll cancel all further shipments.